PSYCHOPATH'S PREY

V.F. MASON

Edited by Hot Tree Editing

Cover Design: Hang Le

Photographer: Olivier Lachance Photographe

Cover Model: Rusty Blade

To the power of love.

PROLOGUE

*E*lla

 The sweat is dripping down my back as I inhale the smell of lavender and roses, and my legs take me farther and farther into the field. The only sounds available are my feet slapping the ground and my gulps of breath while I put all my power, or what is left of it, into running. I ignore my blisters and how hunger almost makes it impossible to move, let alone fight.

I can't let him get me; it will mean he wins.

Not noticing the slippery wet spot in front of me, I fall down on my ass, causing pain to burst through my body. Biting down on my lip, I allow the metallic taste of blood to enter my dry mouth that hasn't had water or anything else to drink for ten hours straight now.

Maybe I shouldn't have been that stubborn.

Placing my hand on the ground, I glance down to study the bloody fingers and stubby fingernails on them while I wonder if the escape and future is worth it.

Slowly, black leather shoes come into view right under my nose as a man's sadistic chuckle echoes through the garden. "Little spitfire, aren't you? Quite the fight you gave me for your life." He kneels and grabs my chin, while I struggle from his hold, but it's useless.

My strength is nothing against his.

Raising my chin, our gazes clash and I can't help but whimper in despair as his unmasked face reminds me once again of the fool I've been.

Because during all the weeks of chasing the psychopath, I never once anticipated it would be him.

And now he has come to collect the most valuable thing I have to offer.

My life.

"You are mine now, Ella. The hunter has won his prey," he murmurs, as he leans down and licks the blood from my lips.

Part of me feels sorry for everything he's had to endure in the life that led him to this.

Not that it matters.

The end will be the same.

Either I'll kill him, or he'll kill me.

Till death do us part after all.

CHAPTER ONE

New York, New York

Psychopath

Monday
Leaning on the brick wall, my eyes scan the neighborhood around me as I admire the beauty of suburban life.

Neatly cut grass covered in light snowflakes, toys lying around for kids to play with and not have a care in the world. Some porches have swings and other comfortable furniture to rest on after a hard day of work.

People laugh loudly at something their friends say while kids run around in the snow, engaging in snowball wars or sledding down the icy road.

Dogs bark loudly while jumping in happiness around their owners who treat them as part of the family.

What's not to like about this life?

Especially when it gives me enough victims to hunt, as no one has more secrets than those living in the suburbs.

Mark my words.

Finally, my eyes rest on the tall, blond man who drinks his coffee while he watches his pregnant wife on the swing. A smile spreads across his mouth and happiness clearly shines brightly on his face. He sets his mug on the floor and leans down to give her a deep kiss while she clings to him tightly.

They don't seem older than thirty; recently moved here, if the various boxes around are anything to go by.

Then my mind clicks as I reach a decision.

He is perfect.

Who is a better victim than the one completely in love with his spouse?

*T*uesday
The man exits the bar while several guys call after him. "See you around, man." He waves at them, slightly swaying to the side as he digs for his phone in the back of his pants, then curses loudly when the thing drops on the concrete with a loud clatter.

Sometimes fools create an easy opportunity to catch them. I don't even have to try.

He looks around and huffs in frustration, running his fingers through his hair as he tries to turn on his phone, but it's useless.

I get out of the car, bored with all this. When my shoes make an unmistakable sound in the otherwise silent night, he raises his eyes to me as relief crosses his face. "Hey, man! Can I use your phone? Mine is broken, so I can't call a cab."

The bar is located on the outskirts of the city in a secluded area, which allows people to relax without listening to cars constantly passing.

Instead of answering him, I grab him by the neck, as he exclaims, "What the hell—" His words die on his lips as I press on his artery until he passes out, sagging in my arms. Then I pick him up and throw him into my trunk.

Not a soul is in sight near my car, which is parked in the darkest place here.

Whistling, I get inside and start the engine, as electricity zaps through me, reminding me of the satisfaction I will soon get.

Wednesday

"Please, I have a wife. We're expecting a baby," begs the man, while I silently lash him to a metal table, securing his arms and legs with leather straps. Not that he'll have much strength, since he has been injected with a serum to keep him awake for the torture but prevent him from moving a muscle or talking.

Gone are the days when I beat the crap out of them before inflicting my dark desires on their flesh. I've learned the art of destroying their body in ways they never see coming, all while they're awake for the torture. At least my ears don't have to bleed listening to their shitty cries.

I almost chuckle when I think about it. But it'll work in a few minutes; until then, I can have my fun.

I take a pair of blue latex gloves from the nearby surgical table. I love the sound of them snapping on my wrists as his eyes widen and he whimpers in fear.

My brows furrow at his cowardice. If you are stupid enough to get caught by me, at least act like a man.

I've never cried while experiencing pain—guess that comes with practice.

"Please." He tries again, but as before, I ignore his words and slide my finger through the many devices displayed for all kinds of torture. I usually like to switch around my methods, but this time I decide to start with the scalpel.

I place it over his liver, the skin dipping with the pressure, and the first drop of blood appears while his screams echo through the room. I've already broken his ribs, so I'd have easy access.

I zone out as adrenaline rushes through my body, awakening everything inside me to the point of goosebumps showing on my skin and pleasure consuming me.

Finally, the smell of a fresh kill.

"What are you going to do? What?" He breathes heavily and winces in pain.

This time, I decide to indulge him.

"I'll cut you up... piece by piece." Before another scream issues from his mouth, I place tape over it so he'll shut up and let me enjoy this moment.

These kinds of moments are everything I have.

Thursday
Placing the last parts into a black garbage bag, I load it into the truck and come back inside to open the windows and clean everything with antiseptic. I take my time with my devices and table, using bleach everywhere, because I don't want any evidence of what has happened here to come back at me.

DNA is everything, after all.

Finally, once it's done, I place the Polaroid picture I took in a metal box. I don't collect trophies as most of those like me do, but time to time, I love to gaze at my collection of killings and remember the thrills they brought me. Then I snap it shut, hide it under the table in the special case that no one can crack, and leave the place that brings me the most joy.

Once I'm behind the wheel, I dial the phone as I drive down the narrow path that leads to the woods where the animals will take care of the rest of the work for me.

"Finally, you called me back!" My friend's voice fills the space in the car and a smirk tugs on my lips.

"I'm sorry. I got held up with work."

He sighs heavily. "Don't tell me you won't be able to make it tonight?" he asks, displeasure lacing his tone. I barely restrain myself from bursting out laughing.

I'm crazy, but not to the point of missing a meeting with him. "I'll be there in two hours."

"Sure, see you there." He hangs up, clearly done with this conversation.

Soon, I stop at my destination, get all the parts out, and scatter them around the place.

I quickly stop by my apartment, take a shower, and arrive right on time for dinner.

It's interesting how people talk with serial killers and never know about them, isn't it?

*F*riday

The phone buzzing snaps me out of sleep; annoyance fills my mind when a woman next to me groans in displeasure.

Her warm body presses against me harder, her hand traveling across my chest and sliding lower, but I push her back, sending a warning stare that causes her eyes to widen.

I fucked her, but the fun is over now. She is gorgeous as fuck with unbelievable tits and ass, but I don't dip my dick into the same pussy twice.

Rising, I turn on the light on the nightstand, wondering how the fuck I ended up sleeping with her, because I never let them stay longer than the sex.

Probably all the booze we consumed last night. Then Jo—I think that's her name—proceeded to show me the various talents she possessed.

Not that her way of fucking is anything to phone home about.

"Yes," I bark into the cell, while the person on the other end of the line barks right back at me.

"Where the fuck are you? I've messaged you like a thousand times." The person continues to scream, so I remove myself from the arms of the naked woman as she slides her fingers down her stomach, still not giving up on turning me on.

Stupidity will end human kind, mark my words. "Get out." She opens her mouth to protest as a grimace crosses her face, but then thinks better of it, and with a loud huff, she grabs her clothes and disappears behind the bathroom door.

"What's going on?" I ask, grabbing a bottle of water from the fridge and welcoming the cooling sensations it provides.

"We have a case. Bring your ass to the office."

Oh, did I forget to mention?

I'm one of the team members of the behavior analysis unit of the FBI.

Brilliant, isn't it?

*S*unday
The music is blasting from the headphones in my ears as I breathe evenly, running with good speed through Central Park. My aching muscles protest at the effort, but I don't listen, instead pushing myself harder while inhaling the frigid air into my lungs, welcoming the burn it brings.

My hoodie and sunglasses hide me from the penetrating stares of people walking around me, and I find relief in that.

I can't stand them while the kill is so fresh.

Everything annoys me at times like this. I speed up, my sneakers constantly slapping against the concrete, and I close my eyes for a moment, exhaling heavily, and instantly slam into someone. The person bounces back from the impact and lands on the snow-covered grass, right on the ass.

Fuck.

I hear a groan, and my eyes focus on the woman in front of me. She sits up, laughing carelessly as she rubs her backside while removing the dark strands of hair from her face, and then her brown eyes look up to meet mine.

I don't say anything while she smiles at me. "Sorry, I'm so clumsy during my morning runs." She gets up, groaning again, and oddly enough, this sound sends different sensations down my spine. "Okay then, bye." With that, she adjusts her headphones and resumes her exercise while still rubbing her spine.

Breathing heavily, I try to block out the images playing in my head, the memories I always try to run away from but can't.

Memories that never come to me when I look at women.

I fist my hands and count to ten, hoping this desire will pass and I can forget about this encounter. Confusing emotions rush through me, and I spin around and trail after her, determined to find out why those fucking eyes of hers remind me of someone I used to know.

*M*onday

I have her file in my hands but throw it on the floor as I walk to the balcony door and drink in the magnificent view of the sunset in front of me.

Slowly sipping my drink, I understand with clarity why I need to hunt her and the pleasure it will bring me.

I don't touch women as a rule, but she will be my exception.

The hunter has found his prey, and nothing will stop him until he gets her.

But first, I have to lure her into my trap.

CHAPTER TWO

*R*ichmond, Virginia

*E*lla, 17 years old
    "This was such a mistake," I murmur, as Chloe rolls her eyes, applying one more layer of mascara on her lashes while Simone drives the car faster, ignoring the speed limit. "Simone."

She shrugs and pats my shoulder.

"Relax, girl! We'll get you home on time." She glances quickly at the clock. "It's barely eleven, for heaven's sake."

Palming my face, I rest my elbows on my knees, as I murmur, "Easy for you to say. You know my parents."

"Don't we all?" Chloe snorts, this time using the lipstick. Why the hell is she even doing it if we left the party a few minutes ago?

Unless they want to go somewhere else after they take the prudish Ella back home.

Fuck my life, seriously.

"They just want to protect me." I try to defend my parents, even though it's

hard when they practically forbid everything, closing me off from life completely.

"Yeah, I know. They're keeping you a saint and stuff." Chloe leans forward, resting her cheek on the car seat. "It's a wonder you even hang out with us."

Yeah, they are both the so-called bad girls of high school, not that my parents know about their reputation.

I keep that tidbit of information to myself.

"What are you going to do for the prom?" Simone asks, while turning right so fast I'm barely able to hold onto the seat without falling back.

This girl drives like crazy!

"I'm not going." There is no way they will buy me a dress or anything else, so the conversation is a moot point to say the least.

The horrified expression on my father's face when I mention going to a dance with a boy, even if it's a nerdy kid from my science class, is enough to crush all my dreams.

He has good reasons to be protective, but I'm so tired of living in a cage.

"That is so fucking sad, girl!"

"Don't swear," I add, as Chloe once again rolls her eyes, but thankfully at this point, the car stops right near the back door of my house, and the lights are off.

Exhaling in relief, I unbuckle myself and kiss my girls goodbye. "Sneak in quickly before they know. Otherwise, you'll miss the picnic too," Simone advises, and nodding, I rush inside, removing my shoes so I won't make a sound.

I tiptoe in complete darkness to the stairs, and then I step on something sticky and slip a little. I almost curse, as it has to be my baby sister and her crazy orange juice obsession. She's been scattering this stuff all over the freaking place.

I go on, ignoring the unpleasant stuff on my feet, and reach my door, quickly sliding inside and shutting it behind me. I'm so lucky that my parents' door is not open. They usually keep track of my sister and me to make sure we are sleeping and not doing any other stuff.

Closing my eyes and resting my head on the wood behind me, I exhale loudly. A light breeze hitting me on the face has me snapping my eyes back open to see my window with the white-as-snow curtains blowing in different directions.

I can't believe I left it open when I sneaked out earlier to meet the girls!

When I turn on the light, hoping to get a quick shower, I notice the red stains on my wooden floor.

"What the hell?" I murmur, then sigh in exasperation about my sister's drawing classes and, as a result, the paints that constantly stain everything. I'm the one doing the cleaning here, so I always spend hours making sure she doesn't permanently damage anything. However, she loves it, and since my room has the best view, or so she claims, she mostly paints here. Which is annoying, but what can I do when I love her so much?

Grabbing my pajamas, I remove any trace of makeup, take a quick shower, and get dressed before thirst gets the better of me.

Deciding it won't hurt to go downstairs, since my parents don't mind that, I tiptoe back into the hallway, and the faint, disgusting smell of something odd penetrates my nose and I almost vomit from it. I didn't smell it when I came home.

What have they been cooking?

This time, I avoid the liquid on the step and go to the kitchen sink, filling myself a glass of water and drinking from it greedily, while wondering if maybe I should give this whole prom conversation another go.

After all, we only live once, right? Shouldn't I fight more for my rights? It's not as if my parents are monsters; they love us and want to give us the best. So they are a little bit overprotective, so what?

With positivity filling me, I turn around and head back, when I stumble on something solid but soft and almost fall down.

Uneasiness sweeps over me, because the object doesn't remind me of one of Sarah's toys. Placing my hand on the wall, I search for the light dimmer switch, since I really don't want to wake up my parents. I rub my eyes as the light blurs my vision for a second.

Once it clears, the air sticks inside my lungs as the picture that greets me stops me dead in my tracks.

An agonized scream of pain echoes through the night, and it takes a while until I understand it escaped my mouth.

Mechanically, I pick up the phone from the kitchen bar and dial, concentrating only on the ringing sounds on the other end of the line. I open and close my eyes, hoping the image will disappear, but it doesn't.

"Nine-one-one, what's your emergency?" the lady asks, and swallowing down the bile in my throat, I look one more time.

My father's lying on the floor in a pool of blood from his cut throat. My mother is nearby with her head blown off, and my little sister... I can't locate, but her bloody pink dress is on the sofa, as if removed in haste.

"Nine-one-one, what's your emergency?" the lady repeats, and I find my voice.

"My parents are dead, and I can't find my sister," I whisper into the phone, cries shaking my body while I barely stand straight.

Life I so desperately wanted to get away from, no longer exists.

*E*lla

"You've got to be kidding me!" I mutter, sighing in exasperation while the sticky, hot liquid spreads into a bigger stain on my perfectly white shirt. The guy who bumped his shoulder into me doesn't even turn back to apologize as he leaves me standing on the road looking like an idiot.

Taking a deep breath, I take out wet wipes to try to somehow salvage the situation, but I'm probably making it worse.

Suddenly, a janitor lady screams right into my ear, "We ain't a resort here, lady! Clean up!" She points at the empty coffee cup that fell on the ground, which still lies in the pool of my morning espresso.

"I'm sorry. It was an accident." I smile softly, hoping it will appease her, but all she does is raise her eyebrow, clearly not impressed with my explanation. Not wanting to get into a fight over the incident on such an important day, I quickly pick it up and throw it away in the nearest trash can. My phone buzzes in my pocket, and I answer it while cursing inwardly over the timing.

"I'm so dead," I say into the phone, while hurrying my steps to the other side of the road to the massive building in front of me, which seems more guarded than the freaking president.

"You sound just fine to me." Chloe snickers while a soft mantra song can be heard in the background.

Great, she's doing yoga again. God knows why, she thinks my voice calms her down and puts her in the special mood.

"My espresso is all over my shirt, and I'm ten minutes late to my new job. I'm so dead." I can practically imagine her shrugging as if it's no big deal.

"Shit happens." Her standard reply whenever something is wrong; she never cares much about it or stresses out. Maybe I should have watched more *Forrest Gump* in my teens as she did. Clearly it changed her entire perspective on life. "Why are you breathing so heavily?"

Almost doing a victory dance, I finally reach the mirrored doors and enter, my black heels clicking loudly on the marble floor, the only sound in the otherwise silent hallway.

The security guard who occupies the administrative desk stands up the minute he sees me while he scans my appearance.

"Excuse me, ma'am?"

"Because I'm late! Gotta go," I say to Chloe and hang up. She can talk for hours without caring about a thing, and I don't have time for that. She is my best friend, but her breezy attitude won't calm me down.

I flash my ID to the security, and he nods and gives me a company access card.

"Your boss informed me that you were coming. You need to go to the eighteenth floor."

"Thanks!" I rush through a closing elevator door as a nerdy-looking guy with his glasses sliding down the bridge of his nose frantically presses the button for the same floor I want.

Guess I'm not the only one late today.

Resting my head on the glass behind me, I close my eyes for a second, allowing the thrilling sensation of victory to run through me, as a bubble of laughter almost escapes my mouth. Despite all the things that went wrong today, including my car breaking down, I can't help the excitement building inside me at the prospect of finally accomplishing my lifelong dream!

Wrapping my hand tight around the gold necklace, Dean Holt's voice washes over me, reminding me of the time she came to my graduation and gave it to me.

"You'll get there, Ella. Mark my words."

I hope that wherever she is in heaven, she is proud of me, despite the fact she didn't support my decision to go into the field.

Once the elevator dings on our floor and the doors slide open, I get out, noticing how the guy still just stands there and does nothing, although his fingers are about to press number eighteen again.

"Hey," I say gently, and he snaps out of his haze. My eyes lock with his, not missing that something flashes through them before he covers it up. "You okay?" He frowns at my question, straightens up, and gets out. He doesn't even bother to answer me as he speeds past, and before I can even blink, he disappears between the sliding mirrored doors that lead toward the main office of Blake Harrington, the CEO and owner of his own security company, Blake Enterprises.

Groaning inwardly at my reflection in the glass door, I shake my head at my ridiculous outfit and go in after the guy. I'm greeted by the cheerful secretary who stands up the minute he notices me. He wears a green polo shirt and white shorts along with slippers, which surprises the hell out of me. Don't they have dress codes in such establishments? "Yes?"

"My name is Ella Gadot." His blank face shows me he has no clue who I am, so I try again. "My boss was supposed to inform you about my visit."

"One second," he mutters, grabbing the phone and dialing five. A second later, he speaks into it. "Blake, hi. An Ella Gadot is here, she claims that... got it." He hangs up and for the first time graces me with his smile. "They are waiting for you."

"Great." I mentally go over all the successful milestones in my life to give me more confidence to take the step, and with a firm knock, I enter the office where a deep discussion appears to be happening, if the loud voices coming from there are any indication.

They all stop though, the minute their eyes land on me, and it's at times like this I wish the universe would just listen to me for once and swallow me whole.

The office is a large space with a huge window that displays the beauty of New York City. Based on the picture I've seen in various magazines, you can see the Empire State Building in all its glory while people walk on the sidewalks and seem the size of small fruit. The sky opens up magnificently, so much you can look into it and forget everything in the world exists.

There is a sense of freedom in that.

I wish I had the opportunity to see it at night, but my job doesn't pay me to gaze at the skies.

It pays me to get into the minds of serial killers.

"Ella, you finally decided to join us." Noah scans my appearance, lingering for a bit on my shirt before he addresses Blake. "Ella Gadot, the newest member of our team." He introduces me with an indifferent expression, but I can't miss his sarcasm. He clearly doesn't appreciate my lateness.

"I'm sorry. I got a little lost on the way here." I try to justify it, and barely restrain myself from slapping myself. There can be no excuse for being late on your first day. I have to own it instead.

He leaves my words with no reply as he turns back to Blake, a handsome blond man who sits behind his desk while his watchful green eyes light up with fury.

What the hell?

Noah motions to the nearby chair, and I sit down while secretly studying the office. Not because I'm in awe of all the luxury, but because Blake is under investigation.

For murdering his ex-wife.

So I scan his bare walls, the expensive leather furniture, which is comfortable as hell, and the expensive Persian carpet in the middle of the room. The heavy, black, wooden desk has very detailed figures carved into the sides. He has a lot of hunting trophies gracing his walls, which I find out of place, considering it's his office. No framed photographs of the loved ones, nothing personal to give a clue where his loyalties lie. Blake exudes power and dominance, but with his military background, it's understandable.

Detailing all this in my mind, I take out my notebook and make several notes for myself while snapping my attention back to Blake, who is still in deep conversation with Noah, talking about his alibi.

"Look, agent, get this straight, I didn't kill my wife. I was home, resting after my last assignment." He sounds irritated, while Noah just raises his brow.

"Is there anyone who can confirm this, sir?" His lips thin as he shakes his head, and he snaps, hitting the table with his fist while I jump on my seat.

"This is fucking bullshit. I have proof I was on assignment, the cameras showed when I entered my building. I'm supposed to have a babysitter all the time so you'll believe… or what?" He rises from his seat, and Noah follows him while they both face each other.

Noah has a buzzed haircut; his muscled body, encased in a black suit, emphasizes his strength and experience in field work for the last ten years. He has brown eyes that don't betray any emotion, and I suspect he doesn't have many friends. The file I got on him is short, so I have no clue about the details of his life.

But no matter how much I try, I can't turn off my instinct or psychological mind from studying people around me.

It is in my blood.

"No one is charging you with anything so far, sir," Noah says, then leans forward. "So control yourself," he warns, and then continues, "Don't leave town, or the country, before the case is closed. We will stay in touch." With that said, he gathers his files, picks up his phone, and moves in the direction of the door. Although I rush after him, he walks so fast he is almost back at the elevator.

He clicks on the button as the man from earlier joins us. I have a second to react, when Noah asks him, "You found anything, Preston?" The guy shakes his head and Noah just mutters something under his breath. The elevator opens with a loud ding and we all get inside, and I can't help but feel odd about all this.

Not exactly how I imagined my first day at my dream job.

"Don't ever be late again, or you'll be dismissed from my team."

My eyes widen at Noah's words, and I snap my attention back to him where he holds my gaze. Swallowing down the bile in my throat from his stare—I sense something dangerous is hidden there—I nod without saying anything. Seconds later, we get out, but not before I notice a Greek symbol on his hand that traces up to his sleeve.

My brows furrow as I search my memory. I've seen it somewhere, but where?

"What do you think of him?" he asks me suddenly, and I bump into his back because I don't expect him to stop.

Slightly taken aback and acting like the idiot I am, I blurt, "He isn't guilty." From the corner of my eye, I notice Preston on his phone as he continues his walk to a black car located in front of the building.

Noah spins around to face me, and questions, "Why?"

"He doesn't have any photos in his office, which means he doesn't hold much affection for his family or friends. It's void of any kind of emotion. The case you presented me shows there was rage when the person was killed. A man like him, who likes to hunt, would have planned everything and never done something like that in rage." His wife was found in a pool of her own blood. She had been stabbed thirty times in the chest, as if the person hated everything about her.

"She could have provoked him and his control snapped, just like back at the office," Noah says, crossing his arms.

I shake my head. "With all due respect, sir, a psychopath or sociopath didn't kill her. The evidence, the scene of the crime, and the crime itself shows that the act was spur of the moment. And this could have only been done by a person who is highly emotional in everything. Blake has a military background, not to mention he owns a security firm. If he had done it, we wouldn't have found her body," I finish, taking a deep breath, hoping I didn't screw up my future.

A beat and then his mouth spreads in a smile, making him almost approachable, and it stills me for a moment. "Welcome to the team, Ella Gadot." Then he motions to the car and I get in the back seat with Preston, who already has his laptop open, typing away furiously on it.

"Where are we going?" I ask, while declining one more call from Chloe. This girl... seriously. I love her to pieces, but she has no idea about personal space or the importance of keeping a job. She doesn't have to with her talent for design work.

"To FBI headquarters. You need to meet the rest of the team."

Finally!

CHAPTER THREE

*R*ichmond, Virginia

*E*lla, 17 years old

A soft blanket wraps around my shoulders as the woman with a cup of steaming tea in her hand kneels in front of me while she tries to give me a reassuring smile.

What can be reassuring in this situation? The nightmares will haunt me till the end of my life.

I try to control my breathing without gulping air, because I don't want them to bring back that psychologist who wants to help me. I don't need therapy, especially from a person who keeps repeating that in time everything will be all right. What does she fucking know anyway?

"Here you go, honey," she murmurs, but I just blink and make no move to take it from her hands, even though I tremble so much I can hear my teeth chattering against each other.

The images just keep playing in my head, no matter how hard I will myself to forget them.

Blood.

Dead bodies.

My lifeless parents with no hope of surviving.

And finally, my little sister.

Thoughts of her snap me out of my stupor and I finally make eye contact with the officer lady, concern lacing her features. "Sarah... did you find her?" My sister is the only hope I have left. Surely life is not that cruel to take her away from me too?

She opens her mouth to say something, when another officer steps in, giving her a stern look. She nods, and with one last pat on my knee, rises and leaves me alone with the man who exhales heavily.

He is different from anyone else; he wears a black suit and oozes the confidence of a man who doesn't take shit from anyone. I've noticed him before, when he ordered around several people who look like him.

"My name is Agent Bates." He shows me his badge, and my brows rise at the FBI insignia. This required the feds to come?

He grabs the chair nearby and sits in front of me, while I repeat my question. "Did you find my sister?" His lips thin as he leans forward and reaches for my hands, but I move them away.

I don't need comfort if it means he doesn't have a good answer for me. Finally, he speaks, and part of me wants to shut him up.

To not have this finality in my life, the truth I will never be able to run away from.

But I can't, so all that's left is for me to listen. "We found Sarah in your basement. She was... she was hurt." He swallows as if he is shocked himself by what the monster did to her. "She died a few hours ago. I'm so sorry, Ella," he says, as if it will make everything better.

My entire family was murdered tonight.

How can anything ever be better again?

As tears stream down my cheeks, I close my eyes and fist my hands so the sobs will not escape me. I glance to his lap, where there is an open folder with several pictures, and bile rises in my throat. "What is this?"

He curses and tries to close it. "You shouldn't have seen this." He can't stop me before I grab the folder and scan pictures of people who had the same things done to them as my parents.

And then I find the last picture, this one with a little girl.

I stand up quickly, rushing toward the bathroom. I make it just in time before I vomit the water I drank earlier. The monstrous things keep on playing in my mind along with the smell from my house that I know is seared into my brain for life.

I feel Agent Parker's presence behind me, and whisper, "That's what he did to Sarah?"

A beat of silence, and then, "Yes." I find the strength to get up and wash my hands in the sink as he gives me a hand towel. "He is a serial killer who has done this to several families."

I lean on the sink, still dizzy, and I'm afraid I'm going to barf again.

What kind of sick, twisted monster does he have to be to do that?

"So there are more people like me? Kids?"

He shakes his head. "You are the only one he kept alive."

What? Why?

"Do you remember anything, Ella? Any detail will help us."

"No," I whisper, because I'd been at the party while he did what he did to my family.

Well, I have all the freedom in the world now.

Unfortunately, it has a high price.

*E*lla

The car moves smoothly through the traffic of New York while I pick up the folders next to me and study the list of all the people who could have hurt Claire Hendricks. The woman sure got around, from one powerful man to another, although most had nothing but nice things to say about her. No enemies or scandals either, so who could have killed her in such rage?

Maybe a rejected admirer?

Preston continues to type while frowning and wiping away the sweat from his forehead. I take out a tissue from my purse and extend it to him. He gives it one glance, pauses, but then resumes doing his thing, ignoring me once again.

Seriously, what's up with this guy?

"Your recommendations are splendid, Ella." Noah drives the car and catches my gaze in the rearview mirror. "Hope you can live up to them."

I rub my forehead, wondering if this is what it's like to work for the FBI.

Will I have to face constant smirks and jokes? Although Dean Holt warned me it's not an easy job, with people constantly facing danger and psychos. They need to find fun in something, unless they want to go insane.

I just never thought I'd be the one they made fun of.

The car stops abruptly and I glance through the open window at the Federal Bureau building, the New York field location of the FBI. The building has impossibly high glass walls with a clean appearance all around.

Noah shows his badge to security, who nods and opens the gate for us, while several other cars wait their turn. The territory is highly guarded.

"Why did you choose our office?"

I'm slightly taken aback by the question from Preston, who has shifted his attention to me. He keeps his locked hands on his laptop while Noah searches for a parking space.

"As in the Behavioral Analysis Unit?"

He shakes his head, moving the hair from his forehead, which makes him almost cute and not like a jerk. "Our office. The headquarters are at Quantico. You'd have a wider scope of experience there."

The main headquarters of the FBI is located in Quantico, Virginia. They train the academy students there, handle the most important cases, and generally work hard. Other offices in the country are just field offices that handle cases where they have jurisdiction.

"Oh, I studied here, and all my family is here."

I choose not to mention that Virginia is my home state and I don't want to go back there, ever. It holds too many memories, memories I try to forget every night. Not that I have much success though.

"I heard people have fun there," Preston says, and I just blink, because this guy is so freaking random.

Noah finally parks the car and we get out, as he orders someone on the phone. "Make sure everyone is in the conference room in five minutes. We have a lot to discuss." The way he says it, the tone of his voice, leaves no room for questions or the desire to disobey the guy.

As we ride the elevator to our floor, Preston mumbles something, Noah acts like a statue, and I think about how monumental this moment is in my career.

All the years I've worked so hard for this, through constant rejections and sleepless nights, working three jobs at a time to support myself in college just to be able to stand here today and help catch those people who hurt families.

Who destroy lives.

I've learned everything there is to know about them, studied their psychology and behavior. Gotten to know what makes them who they are and what their triggers are. How they try to justify their actions because of their upbringing or life circumstances.

The knowledge still doesn't dull the pain of losing my family. But maybe once I save other families, it can shift. I'm not sure I can afford waking up with nightmares for the rest of my life.

"Ella?"

I snap back from my memories to see Noah holding the elevator door for me since Preston has already rushed outside.

"Sorry," I mumble, and his gaze softens for a second but quickly passes, so it must have been my imagination. "I was lost in my head for a second there."

"Happens," he says, and we go through more glass doors that open wide to countless desks with computers where people click on them or drink coffee while talking with their coworkers or studying folders. Noah has a certain direction in mind as he guides me to the right corner where stairs go down a level, sort of like a wing, and several people pass by and greet him.

Finally, we reach a spacious conference room with a huge TV in the middle along with a round table that holds several iPads. People occupy most of the chairs. A couch that has seen better days sits in the background, and the smell of coffee is strong.

At least we all share love for coffee.

"Everyone, meet our new team member, Ella Gadot." Noah introduces me as they stand up, each one of them extending a hand to shake.

"Andrea." The only female member is first, bold in her approach.

Her long blonde locks go with her sapphire eyes as she winks at me. "I'm the only sane one here. Girl power!" She raises her fist while the guys roll their eyes; a smile tugs at my lips. I can be friends with her. Her gray suit showcases her fit body nicely, and I suspect she probably is a hit here. The woman is beautiful. "I'm a profiler."

"Jacob Ford." The man has insane muscles and strained veins on his neck. His James Dean haircut gives him a naughty look while his assertive green eyes don't appear to miss a thing. "Welcome." Something about him unsettles me, but I return the grin. Although he speaks the word, I don't think he likes having me here very much.

"Preston is our computer science specialist, so he mostly stays here. We rarely need his presence in the field," Noah informs me while Preston drinks his coffee and doesn't pay attention to anyone.

They act friendly, but I know better. In such professions, you have to prove your worth first. They trust their team members with their lives, and such trust is not easily given.

"And Kierian who is late." Noah sounds angry as his eyes focus on the door behind me. I turn around to see one of the most handsome men in the room.

Although he has muscles, he is more on the lean side with a defined six-pack that his black T-shirt emphasizes while his black jeans give him a rather dangerous posture. His black hair is done in a man bun while his five o'clock shadow gives him a brutal yet hot look. But the most mesmerizing part of him is his beautiful exotic silver eyes that oddly enough do not go with everything else. They appear to hold so many secrets, not that anyone will likely ever find out what they are.

I should know, since I had a one-night stand with him two weeks ago.

Groaning inwardly, I really hope he never mentions it to anyone, because there is nothing like starting work with that kind of reputation.

Hooking up with a coworker!

My brows furrow at his looks, because FBI agents mostly keep haircuts short and no facial hair. In other words, they don't stand out so no one pays them attention. Exceptions are undercover agents.

Then it dawns on me that Noah mentioned one of his team

members has recently been undercover working on an important case for locating a serial killer who targeted people in small towns. He must be that agent.

Kierian smirks at Noah while he salutes him with his coffee cup.

"Good morning to you too." He then gives me his hand. "Welcome to the team. I'm the only nice one here," he jokes, while the others groan, clearly used to his behavior.

My eyes narrow at his words, his handsomeness diminishing rapidly. So he is going to act as if we don't know each other.

Good, but it doesn't mean he is allowed to speak to me with such familiarity. I open my mouth to give him a piece of my mind, when Andrea does it for me.

"Kierian, no need to show you are an asshole from day one." But they share a smile, so she doesn't mean the heat of her words.

Well, okay.

The team sure is an interesting bunch of people.

"I need to speak with Eva. Once I'm back, Preston will present the new case to us. It's urgent, so no slacking," he warns, and everyone nods, while Andrea pats the seat next to her. "Come sit with us till we wait for the case to land here. You want coffee?"

Oh my God, am I really about to get my first case?

*P*sychopath

She smiles at something Andrea says while picking up her coffee, and her eyes close in pleasure as she takes her first sip. She twirls a dark curl with her index finger as she listens attentively to all the information on the previous case. Although she acts at ease, I can see tension in her shoulders as if she doesn't know if they accept her.

She almost reminds me of a doll with her pale, clear skin that will probably look magnificent with blood smeared all over it while her beautiful brown pools fill with tears and fear from what I make her feel.

I always preferred blonde hair on women, but her dark locks somehow dimmed the purity of her demeanor and made her more approachable to me.

To my desires.

My cocks hardens against the zipper of my jeans as my hand tightens on the pen I sign the reports with, but not from the images of her taking my dick while she is spread on my bed.

Oh, no.

It's from the idea of her spread on my bed while I use my favorite knife on her skin, to mark it with different cuts that will give me her moans and screams. Then I'll fuck her with all the blood spread between us, forever binding us in a divine way.

Her picture alone as my trophy won't do her justice.

She should have stayed in the center and worked with cognitive psychology, not stepped into my world.

Because she became my prey, and sooner rather than later, I will get her.

I just have to play my cards right.

CHAPTER FOUR

*R*ichmond, Virginia

*E*lla, *17 years old*
     The sun shines brightly, lighting up the entire field while birds chirp in the trees. A light breeze touches my skin, but I want to snap it away as it reminds me of my whereabouts, and I hate nothing more than the fact this weather is amazing for such a day.

The velvet jacket scratches my skin because it's too hot for such clothes, but I don't care. The priest continues to read passages that seem related to the situation, while people are sniffing or crying and sending pitying glances my way in the process.

Not that I focus on them, numbly watching the three coffins in front of me that hold the people dearest to my heart.

Their lifeless bodies are cold, so cold I can't even remember their warmth anymore, even though it has been only five days.

My nails dig in my palm, shooting pain to my brain, which I welcome, because it's the only thing keeping me alive. The only thing that allows me to be brave enough to face each new day, even though everything in me screams to run, to beg someone to kill me. So I won't be alone, so I won't feel the exhausting desperation as my world crumbles around me.

The majority of newspapers and TV reporters call me lucky because I'm the one person who managed to escape the serial killer.

Lucky.

How ironic.

The priest must have finished at some point and the men come to lower the coffins into the ground as people stand to say their final goodbyes. Most of them are my parents' coworkers, neighbors, parents from Sarah's school. Even my school's teachers showed up, giving me their support.

I slowly walk to the coffins, knowing full well everyone's eyes are on me as the thorns of the roses hurt my skin. I plucked them from our garden, because they are my mom's favorite.

Were.

I should learn to use past tense when thinking about them.

I taste the salty tears streaming down my cheeks as sobs threaten to escape, but I can't allow it.

Not here, not now, maybe not ever.

"I love you," I whisper, and throw the roses on each of their graves, wiping my face while Agent Bates comes closer, placing his hand on my shoulder.

"I'm sorry," he says, and I just shrug, not wanting to nod or give any other reaction.

Why don't they understand their words don't bring comfort to me? I don't feel bad for acting this way; they should know better.

"Ella, none of your family wants to take you in," he states, and I snort, although it lacks any humor. He wants to have this conversation here?

As if it's a surprise. My dad's side never liked my mother, so it is no wonder they've refused. "Normally, it would have meant that you'd have to go to foster care until you turn eighteen." I frown at this information, finally meeting his eyes as he continues. "But the Donovan family offered to take you in until your graduation, and this way you will not have to move or jeopardize your future."

What?

On instinct, my head moves in the direction of Chloe's family, who stare at us tentatively, as if searching for my reaction to this news.

Nothing in my life will ever be normal again, and I'm not sure what I want to do with my future. But for them to honor their friendship with my parents like this and be willing to give me a roof over my head when they don't have to?

At this vulnerable moment in my life, it means everything.

Ignoring the agent, I rush to Chloe, and in a second, I end up in her arms, sobs shaking my body while she holds me tight, not letting me fall. She soothes my back with her pats, while I cling to her. She is the only thing left in my life.

"They are gone, Chloe," I say hoarsely into her neck as she whimpers in pain.

"I know, honey. I know." And because she doesn't try to reassure me or give me bullshit that someday it will be better, I hold her tight, hoping that someday life will not be a never-ending nightmare.

*E*lla
        I continue to sip my coffee, while Andrea asks, "So what's your experience in the field?"

"I worked for a few years with a private investigator." My reply doesn't impress Jacob as he raises his brow.

"To land a job here, you've got to have at least seven to fifteen years of experience in law enforcement. The only exception among us is our man Preston." He points at the guy who shuffles channels on the TV while checking something on his iPad and then huffing in frustration. "He got in because he hacked someone he shouldn't, and the FBI always keeps impressive talent." Yeah, this information is common knowledge. People sort of don't have a choice but to work for the government, unless they prefer to spend time in jail.

"Well then I was an exception." I try to lighten up the mood, but none of them seems impressed. Andrea just plays with the spoon in her cup while Kierian leans forward, resting his elbows on the table, his gaze never leaving mine.

"What makes you so special?"

Before I can answer his question, Jacob rudely interrupts me.

"So we lost Jenny because you are someone's daughter or have a connection here?" He squeezes the cup harshly, and I'm surprised he doesn't break the thing.

So that's the source of his anger? I should have expected that.

They informed me a few weeks ago that their agent Jenny was

injured during one of the cases, and she couldn't come back to work due to psychological trauma. They gave her several chances, but at some point, they had to give up. She had worked with these people for around five years, so no wonder they see me as an enemy now.

Their loyalty lies with their friend.

"I don't have any family working in FBI." Any thought or mention of my family unsettles me as it takes me back to all those awful moments I've experienced. None of them misses my breath hitching, and even Preston turns around to give me a curious look. "Like I said to Andrea earlier, I worked in cognitive psychology while also helping a private investigator get to the bottom of psychological crimes. I applied several times to work with the police, but they declined." I don't feel like sharing with them about my past, so I keep it vague like that. "But then—"

Noah enters the conference room, takes the situation in, and finishes for me. "She was the one who caught Smith."

A shudder runs through me as memories of that day wash over me like an ocean wave, the images playing like a movie in front of my eyes.

The crazy person who entered the train and claimed he had a bomb, the panic among people, his demands to the law. Thankfully, I convinced him not to do anything drastic, and the police came in time to save us all.

All because I could recognize the signs of a psychopath in him so easily; it was like a natural-born talent in me. That gained the attention of the FBI, and since I'd applied for years for any kind of position in BAU, Noah's call was a gift from heaven.

Preston whistles and then turns on the monitor while the lights go off, and everyone forgets about me and focuses their attention on the case. "Yesterday, the New York police department got a call from the Hudson River area. A body was found, or what was left of it anyway."

He clicks and several pictures of scattered and chopped flesh appear, and I almost spit my coffee even though the rest of the team has no reaction.

They are probably used to it by now, but holy crap! Kierian even manages to grab a bite of his doughnut. How can he eat while looking at this?

"Animals already ate most of it, but it's clear that someone just destroyed certain pieces, keeping the body intact as a whole." He clicks again and we have a zoom in on the pieces. Everything is smeared in blood, while one piece of a person's hand lies in the middle of the forest floor. The fingers are chopped and fingernails are gone. "Oddly enough, wolves or coyotes did more damage than the unsub. At least on the outside it seems that way. They scanned the teeth, and the victim is thirty-five-year-old Thomas Parker. He didn't return home from work four months ago, and his wife filed a missing person report."

"Why did they call us?" Jacob asks, as he zooms in even more on his iPad to study the details. "For us to take the case, we'd need more bodies than this one."

"That's the thing." Preston clicks again and the screen changes to a few other slides that hold similar pictures, but the pieces on them look older, and the find consists more of bones. "They found one more body, several feet away from the first one." He huffs in exasperation as several slides mix up before he settles on the right one. "They're searching the place for more. Quite an odd place to bury your victims, but something must've driven him there."

Jacob leans back in his chair, disgust written all over him. "We are dealing with a serial killer then."

"A dangerous serial killer." Kierian finally speaks while he points at the body. "Look at all this work. That takes time and dedication. He planned this. It's not spur of the moment."

"No sign of remorse either. He doesn't respect the victims, based on how he threw them away. For him, they deserved it," I murmur, making a mental note to myself.

A serial killer without remorse equals a smart serial killer. They don't have emotions clouding their judgment, and everything is for their personal gain only. They will use everything from manipulation to torture to get what they want.

"Do they know how long ago the other crime was?" Andrea bites on her pen. "How did he escape our radar for so long?"

"The autopsy should be ready soon, but my guess? Around a year based on the condition of the bones."

"Two victims at least in the span of a few months." Noah finally speaks. "He is evolving."

Preston nods. "And doesn't think anyone can stop him."

I agree with his conclusion, because he doesn't even bother to hide the bodies properly. "Any information on the other victim? Are they connected in any way?"

Preston shakes his head. "Ken Aldridge was a middle-aged man who taught music at a school, and had a loving marriage and two kids. Thomas was a lawyer with a kid on the way. No mutual friends, hobbies, or anything else. Never crossed paths."

"For a serial killer like this guy, there must be a pattern that triggers his MO," Jacob muses. "He doesn't randomly pick them. But what is it?"

"That's why they invited us. Okay, get in the cars. We need to see the crime scene as soon as possible. Maybe we'll find something useful. Andrea and Jacob, you go to the morgue and study the pieces. I'll speak with the detective assigned to the case. Preston, check for similar crimes in any other cities or states. Solved or not. Kierian, take Ella with you and check out the crime scene. They're still scanning the place." Noah barks orders quickly and everyone spins into action.

Of all things, he chose for me to see the crime scene on my first day.

Why?

*P*sychopath

She nervously bites her nail as she gets her stuff ready to go, and I can barely contain the sinister smile that threatens to spill out at the prospect of her fear.

The wince, the horror flashing in her eyes during the presentation. I long to show her more, for her to see how a man can go insane.

And also pride... she needs to see what I'm capable of so she'll forever understand.

There is no escape from me.

But first, she needs to know. She needs to show me she is worthy for me to spill my secret to her.

Unfortunately for her, it means solving a crime.

My fingers prickle as familiar excitement rushes through me, but I fist my hand and keep the indifferent expression, because the time hasn't come yet.

Anniversary be fucking damned.

CHAPTER FIVE

*R*ichmond, Virginia

*E*lla, 18 years old
  "Ella Gadot!" the principal says into the mic as the audience hollers, clapping fiercely.

Chloe's family gets up to whistle and send smiles my way as I go to get my diploma during graduation. All the teachers shake my hand while praising my intelligence and predicting I'll make our city proud someday.

I quickly grab my diploma while winking at the principal, who is still disappointed with me for not wanting to give the valedictorian speech. He passed it to Kyle, who has a slightly lower GPA than mine and gets off on the attention.

For me, it means nothing, so whatever. Besides, the three most important people will never hear it, so what's the point?

I look up to the sky, and murmur, "I did it, Mom... Dad... Sarah. I love you." And although it's been a year, the pain doesn't go away.

Not a raging inferno anymore, but rather a scar that will never heal.

I join Chloe back at the seat as she wiggles her brows. "Who are fucking *college students now? We are!" She shoots her fist in the air in a victory gesture and then hugs me and Simone at the same time while we groan.*

"We're not even going to the same college, girl," Simone says. I silently laugh while she shares my amusement, but Chloe just shrugs.

"Our colleges are only like a few hours away. So I expect you two to be there for me in case I have a crisis," she warns, while I just roll my eyes.

"I'm studying in New York and you'll be in Texas. How is that a few hours away?" I wonder sometimes if Chloe lives in her makeshift reality.

"I meant flying," she says, wiggling her fingers at us while her shoe keeps digging into the chair in front of us.

Yeah, like that will be possible with my law degree while holding down a waitressing job. Although I have insurance money and a scholarship to the university, for the past year, I've busted my ass at the local diner to have enough for my spending money. Chloe's parents constantly try to buy stuff for me, but I refuse. They have two more kids to feed and clothe. I'm not their responsibility, although I will be forever grateful for this past year.

Never once have they made me an outsider. They've tried their best to integrate me in their family. But unfortunately, it didn't change the variables in my life's equation.

"News flash, we aren't rich," Simone adds, but Chloe has none of that.

"That's not freaking true—" Whatever she says next escapes my notice as my eyes widen when far away, emerging from a car, I recognize Agent Bates.

The man who investigated my parents' death.

I rise swiftly, ignoring the surprised looks thrown my way, and almost run to the guy who holds a box with a red bow.

"Hi," I say, while he just nods and gives me the gift. While I take it, I can't care less for it. "Thank you. Why are you here?" A year ago, they couldn't find the person who killed my parents, so they wrapped up the case and left.

He told me there is just so much profiling they can do, and I hate knowing the monster is out there, terrorizing other families. Although I never found anything in the crime section of the newspaper, I still kept tabs on those constantly.

But he is here now, so it means something, right? No point in stalling.

"Yes, we found the man responsible for what happened to your family. And we are sorry."

"Sorry?" I repeat like a parrot, confused as hell.

They should be proud and happy! Now I can finally spit in the face of that awful man for what he has done.

Before he can elaborate, chaos erupts around us.

A SWAT team surrounds us, and a moment later, I hear a scream behind me and spin quickly, only to see Chloe's dad being held down on the ground as the officer recites his rights to him.

No.

No. No.

But Agent Bates doesn't let me live in denial. "He is the one, Ella. And I'm so sorry."

This couldn't have been a bigger nightmare, could it?

But as I watch Uncle Benjamin get cuffed by the police officers while complete indifference is reflected on his face, the horror becomes my reality.

And I do the only thing I can think of.

I run in the opposite direction before anyone can stop me.

*E*lla

The car stops abruptly and I startle awake, sitting straight at once.

"We're here," Kierian says, while chuckling. "Partied hard last night, huh?"

Frowning at his humor, I just shake my head and check my phone along with my tablet to make sure I can snap pictures if needed.

As hot and man-whorish as the guy seemed back in the club, he hasn't spoken a word since we got the order. He just pointed at the car, telling me to hop in, and turned on classical music that immediately filled the space.

I find it weird, but then it seems everyone has issues in this job, so I'm not really surprised. I just wish I hadn't slept with the guy two weeks ago, even if it was the best sex of my life. Maybe he doesn't even remember us hooking up.

And at that, anger swipes through me, because the idea tastes bitter in my mouth.

Moving on.

I'm about to hop down, when his hand on my arm stills me. "Have you seen a crime scene before?"

"Yeah." Back during my internship with the FBI and the police academy, the only reason I felt bad during the presentation of a case was because I'd never seen parts of bodies just randomly lying around. I think it can unsettle anybody.

"Dead bodies too?" He presses the issue and I nod, even though that's only partially true.

While I've seen them, I've never come close or touched them willingly, but I know it's part of the job. "You think we might find something?"

He shrugs and we get out of the car, while he murmurs, "You never know. I'm just making sure you know what to expect. This job won't be for you if you turn green every time."

I don't have the chance to reply or defend myself against what feels like a personal attack, when a police officer greets us. "Agents." He shakes our hands. "Thank you for coming."

"Did you find anything?"

The man exhales heavily. "Part of the first victim, and the second, legs. But other than that, no. I think it was just these two bodies." Kierian doesn't seem convinced, though, as he grabs the gloves, gives me a pair, and puts on the other.

While he hunts for more clues, I look around the forest, registering several details in my mind, trying to build a complete picture that will give me better insight into the unsub's mind.

The forest is located halfway up the hill, with the road several miles from here and the lake. Besides a few hunting shacks, the area is undeveloped despite being situated between two cities. However, it's an open space and not a secluded area, so anyone passing by could have seen the person dropping bodies or driving up here.

So the unsub must have been strong, have a driver's license, and good knowledge of the city and its outskirts. Not to mention he knew the exact place where wolves or coyotes would be searching for food.

But even those animals don't typically feast much on human flesh, just destroy the bodies. It's like the unsub punished the victims even after death, basically showing them one, giant middle finger.

Taking out my phone, I dial the shortcut for Preston's number, and he answers on the first ring. "Yes?"

"Can you check something for me? What's closer to the crime scene? New York or New Jersey?" Maybe we've searched in the wrong location, but we had to narrow it down.

If a different state seems like the stronger possibility, we'll have to transfer the case. "One second." Preston's clicks on his keyboard echo in my ear, and in a second, he replies, "Definitely New York. It's around an hour's ride, give or take ten minutes. It's around two hours to New Jersey."

"The unsub is from New York."

"Right, his MO shows no respect for victims, so he wouldn't spend more time with them than necessary. In his mind, it means giving them attention they don't deserve."

At least we narrowed it down to the city. "Check everyone who recently got out of prison or a psychiatric facility, please."

"Sure." Then he disconnects the call, and I walk down the narrow path among dogs sniffing around for clues.

Kierian kneels, tracing his fingers on the ground and looking closely. I recognize the barely visible tire track. "Police cars?"

He shakes his head. "They won't drive this close to a crime scene."

"But it can't be him. The bodies are several months old and we've had some heavy rains."

"Unless he comes here on a weekly basis." Sometimes serial killers love to visit their crime scenes; they get a special high from the place that fueled their sick desires. It usually works for them until the longing for fresh blood overpowers their pleasure in knowing someone lies in the ground.

That is usually the time they choose new victims, and it becomes a never-ending circle.

Except I don't think that's what drives our unsub; I don't have an explanation for it yet, but something is not adding up for me.

Kierian rises, while shouting to the men nearby. "Check those tracks. We need information on them as soon as possible." Then he briefly glances at me and resumes scanning the environment. "What's going on in that head of yours?"

"It's easier for him to kill than come here."

"Why?"

"He clearly hated those men. He wouldn't give them the time of day after the killing."

"Interesting theory, but we shall see." Narrowing my eyes on his dismissive tone, I'm about to speak a few not-so-nice words to him when we turn in the direction of a huge-ass tree that stands a few feet away from us, as a police officer shouts, "We found something."

We rush over there, and when the criminalist scoots aside, scattered flesh and body parts come into view.

A festered leg and hand, smeared with dirt, have bite marks visible on the skin. The smell coming from them is so offensive stomach acid rushes up my throat. I count to ten in my head to control my natural reaction and then swallow back the bitter taste.

Kierian stands closer to me, bumping his shoulder against mine, and I blink in surprise at his silent support. He can't do much else with his gloved hands. "Are these similar to what you found earlier?" The criminalist nods.

"Yes, they appear to belong to the last victim." And the man proceeds to put them in a bag, while carefully preparing to take fingerprints in case he finds them.

Kierian dials someone, and in a second, Noah's voice echoes between us on loudspeaker. "What is it?"

"We found two more body pieces, but they all appear the same. Looks like only two victims were here."

Noah stays silent, and then asks, "Preston, do you have anything for me?" He is on the line too?

My brows furrow, while Kierian mouths, "Conference call." And then we hear Preston's voice. "No debts or loans, and no illegal stuff. So it's not a revenge or professional kill."

Well, we can cross mafia off the list, but it doesn't suit the unsub anyway.

He won't work for anyone else.

"Can it be Sociopath?" The notorious serial killer who cleaned up half the elite around seven years ago. "Maybe he's back?" Noah asks.

Before any of the guys can reply, I pitch in, "He hasn't been active in years. And the victimology is different."

"I agree with Ella," Kierian says.

Noah orders, "Come back here. We need to review the information before proceeding."

Kierian nods to the police officer. "We're going to head out. Thanks!" We remove our gloves and throw them into the trash. Then he grabs my arm and pulls me to the car.

"What are you doing?" I try to tug my arm away, but it's useless. He doesn't react except to press me to the car, blocking the view of me from everyone else.

"Are you all right?" He scans me from head to toe, and I blink, surprised at the surge of energy between us as he transforms from cold coworker to dominating man who awakens my body with new desires with a single touch.

"Yes." Licking my dry lips, I exhale heavily. "I just don't see... well... *that* on a daily basis. But I'll adjust with practice." Not wanting to create an uncomfortable situation for both of us, I say, "Let's just forget about it." Stepping away from him, I go to my side of the car and get in as he does the same.

My hands freeze on the seatbelt, when he tells me, "You don't run from dead bodies, but you do run from men." Well, apparently, he does remember our one-night stand.

I don't know what annoys me more, the relief flashing through me, or fear where this conversation might lead.

Or rather how I sneaked out of his apartment after he fell asleep, so I wouldn't have to face him the morning after.

In one single night, he made me feel more alive than I've ever been. The emotions he awakened inside me have no place in my life.

"I didn't run." Clearing my throat, I add, "Even the term one-night stand means two people for just one night."

"Thank you for explaining the phrase to me. Here I went through life, letting women walk all over me," he replies cockily, and I want to smack him on the back of his head.

None of it is funny.

"This is not funny, Kierian."

"I beg to differ."

Huffing in exasperation, I take a deep breath, willing myself to calm down. "It doesn't matter anyway. We work together now, so it's better we never discuss it again, okay? There is no point." Since he stays silent, smoothly navigating the car through different turns, I finish with, "We are coworkers." Oddly enough though, the word tastes bitter in my mouth.

What the hell is wrong with me? I shouldn't be this emotional over some guy I just met two weeks ago and shared a few hours of sex with.

Especially not when there are people dying because of a serial killer.

"And nothing else?" He catches my gaze as we stop at a traffic light. "You'll be able to look at me and not think about that night?" he asks, and instantly a flashback hits me, as vivid images dance in front of me.

Biting a pillow to muffle my screams, I close my eyes, my back lifting as Kierian scoots me closer to the edge of the bed, his fingers digging painfully into my ass, probably leaving marks that will last for days.

He opens me up for his assault, sucking on my inner thigh and sending ripples of pleasure through me as his whiskers scratch my skin.

He breathes me in, before asking, "Have you ever been properly fucked by a man's tongue, Ella?" But he doesn't care for my answer, as his tongue pushes into my opening, licking me deep, at once making me aware of every single breath and sensation in my body.

He slides his tongue from one lip to the other then growls against my core, causing a vibration that spreads fire through my entire system.

A moan tears from my throat as I throw the pillow to the side and lace my hand into his hair, pressing him closer to my center, seeking the pleasure he's promised me.

Shaking my head from the memory, I lean back on the seat, my cheeks flushing and heart beating rapidly against my ribcage. I long to gulp air, but I can't with him so close to me.

He chuckles, although it lacks humor, as he speeds up on the road. "That's what I thought, darling." He changes gears and flashes me a determined look. "We are far from over."

As I discovered during our night, Kierian is very good at keeping his promises.

God, what am I going to do now?

*P*sychopath

Unfamiliar emotions swirl through me—although, I'm not sure a euphoric rush of adrenaline at remembering her fear-filled voice could be considered an emotion.

But what brought even more anticipation?

Her mind.

Her desire to catch me is so strong. She sees outside the box and digs into details other people might never notice.

How can I not enjoy playing a game with her?

She would have been a great asset to the team helping catch the likes of me.

Too bad my case will be the first and last she'll ever have.

*E*lla

"Kierian, you look too smug for your own good," Andrea muses while pouring herself a cup of coffee and sending us a smile as the rest of the team hangs around her table, sitting silently deep in thought.

Kierian winks at her, placing his hand on his chest as he sighs dreamily. "Why now, Andrea, is that a compliment? Flattered." She punches him in the stomach, and he lets her, quietly laughing as his gaze catches mine, but I quickly evade his drilling stare.

After our conversation in the car ended, I put on my headphones and blasted music on high so he wouldn't bother me anymore with conversations that confused me.

He didn't push though, just kept whistling under his breath, and I don't know why, but it pissed me off.

No matter how much my body craves him, or how much we have in common, I've learned that nothing but a one-night stand works out in my life. So why does he insist on trying to make things complicated?

My head should be busy with our unsub, not men. Thankfully, I don't have to wait long for a distraction.

"So what do we have so far?" Noah fires a question, drumming his fingers on the desk while looking at the pictures spread before him.

"Not much besides the two dead bodies, with the same MO and nothing connecting them. Both hidden in the same spot."

"Similar crimes outside the state?"

Preston clacks with his tongue. "Nothing."

"The autopsy showed the unsub most likely used scalpels and knives in certain places to torture. Like the liver, stomach, back, and neck. Based on the criminalist's report, they wouldn't lose much blood, but the pain would have been unbearable. Their ribs were broken. He also detected serum in their system." Jacob reads the last part, sliding it to Noah.

"Awake for the torture," he states. "So we're dealing with a sadist?"

"Except—" I snap my mouth shut, not knowing if I should continue my thought, but since everyone looks at me expectantly, I elaborate. "I don't think he's a sadist."

"He is inflicting pain on their bodies. And then lets animals eat the remains. Clearly, he wants them to suffer even after death," Andrea states.

"Or he is punishing them." Preston blinks at my words. "It's like he is getting revenge on something. Both bodies have similar marks. Both male. But they are not connected. What if it's not them he is punishing?"

She rubs her chin. "Surrogates for someone else?"

"Most probably his father." Usually all traumas came from childhood, especially such violence.

"Then both the victims have something in common that reminds him of his father," Kierian supplies, and I nod, but Jacob just curses.

"It still gives us nothing. Not even a hint of where to begin this investigation or create a profile."

Noah scans the board from side to side and then points at me. "Ella, speak with Mary Parker. Maybe she can clue us in on her husband. Andrea, talk with the other family. If we know more about the victims, we will know more about the unsub." Then he shifts to the guys. "Preston, dig deeper, maybe there were cases of similar body dumping? He could have developed a stronger MO over the years."

True. Serial killers learn as they gain experience. Their very first victims rarely undergo the same torture as everyone after them. They try to play with firsts, exploring what answers their desires.

"Jacob, you, Kierian, and I will investigate their workplaces."

Everyone spurs into action, but his defeated expression nags on my mind.

So before he can exit, I call his name, and he turns to me. "What happens if we find nothing?"

"Police will still investigate. Unfortunately, the case for us will be closed. There is only so much we can do."

It can't happen.

It means evil wins, and I didn't come here to let monsters ruin innocent lives.

I will find him.

One hour later

*E*lla

Entering the common room, I notice a beautiful young woman sitting on the couch, drinking water as she holds a small baby sleeping in her arms.

She licks her lips while breathing heavily, and her shoe taps the floor in a nervous manner, like she doesn't know what to expect.

Oddly enough, I don't see sadness or pain in her features; they're usually present during this kind of meeting.

I speak as gently and quietly as possible, not wanting to wake the baby. "Mrs. Parker? Hi. I'm Agent Ella Gadot."

She freezes as she looks at my extended hand, seeming lost for what to do next. She eventually nods and sips a bit more of her water. I've seen many women in my line of work, and her hesitation to take my hand unsettles me. I plaster a smile on my face, hoping it'll ease her a little bit.

"Do you want to put the baby in the stroller?"

She shakes her head, bringing her son closer to her chest. "No, I prefer to hold him." Exhaustion laces her voice, but also fear. Why is she afraid of this? Surely she doesn't think we have her under investigation?

"I'm so sorry for your loss."

She rocks the baby from side to side, as she finally asks, "He's really dead?"

There is no easy way to say it to loved ones. I still remember how an agent delivered the news to me and how it shook me to my core.

A monster killed her husband, the father of their child. He'll never get the chance to see his baby. How can anyone do that?

"I'm so sorry," I repeat and clear my throat. "It's him." She blinks and looks to the side, avoiding my gaze.

Maybe she doesn't want me to see the tears in her eyes? I hate to continue this conversation with a woman who probably still had hope her husband would come back, but work is work. The faster we catch the unsub, the fewer families who will fall to his monstrous ways. "Mrs. Parker, was he acting differently before he was kidnapped? Any weird phone calls? Friendships?"

"No. We'd just moved to the neighborhood. He didn't have time to talk with anyone much. He had no friends here." She pauses, something flashing in her eyes but quickly disappearing. "He just started a new job. He was a lawyer." She pats the baby. "Our son was about to be born. Everything was normal."

"Did he have any changes in temperament? More nervous, aggressive? Any anger issues?" Sometimes great fear in the wake of something provokes aggressive behavior, so maybe he just hid his problems from her.

And based on our records, he didn't have a job, so he must have lied to his wife. Why?

Self-disgust crosses her face, but she replies steadily, "No, he was the same."

Something isn't adding up here, but I see Noah motioning for me to finish it. Clearly the wife doesn't know much, so keeping her here with a child is useless.

"Thank you, I guess there are no other questions." I stand up, but she is still glued to her couch as she raises her brown eyes to me, filled with curiosity.

"Do you know who did this?"

I wish I had an answer to her question; it's the most valid one when this kind of tragedy strikes.

Who and why, and in most cases *why* isn't satisfying or fair, but you learn to live with it.

"No, but I promise we will do our best to catch him."

She turns around to pick up her diaper bag and her shirt tugs on the side, exposing a little of her back. I blink in surprise, noticing several faint scars under the harsh light. Once she is done, she gives me a weak smile. "Thank you for telling me." With that, she leaves, and for a second, I wonder if I've imagined the relief coming from her.

That's not possible, right?

"You all right?" Andrea joins me inside, holding her mug of coffee and offering me mine.

"There is something fishy about this situation."

She pauses with her mug midway to her mouth. "The wife couldn't have killed him."

"No, it's not about that. It's like she wasn't even sad."

"She is probably in shock."

"Or doesn't mourn him much," I mutter, the bitter taste in my mouth staying while I think about this more. "How about Ken's wife?"

"Surprisingly, she stayed calm, just kept repeating that it was over. She seemed relieved actually, but I think it's easier to know for sure he is dead, instead of spending her life with what ifs."

Or when you don't really feel bad for someone killing your husband and can't hide it very well.

I go back to the case, studying the different body parts, but still they have no answers for me.

Why would a wife not mourn the loss of her husband?

What could he possibly do?

What?

And more importantly... did the unsub know?

. . .

P sychopath

Sitting on the school bleachers, I rest my back on the seat behind me as I watch the football practice in full swing. Young guys scream at each other, some pushing and flexing muscles while others keep all their attention on the game, running back and forth even though they don't know the plays yet.

Cheerleaders giggle as guys wink at them, and they murmur things to each other, while stretching and bouncing in place.

A loud whistle erupts and their coach, a muscled man, joins them on the field while waving at everyone.

Instantly, all activity ceases, and the football players stand straight as he watches them approvingly. Especially his son, the captain of the team, who hides from his gaze yet puffs up his chest proudly for people to see.

He is the best on field; his nickname is "machine." He's already gotten several scholarship offers, while his father posed in all the photos with him, preaching that hard work and discipline helps you achieve success.

Kids look at him with adoration and respect. After all, what's there not to like about the guy?

Two kids. Long-lasting marriage. Favorite coach of the year twice and works at the local shelter once a month to help those in need. The community values him deeply and no one gets on the team without his approval. He loves his team dearly, giving them the best, and always protects them.

"All right, kids. Stop staring at the girls and keep your mind on the game." Little snickers echo through the team as he clasps his hands. "We have the most important game coming up. Let's show them who's the best." He swings his gaze through them. "I don't hear your support."

The roar erupts, and everyone jumps to do their stuff as the coach calls to one of the girls who happens to be his daughter.

"Lina, come here." He murmurs something to her, and because they are too fucking busy with their lives, most people won't notice as fear enters her eyes and she winces nervously, her shoulders sagging with each word.

Adjusting my sunglasses better on my nose, I make a decision as a smile spreads across my face.

He'll be perfect.

I don't usually kill so fast, preferring to take my time between victims. I get more of a high from anticipation, and besides, my mentor taught me better. They'll probably close the case since there is nothing connecting my killings on the surface and move on to another one. That's how profiling procedures work. But if I give them more bodies, they'll have no choice but to work on them.

How can I refuse to create one more case for Ella to find the truth faster?

When she finally figures it out, she'll be at my mercy.

I can't fucking wait for that.

*E*lla
Yawning loudly, I stretch my arms while sighing heavily. No clues pop up no matter how many times I read through all the files.

We've spent the rest of the day studying cases that could fit the unsub but come up blank. The guys didn't get much information from coworkers or other people either, only that they were great, all-around men and everyone felt sorry someone killed them.

On the surface, it seems the unsub doesn't have clear preferences when it comes to victims, since one victim was a young man in his thirties and the other was a man in his fifties.

I'm so deep in thought that a voice next to me startles me and my coffee almost spills on the table. "The workday is over." I look up to see Kierian, his gaze sweeping over me.

Only then does it register we are alone in the office, most of the people gone. Normally when the team travels all over the country, they work on the case twenty-four seven until it's solved, but when you work in your own local area, you can go home and regroup.

"I've got nothing."

"Staying here won't solve the problem." He motions to the door with his head. "A fresh perspective in the morning will be better."

It's hard to argue with that statement.

"You're right." I stand up, shut off my laptop, and scoop all the paperwork into my bag. "Crap!" I exclaim, searching for my phone in my pocket. "I need to grab a cab home. My car is in for repair; the thing had to break down today of all days," I mutter, and blink in surprise as his hand halts my movement.

"I'll drop you at home." If it came from any other person, I would gladly agree, but in this case, it's too weird.

Especially with his earlier statement.

"I don't think—"

"Let's go, Ella. It's not safe wandering around the city. I promise you this wolf doesn't bite." I lift my brows, and he chuckles. "At least not outside the bedroom."

"I don't remember much biting." I groan inwardly. Why did I have to go there? I shouldn't encourage his playful behavior. "And for your information, I've been on my own for a long time. I don't need a protector." He doesn't appear impressed with my words; he just holds the door for me, and I quickly slide in and press the elevator button, feeling exhaustion run through me.

"Tired?"

"Like you wouldn't believe." Finally, the doors open, we step inside and ride down, and then he leads me to his car.

"I'd offer dinner, but I suspect my offer would be met with a refusal."

Hilarious.

"Definitely." He chuckles again and we hop inside. A few minutes later, we're heading in the direction of my house, which is located around thirty minutes from the office.

Then it dawns on me.

"You didn't ask where I live." My brows furrow, uneasiness washing over me. I don't think he is dangerous per se, but a girl can get ideas.

"It's in your file, Ella. Relax." He makes a hard turn, and I sway to the side, bumping shoulders with him. Instantly, electricity sizzles between us, but I quickly lean back, avoiding the touch.

He doesn't comment on it, just squeezes the steering wheel tighter.

Topic. We desperately need a topic that can distract us from the sexual tension running high in this freaking car!

"So how long have you been working here?"

"Around three years. I was on the police force before that."

"What made you choose criminal psychology?"

He shrugs and stops at a traffic light, shifting his attention to me, and once again, I'm on the receiving end of his silver eyes. "Because I felt this way I could stop criminals before they did more damage. It felt right at the time."

The way he says this confuses me, so I ask, "It doesn't anymore?"

"There is always frustration when we can't solve a case or someone dies while trying to solve it, even though we are doing all we can. The constant guilt. But then again, I think everyone in law enforcement has the same frustration, one way or the other."

True.

"Any family?"

He flashes me a grin. "Why? Suddenly curious about my life, sweetheart?"

"Don't call me that," I snap, because I hate all this shit. God knows how many women guys call that name, and I feel like when you address someone, it should be a nickname designed specifically for them.

I can hear Chloe laughing in my ear as she called me an idiot while Simone nodded in agreement. They didn't understand my little quirks like that.

"Actually, forget I said anything."

He meets my murmur with a sarcastic comeback. "Apparently, 'forget it, Kierian' are your favorite words thrown my way."

"Do you harass all your one-night stands?" Not that I ever want to think about him with other women, as it creates a deep, red rage inside me.

"I'm hardly harassing you, Ella. And it wasn't a one-night stand."

Oh my God. He's impossible!

He threatens my sanity, and no person should do that. I want to sacrifice my life to catch serial killers, and I won't be able to form any kind of relationship with someone if my head is busy worrying about them.

In normal circumstances, I wouldn't bother explaining or justifying my actions, but I feel like Kierian deserves that. It's not his fault I'm fucked up. "My family was killed by Benjamin Donovan."

He freezes, muttering quietly, "Fuck."

Talking about my family always brings me pain, but it needs to be said so he can put all this crap to rest. So I continue. "It changed my whole life, okay? I don't ever want to come home to find my family dead... again. I don't do relationships. Frankly, I have no clue why I'm telling you all this, considering we had a one-night stand, but there you go. Please drop the subject, Kierian."

"You are the only living victim of his crimes."

"Right. The lucky one." Sarcasm laces my voice. "Someone even offered me a contract to write a book." I shut the door in their face and got a restraining order. How stupid can someone be to be so insensitive to a tragedy?

I expect him to reassure me or tell me he's sorry; that's what people usually do and why I hate to share this tidbit of information.

Instead, he turns the radio louder and continues our ride in silence while I'm slightly taken aback by this attitude. Shouldn't he have additional questions for me? Anything to break the silence that's fallen over us.

And while my initial plan was for him to step back, I can't help the disappointment deep in the pit of my stomach that my fucked-up teenage trauma changed his mind.

Go figure.

Finally, my building comes into the view and he pulls over to the side, the engine running as he gets out, and my brows furrow.

What is he doing?

I follow suit, only to be immediately pressed to the closed door behind me without even an inch between us.

"What are you—" My words die on my lips as he covers my mouth with his, and I gasp in surprise, giving him the perfect opening to push his tongue inside. One hand fists my hair while the other locks tightly around my waist.

All common sense flies from my mind, and instead of freeing myself, I angle my head, giving him deeper access, and we both groan. I can't help but grab his jacket, bringing us closer, although closer is impossible at this point.

No one in this world in my memory kisses as good as Kierian McAvoy. With him, I don't have to think about anything, because only we exist in the cocoon he creates.

He dominates my mouth in a way that makes a promise and stakes a claim, and even though I know it's not meant to be, I give all of myself to this kiss.

My lungs burn, and with a moan I tear my mouth away as we both breathe heavily, gulping air. He runs his nose along the crook of my neck, breathing me in, as I whisper, "Thanks for the goodbye kiss." He bites a little on my skin, sending a hot flash straight through me, and thank God he parked in a secluded area, so no one will see this public display of affection.

He leans back and our gazes clash; his heated one drills into me as if he wants to know my darkest secrets, but I don't have any. "At work, we work. But when we're outside it? We'll explore this. Understood?"

The haze of the kiss doesn't overshadow my determination as I pull away, and surprisingly, he lets me. "Kierian, you don't get to order me around."

"No, but I get to push you out of those chains you've placed on yourself." With that, he gives me one last peck, and murmurs, "Good-night, Ella."

I stand there speechless as he hops in the car and drives away, leaving me alone while confusing emotions swirl in my mind.

Placing my fingers on my burning lips, I wonder just how determined Kierian can be.

CHAPTER SIX

*R*ichmond, Virginia

*E*lla, 18 years old
  "*This is insane,*" *Agent Jordan screams in my face, but I don't budge under his harsh voice. He looks in the direction of Agent Bates, gesturing with his hand to do something with me.*

The agent turns to me, and we hold each other's stare for a short while. He must read my stubbornness, because with a heavy sigh he nods.

"She needs it," he says as if he knows what I'm going through, but I doubt it. To understand my nightmare, you have to live it.

Agent Jordan presses the button on the door, and we step into the prison hall where each move echoes through the space filled with dangerous energy. Goose bumps break out on my skin as the prison officer greets us and motions to the long hall studded with gated doors.

He takes us deeper inside, where we pass several rooms with inmates.

Agent Jordan's hand on my arm tightens as he pushes me forward, not letting me sink into despair, fear, and doom.

After a few more steps, we reach the guarded interrogation room, and with the press of another button, the door slides open while two more officers meet us there.

"He's already inside," one of them says, turning on the screen. My breath hitches as I see Ben for the first time since my graduation.

The room has only one metal table along with two chairs with a two-way glass mirror. He wears an orange jumpsuit. His normally long hair is buzz-cut almost bald. Anticipation is written all over his features. His fingers drum impatiently while he jiggles his legs, clearly barely containing his excitement.

"He is handcuffed to the table, so there is no way he can get to you. However, we will be here the entire time, and if he even attempts to stand or try to hurt you, we'll be by your side," Agent Bates promises while pressing one more button so the doors next to him slide open.

His reassurance does little to soothe me, but I have no one else but myself to blame for this situation.

With fear, though, comes determination. Chloe's father is to be executed in a few days, and I can't let him go without getting an answer to my question.

Just one fucking question, and he can go rot in hell.

Taking a deep breath, I stop there while Ben's attention immediately focuses on me and his mouth spreads in a wide grin.

He tries to stand, but the chains won't let him, clanging against the metal as he angrily pulls on them.

Then he calms down, and says with wonder and joy lacing his voice, "Ella."

Sitting down opposite him, I hold his stare while different thoughts run through my mind.

I've been preparing for this meeting for the last two months, playing it over in my mind hundreds of times, imagining spitting in his face and demanding answers. I cut off everyone from my life, even Chloe, who suffers her own pain. This man destroyed my life and then pretended to be a good guy, when in fact he was the evil one.

But as I sit here, I can't muster an ounce of emotion except deep regret. And before I can stop myself, I ask the one question that doesn't let me sleep at night and wrecks my soul every day. "Why?"

He frowns. "Why did I kill your parents?" he asks so easily, so carelessly, barely curious. Like we are discussing the weather or the latest gossip. A little grin kicks up the corner of his mouth, reminding me of Chloe when something brings her joy. How can I ever stay friends with her? She shares the same face with him. I used to be jealous of the connection she had with her father, their camping trips and soccer games. My father hadn't let me play or do anything dangerous while he constantly preached to me about the future.

How I wish I could hear his nagging voice one more time; I'd give anything for it.

"It brought me pleasure," Ben says, and it snaps me back. I try to understand what he's talking about. "My victims. How their pulse stops once I slice their throats, the fear in their eyes, and the power high it brought me. I wasn't just a dad or a loser husband there. I was the fucking king and their life belonged to me."

Bile rises in my throat from his description, but he doesn't stop. His gaze is faraway, while he almost zones out of everything but his sensations.

Then it hits me.

He is reliving them all over again. "But the little girls... the little girls and their cries while I showed them how much I loved them were the best. Those were the moments worth living for."

My fists clench, barely containing myself from throwing myself at him and beating the shit out of this sick fucker.

Serial killer and pedophile, I fucking hate him. So many destroyed lives because he was chasing some high none of us could understand.

"You were the most beautiful one of them all." What? "When your parents moved into our neighborhood, you were so pretty. Running around in your yellow dress with your dark pigtails, a careless six-year-old." He licks his lips and almost whimpers, while I turn away as if protecting myself from his words. "I couldn't wait to sink my hands into you and strip you of your childlike inno-cence. But your father always stuck around, and they became great friends with my wife, so I had to back down and find other people." The minute the meaning of his words registers, I gasp in shock as he chuckles. "Getting all those other families? They satisfied my desire to kill. Conquering the dragons who kept me away from the princesses, I won them fair and square." This man is sick; what else can explain his fucked-up way of thinking? "But Sarah... she was too beau-tiful to resist. I couldn't help myself." He tugs his chains and screams in frustra-tion when they don't budge. "She begged me not to do it. Nothing compares to the little cries and whimpers of a small girl. Nothing." He digs his fingers onto the table, his eyes sparkling.

My poor baby sister, how could we have never seen this insanity right under our noses?

Death is too easy a sentence for him. He deserves to rot in prison for life. But even then, I don't think he'd ever regret his actions or feel remorse.

How is it possible to live without remorse? And how good a manipulator do you have to be to live in constant deception, a wolf in sheep's clothes? Although calling this piece of shit a wolf, such a beautiful animal, was an insult to the wild creature itself.

"Why?" I repeat my question, and add, "Why didn't you kill me too?" He blinks in surprise while I await his reply, because that's the only question that interests me.

He is so arrogant and narcissistic he thought I'd come to talk about him or the killings. But as much as it might be futile for police and agents or other families, it's not for me.

I only need to know why he left me to live in this world all alone while he took my loved ones away. He wasn't this cruel to other families, but I had to be the only living victim of all his crimes.

He stays silent, and I can't take it anymore. I rise and slam my fist on the table, ignoring the shot of pain that travels from my knuckles to my shoulder. "Fucking why?" I scream in his face while he just rubs his chin.

"I was in the house when you came back from driving with Chloe. I heard you in the shower. It would have been so easy to come and slide the knife over your artery. Your pale skin is made for blood." A droplet of sweat appears on his forehead, so I bang my hand down again, not allowing him to go into some kind of nirvana only he understands. "But there is something about you, Ella... it brings more pleasure to watch you suffer than to kill you."

"You bastard!" I shout, throwing the chair to the wall and dashing toward him, but strong arms grab me from behind.

Agent Jordan locks me in his embrace while he barks an order. "Take him out of here."

Sobs escape my mouth, as I weep for the life I've lost because of one sick, twisted mind who thought it would be interesting to watch me suffer.

My knees wobble and I sit back down, covering my face with my hands while my shoulders shake from crying and the desperation running through me.

Although I got my answer, it hadn't brought me peace or relief.

If anything, it made my suffering even greater.

He leaves, but not before turning back to me with his final blow. "Maybe if you understood the likes of me, you could relate." After that, he leaves, but his words echo in my brain.

No one can understand monsters.

No one can explain this evil.

No one can ever justify them.

But there are people who can catch them.

*P*sychopath

"Please let me go," the man begs, and I barely restrain myself from rolling my eyes, because all their pleadings consist of the same things. None of them takes it like a real man or tries to.

But then again, cowards don't show bravery.

"I have a family—" The tightly placed tape over his mouth shuts him up before I can snap and kill him in a rage, losing all my control.

He pushes at the restraints that chain him tight to the metal chair located right in the middle of my basement. Sweat drips from his forehead down his nose and to his chin; his shirt is soaking wet. He shakes his head, silently pleading again.

Lately, torture isn't bringing me a high, and I do minimal stuff to make them suffer and then kill. But Ella and her interest... it's brought something back.

Something I thought died with all the years of experience.

A desire to make an art of the process.

Her mind works in a different way; she needs more challenge and interest. More hints and clues without answers, so she can dig deeper.

Understand me better so she can finally find me, and in turn, fall right into my trap.

Trailing my fingers through the various blades and ropes displayed on my shelves, an idea forms in my head as a sinister smile spreads on my mouth.

Perfect.

Putting on brass knuckles, I walk to him slowly, building his anticipation. Nothing drives the mind more than uncertainty.

He shifts to the side, not that it helps his position one bit. Grazing it over his shoulder, I pause. "How does it start?" I ask the fucker, and he freezes, tentatively listening to me, probably thinking it will bring him an escape. "A fist here and there. Tripping. Then comes the belt, right?" His eyes widen, as he mumbles something through the tape, but I don't care to hear it.

I know the answers anyway. Oddly enough, all those assholes have the same signature signs, as if they all formed a fucking club where they exchange their experience.

So I punch him hard in the back, causing him to groan in pain, but I don't give him time to catch his breath and deliver another blow to his stomach. All the places where the shirt will cover everything.

So no one will know.

No one will notice.

No one will care.

Unlocking the chains behind him, I give him a little room to move, and he dashes forward, only to fall on his knees with a loud scream when I kick him hard. "Get up." He does, and I repeat my action, while giving him more blows here and there.

The blood is dripping on the floor, his raspy breath echoing through the space as he starts crying, muffled by tape. "Stop, please stop." I walk across to him, wrapping the end of the leather belt tight around my hand as the buckle clicks against my shoes.

"Would you?" He meets my question with a whimper and frantically rips the tape from his mouth, gulping as much air as possible, and I let him, because he'll sure amuse me with his explanation.

"That's not—" I whip the belt at him, hitting him across the back, and he falls back down, barely staying on his knees. "Sometimes—" He continues to justify his actions.

Hitting his other sides with the belt, I continue to kick him in the stomach.

Groans and pants erupt from him as he crawls back to the chair, holding his hands up. "I'll do whatever you want. Just please let me go. I won't do it again."

Right, and the sky is pink.

They always promise and never keep their word, and no matter how many chances a person gives them, they will continue to do whatever the fuck they please.

Memories of the past assault me, my head bursting in agonizing pain as I do my best to block all the screams and blows, but I fail.

Once again, it reminds me why I've stopped the art and focused only on teaching them a lesson.

Throwing the belt to the side, I pick him up and slam him on the table with a loud thud as he thrashes on it, but my punch to his nose stops him real quick. I inject the serum in his system and strap him down to the table.

With gloves on and blade in my hand, I proceed to do what I always do, but this time my mind doesn't have the clarity it usually has during those moments.

Instead, Ella appears, and I dwell on her reaction once she sees his dead body.

My 'welcome to the team' gift.

*E*lla
An annoying sound penetrates through the haze of my sleep, and I dig deeper into the pillow, hoping to escape it.

I've barely gotten any sleep, still conflicted about my new job and Kierian's kiss. I paced the room from one side to the other, practicing a speech to give him so he'll finally stop being an idiot and insisting on something that is never going to be.

And chopped bodies brought back nightmares, reminding me of those pictures I'd seen by accident. I had to take a pill to get some shut-eye; otherwise, I'd have looked like a walking zombie at work. I need a clear head for the case, or I won't be able to help much, and that's out of the question.

Maybe people are right—be afraid of what you wish for.

The sound doesn't stop, and with an annoyed huff, I throw aside the blanket, sitting up and turning on the bedside lamp.

Only then does my hazy mind finally register the phone, vibrations and ringtone loud on the bedside table. Who the hell calls in the middle of the night?

I quickly pick it up, and Kierian's voice greets me on the other end of the line. "Ella?"

"Yep, I'm here." I clear my throat, shivering slightly under the AC blasting on my bare skin.

"We have a new victim, and we are needed on location. I'll be at your place in ten minutes. Be ready." Before I can reply, he hangs up on me, and I glance at the clock.

It's three in the morning. I had no clue when they hired me that they could call me any time. But then again, serials killers don't wait either, striking when people least expect them. I rush to the bathroom and curse when my reflection shows an exhausted woman with her hair all over the place, but I only have time to wash my face, brush my teeth, then put on my jeans and black sweater.

Grabbing my keys, phone, badge, and gun from the cupboard, I head outside and downstairs in time to see Kierian's car pulling up to the curb.

"Thanks for such advanced notice," I mutter, hopping into the car as he drives straight to the highway, moving slightly faster than his usual speed.

"Hi, Ella." A voice from behind me speaks, and I look back.

Preston is resting his head on the window, a thick book on his lap.

"Hey to you too. So I'm not the only one he picks up at night?" Kierian chuckles, and my cheeks heat up, realizing how ridiculous it sounds. "I mean... Shut up." I nudge Kierian lightly in the side when he stops at the red light.

Preston whispers, "Oh." And I see his eyes zero their attention on my elbow as he cocks his head.

Does he find me touching Kierian offending? Before I can ask though, he resumes his reading, so I guess my question isn't important enough to answer.

"That's his way. Don't pay attention to the kid," Kierian murmurs, his voice low.

"I figured as much. Same place?" Work, our interactions should all stay work related for the sake of my sanity.

"Yeah, the fact that we discovered his special place doesn't seem to deter him from there." Focusing on the road ahead of me, I bite my lip, thinking about this information.

Showing this much confidence with the cops and FBI investigating speaks of his arrogance, and that he doesn't have much regard for our intelligence.

"Psychopath," I conclude, because nothing else fits him. Only they crave power, and in this case, he shows us his power by proclaiming himself immune from our investigation.

Preston pitches in to the conversation. "I've searched through the system for any prisoners who got out lately, but nothing comes up. Either they have an alibi or they have tracking monitors for three miles only. Their parole officers would have known if they left their houses." This is bad, because if he is not in our databases, it means we need to search the entire country to catch even a hint of who he is.

Serial killers are consistent, but it's hard to understand his consistency if we don't know the profile.

And to create the profile, we need to figure out what connects them all. Huffing in frustration, I flip through the file, hoping to find something.

He can't just randomly choose his victims if he shows this much restraint. Something must trigger his reflex or memory to act out. And if he hasn't done it before, then a traumatic event must have caused him to snap, creating the desire to kill.

At this point, we have only questions and not a single answer, and it pisses me off.

"But another kill. He is evolving fast. It was almost a year between the previous two. Why another one?"

"To show us his power," Kierian answers. "That he is not afraid, even though we've found the bodies."

"And that he's never going to stop," Preston adds.

"Until we catch him."

"If, Ella. It's always if, remember that." Steel laces Kierian's voice. "Never promise the family, or anyone else for that matter, that you can catch every fucker out there. Sometimes we can't, no matter how much we try. Do not get attached to the case," he warns while I blink in surprise, but I don't have the chance to reply as he stops the car abruptly.

Getting out, I hope we'll find something useful, because his words don't sit well with me. We are supposed to be efficient and do good, not give up at the smallest of problems.

The cops already have the place secured; dogs bark loudly searching for clues while Jacob talks with a witness and Noah is in discussion with a detective.

Kierian gives me a pair of gloves as we slowly walk to the crime scene.

Criminal experts nod at us while pointing at various body parts. "We're done. All yours."

Ducking under the yellow tape, I kneel in front of the body, investigating the usual torture spots, and sure enough, there is a scalpel wound on the liver, chopped fingernails, and his other tells.

But there's more.

"Do you see this?" I trail a finger over the red marks around his neck. "The unsub choked him." Kierian leans closer. "And punched him in several places. The bruises are still fresh." He traces the belt buckle wounds, while looking under the head. "He didn't touch the head or face though."

"He probably wanted the victim to be conscious for the torture," I conclude. When Preston joins us, he shoots a few pictures from different places and angles while I walk around investigating the soil, but it has no footprints.

How the hell is this possible? Is he some kind of ghost who leaves no trace?

Logically thinking, it's quite odd he decided to commit another crime so soon and to drop it in the same place. And rigor mortis hasn't set in yet, so the body has been here only a couple hours, yet animals have still managed to damage it.

"Do we know who the victim is?" I ask no one in particular, but it's Noah who answers me from behind.

"Coach Tanner Davidson. He was leading a winning high school football team. Perfect husband and father. No records. Preston?"

"I ran a search on him. Nothing dirty or illegal comes up. He is not connected with the other victims."

"Perfect family," I whisper, blink, and then address Noah. "Can that be our link? All of them were happily married men with kids."

"Thomas's wife was pregnant."

"Well, on the way then. He didn't let him enjoy being a father." Kierian rubs his chin while picking up something on the grass. He flips it over, and reads out loud, "Davidson's Christmas. The family picture is torn." Indeed, it's cut in two, right in the middle, separating the father from his kids and wife.

"Maybe the father left the family and now the unsub has a vengeance toward those who have something he didn't?" Andrea and Jacob join us as we dwell on that theory. While he clearly has a problem with family men, I'm not sure it was as easy as a divorce. Unless the mother made his life a living hell after that, but then shouldn't his violence be directed at women?

"Andrea, Jacob, you two go to the morgue, wait for the pathologist, and check the other victims again. Preston, dig for clues. I'll speak with the detective. He needs to give me access to their archived records. Something must drive him to this place." Noah then shifts his focus to us. "Kierian and Ella, work a little more on that theory, but also check all the records from the school on the coach. We can't exclude anyone." Once he is done issuing orders, he walks away as we separate to do our assignments.

"You're not convinced about the divorce?" Kierian asks, and I shake my head. "Me neither. This guy wants something, but that's not it."

That's true. I just wish we could find out what before he kills someone else.

"Let's think about his strategy," Kierian says, stepping back from me and circling the place with a leaf in his hand. "He kills them, then brings them here in the middle of the night and dumps the bodies. No bags, no traces, nothing."

"And animals help him out with the rest. It's as if he knows their location, but aren't those restricted areas? There shouldn't be any wolves." At least not the ones that will go unnoticed.

"Unless it's not a wolf." Furrowing my brows, I shake my head, silently waiting for him to elaborate. "What breed of dog is similar to a wolf in nature?"

Um, what? "I'm not a pet person."

He chuckles at that. "Right. Tamaskan dog. It's created by crossing several breeds and reminds me of the wolves. Easy to train, loyal."

"You think he lets his own dog do that?" This twisted man corrupts pets?

"Yes, I'm positive. He can't predict wolves, but with his dog? He knows exactly when the crime is done." He slides his phone open and quickly writes a message. "Preston will check it out later. I just e-mailed him the name."

"If the breed is rare, then we can check through the breeders for owners." He nods and I sigh in relief, this information is at least something.

"I'm starving. Let's have breakfast." He surprises me with his statement, and I open my mouth to protest while he chuckles. "A breakfast won't kill you, Ella." My stomach chooses this moment to growl loudly, humiliating me on the spot. "I think we have a deal."

He moves toward the car, while I shout, "It better be good!"

He just waves without turning back, when Preston next to me murmurs, "Trust me. That place is the best."

Did we become the three musketeers without me knowing? "Why is Noah dragging you around? Wouldn't it be better for you to sit in the office and provide us information?" At least based on my research, that's what hackers usually do. What good does it do to have him with us in the field if we can't call him to check important stuff for us?

"I have a low tolerance for dead bodies and blood." Blinking a few times at this, because it has nothing to do with my question, I wait for him to elaborate. "So Noah thinks it's good for me to come to crime scenes and see it. This way I don't have to puke all the time."

"Why, then, have they assigned you to BAU?" Surely the FBI could have found another use for his abilities.

"I have a degree in psychology. Plus, it's the only interesting depart-ment for me. Anyway, let's go." With that, he leaves me while I wonder about Noah.

The man sure enjoyed giving tough love.

Noah, Preston, Kierian.

There is something about them that unsettles me, each in a different way.

*P*sychopath

My little prey is not as easily convinced as the others. I can practically see the thoughts swirling in her head as she searches desperately for any clues.

I gave her a hint with the family photo; she just needs to move in the right direction.

Ella Gadot is an interesting woman.

Although interesting isn't a word I'd use.

She is a thing of beauty, even in blue jeans and boots along with that black sweater, which only emphasizes her femininity. I've never touched a female body as my true self.

Is it different inflicting pain on them? Different when the woman knows exactly who touches her as sexual desire combines with fear?

Not that I want to bring her agonizing pain like I do to most of my victims, no.

With her, it's about breaking the spirit in that seductive body.

The only valuable thing Ella has left after life dealt her a shitty hand is her unbreakable spirit that can withstand anything.

And I want to see what it takes to strip her bare of it.

Maybe then, I'll understand why it's so easy to break other people.

The game has officially begun.

*E*lla

Digging into the eggs with my fork, I munch on the toast and moan with pleasure as the taste spreads inside my mouth.

Kierian chuckles next to me, winking. "No regrets about coming here, I assume." Swallowing the delicious bite, I shake my head.

The family establishment located on the outskirts of the city reminds me of the wooden houses from fairytales.

Everything is made out of wood, from the chairs to the tables, except the old jukebox, which blasts rock and roll at its finest. Black-and-white pictures are scattered on the walls with an attractive couple in different stages of their lives with their restaurant in the background.

It's full and homey, and I can't believe I've missed this place after living here for the last decade!

"None at all!" Then I address Preston, who flips his book, concentration written all over his features. "Are you hungry?" He glances down at his pancakes and then shrugs, resuming his reading.

Seriously, this guy has to be seen to be believed. An interesting person for sure, but I wonder how he keeps friends and relationships with this approach. Or does he just say *bon voyage* to whoever decides to leave his ass?

"Pres, food."

Preston gives Kierian a confused look but then nods and puts his book away. He tentatively tries the pancake and then continues to eat it quickly, taking big bites as fast as he can.

"Don't choke on it," I mutter, but I don't have much time to dwell on it as Andrea and Jacob join us, sitting in the nearby seats. Kierian called them on our way here, and since no one had a proper breakfast, they agreed immediately. I've yet to discover the dynamics of the group, but they seem to share a tight need for friendship. Although, based on what Preston said on the way here in the car, they rarely hang out together outside work.

I imagine they want to spend it with normal people who don't remind them of their job that requires always delving into sick minds. Everyone needs to rest, even FBI agents.

"Hey, guys," I say, and Andrea grins at me while Jacob just grunts. How long does it take this guy to accept a new coworker exactly? I don't need new friends, but his attitude annoys me.

"You want the usual?" Jacob asks her, and when she nods, he gets up to order and she shifts her attention to us.

"Okay, this is definitely our unsub." As if there was a doubt. "Although he beat him up, everything else matches like Ella said." She pauses, and then says, "Something must have gotten him angry with the man." Taking the folder out of my purse, I open it to study the pictures of the previous murders and the new one.

"Or he just felt like he needed to punish him more."

Andrea frowns. "But serial killers don't change their signatures." That's true, but it's not adding up to me. Why would he risk so much?

"Unless something triggered him," Jacob pitches in as he sits next to me and points at the last victim, who has belt bruises on his back. "This is provoked violence. These are not controlled."

"A memory." Taking out a pen, I place a blank paper in front of us and then draw several circles. "Here is our unsub and all his victims— well, those we know of. He is consistent with these wounds." I point to the lines on the liver, neck, stomach, and back. "But these are new." Now I point at the knuckles, shoulders, and large bruises that weren't present on the other victims. "What usually inspires this kind of rage in psychopaths who plan everything?"

"The victim may have said something that triggered him," Preston suggests.

"Correct. Something in the coach's life must have reminded him of his own childhood. People usually beg in those situations. What did he say that provoked the violence?" I think a moment, and then add, "We need to speak with his family. I think they can give us better insight on the situation at home."

Jacob nods. "Noah already called them in."

I just hope it will give us some results. Something attracts him to those perfect families, but what?

CHAPTER SEVEN

New York, New York

Ella, 21 years old

Rushing inside the building, I quickly pass by the secretary who gives me a stern look, and with a wink, I knock on the door.

After a second, I hear a loud, "Come in." I enter Dean Holt's office, who sips her morning coffee.

"Ella, lateness certainly becomes you," she says, and I wince, hating the fact that whenever she calls me to her office, I end up late.

In my defense, she always wants to hold our meetings in the morning, and after a nightshift, it's impossible to drag myself away from bed. I always manage to oversleep for five minutes, but those five minutes are crucial as my freaking roommate always hogs the bathroom. Last night, I had only enough strength to crash on the bed, and no way did I want the dean to smell alcohol on me, even though I didn't drink it.

"My signature mark."

She shakes her head at my humor, but I notice how the fine wrinkles at the corner of her eyes deepen, and she motions for me to take a seat.

Dean Holt is one of the sweetest people I've ever known, but she rules the psychology faculty with an iron fist. She will forever help you if you need any help, but fuck with her or her program, and you are screwed.

She usually has meetings with me once a month to discuss my progress on certain projects and evaluate my grades for the scholarship, because I'm also getting a minor in journalism. I love reading, writing, and researching, so I figured, why not? The scholarship doesn't cover minors though, but thanks to my dean, she has managed to snag a deal for me. As long as I tutor new kids in English, the university will grant me my minor.

So, overall, Dean Holt is one of my favorite people.

"What's up, Dean? You never call me more than once a month." We saw each other two weeks ago, so why am I here now?

All humor leaves her as she opens her drawer and takes out a manila envelope. I recognize my transition papers, and my mood lightens. "You approved my specialty?" I finally have the chance to elect my specialty in criminal psychology, although I've already read all the books on the subject, having a friend in the fourth year. I had to apply for cognitive psychology, because they didn't have enough places in the program when I switched my majors.

She locks her hands on the folder, playing with her thumbs, then shifts her attention to me. The excitement dies inside me. "I can't do that, Ella."

"Why?" So it's not a coincidence everyone has tried to get me to change my mind? All the professors are against my decision, claiming I will have greater success in cognitive psychology.

Except that's not the reason I joined the major to begin with.

She pauses again, her face darkens, and realization hits me. "Because of my family." She flinches, but I have no reaction.

In four years, I've learned to live with the truth. To be that special girl who managed to escape the killer, who lived in the same house with him, who was best friends with his daughter.

It's not hard anymore; it's just an annoyance that will always be there, especially with the internet supplying all the information for curious psychology students.

"You don't have to sacrifice your life for this," she says, and I frown while she elaborates. *"You were given a gift when you were allowed to live. It doesn't mean you have to spend your whole life catching serial killers just because you*

didn't know Chloe's father was one." Her words are like cold water thrown on me; they freeze me, and for a second, I can't breathe.

"That has nothing to do with it. I want it."

A humorless chuckle escapes her as she takes out a paper.

"When you applied to this university, you dreamed of being an international journalist who would travel all over the world, snapping beautiful pictures along with writing exciting articles." She shifted in her seat, leaning closer. "Then, after the tragedy struck, you decided being a prosecutor was more interesting. Because you suddenly wanted to catch criminals." I open my mouth to defend my decisions, while she fires more information at me. "And then when Benjamin was caught, you changed to psychology. Ella, you are on your third year of studies. Don't tell me you don't see the psychological pattern here."

Denial rises inside me, and I shout, "No!"

"Yes! The guilt for surviving the attack and for living with him makes you feel responsible for everyone else. Ella, nothing that happened was your fault."

I can't listen to this anymore, can't let this world-famous psychologist analyze me and my behavior. Because acknowledging her words will mean opening myself up to the emotions and memories and pain, and there is no place in my life for that.

I stand up swiftly, the chair crashing against the floor from my push as I adjust my backpack on my shoulder. "I don't have to listen to this." I don't threaten to switch universities, since I'm stuck here with my scholarship. I will get my degree in a master's program then; it will take a little longer, and I'll have to struggle a bit more, but at the end of the day, I'll still get it.

And help those in need.

No one can stop me.

I'm almost out of the office, when Dean Holt speaks one last time to me, and her words stab my heart with an imaginary razor-sharp knife. "No matter how many lives you save, you will never bring them back."

But it's one more truth I don't want to look at, so I silently leave her office while blocking all the thoughts swirling through my brain.

What everyone fails to realize is that I have no choice.

It was taken away from me four years ago.

. . .

*E*lla

The girl is sitting on the couch in the office. The captain of football team is pacing back and forth while running his fingers through his hair nervously, glancing at his mother in another office, a door away from them.

His sister, the cheerleader, scrolls on her phone. Probably without realizing it, she bites her nails, a gesture that suggests nervousness or that something bothers the person, but she cannot speak about it.

I don't have to speak to them to figure out that "perfect family" is not a term suitable for this one.

They both halt their movements and straighten as they notice me entering the space. "Hi, I'm Agent Gadot. I'm so sorry for your loss." They nod, but I don't see an ounce of sorrow on their faces.

Just like I didn't see on Mary Parker's.

"Thanks. So Dad is really dead?" Dylan asks abruptly, and Kira elbows him lightly, fear crossing her features when she glances at me.

"Yes."

He exhales in relief, but quickly clears his throat. "Do you know who did it?"

I shake my head, proceeding gently. "We will do our best to find him. But for that, we'd need your help." He frowns, while his sister yet again stays quiet.

"We don't know anything." Defensiveness laces his tone, which will probably make it almost impossible to get him to listen to me.

"Have you seen anything strange lately in your father's behavior? Like he was absent, quiet, or had flashes of violence?" Basically anything that can indicate if the unsub was communicating with him, threatening his peace.

They shift uncomfortably. "He was his usual self," Dylan replies, focusing his attention over my shoulder. "Nothing special. We were in rigorous training due to the championships, but that's about it. You can ask Mom for more." He rises. "If you don't mind, can we leave now? You'll have much more luck investigating the case without wasting your time with us." He grabs his sister's elbow so she'll get moving. "Come on, Kira."

She doesn't listen; instead, she fires a question at me. "Was his death painful?"

"Kira—"

"I want to know, Dylan," she hisses and looks back at me, waiting.

"Yes, I can't get into the details right now, but it was painful. And he suffered."

"Thank you." She exhales heavily. "For the last few weeks, there has been this guy. He sits on the benches, wearing glasses and a hoodie. He watched us during practice." She bites on her nail. "He always comes at the same time. Never failed to show up."

The unsub.

Methodical about his timing and hunting. So we weren't wrong when we assumed he hunts them down after knowing certain things about them.

But weeks? It's showing great restraint, too great.

"I appreciate this information." They nod, and I hold the door open for them as they rush toward their mom who just left Andrea.

The woman hugs them close, and murmurs, "It's all right." And then I blink in surprise as I see several bruises on her neck.

"How did you get those?"

She has a deer caught in headlights look, but she just shrugs. "The other day, I fell down on the stairs. I-I-I haven't been sleeping well since my husband didn't come home. Nothing serious. We'd like to go if you don't mind. We are really tired." Avoiding my gaze; fumbling with her fingers; stammering.

She is lying to me and thinks she can hide it; unfortunately for her though, I've seen such cases on a daily basis.

All abused women magically become clumsy on the stairs.

They go to the elevator, when Andrea joins me, and murmurs, "Nothing. Perfect marriage."

"And no tears, right?"

"Yep. It's like she is glad he is gone."

"So are the kids."

Our unsub is starting to look more and more like a Robin Hood, at least in his mind.

But to check my theory, I have to dig for more information, but I know one fact for sure.

He saves them all from the perfect family image, giving them freedom.

Freedom he was denied as a child.

*P*sychopath

It's always interesting for me to see the families of my victims, especially those with grown-up kids.

I search for relief on their faces, or happiness, but all I mostly find is confusion. Especially on the wives' faces. It's like they don't know what to do anymore once the monster is gone.

It's different with kids though.

As I watch them pressing on the elevator button, anger comes from the boy in waves as he snaps at his sister, who continues to bite on her nails. She exhales heavily, but hangs her head low while her mother just shakes her head.

He is probably mad he wasn't the one to kill him or that he got off lightly. He won't ever feel what it's like to have the fucker at his complete mercy and be the one in control of the situation.

It's for the best though.

Rubbing my chin, I put the fucking mask back on and turn to my colleagues to solve this case.

*E*lla

A pile of folders lands on my desk, and I raise my eyes to meet Preston's, who exhales in exhaustion. "Man, those were heavy." He wipes his forehead and then explains. "Noah wants you to check those out."

"What are those?" Isn't it easier to check everything through a computer?

"Messages from victim's phones. Maybe something will catch your attention, some similarities. I ran a quick check; no related numbers show up, but based on messages, we might find some clues."

I'm not sure how this can help the investigation, and it looks more like a waste of time, considering nothing connects them, but I nod anyway.

Can't argue with the boss!

"Sure. Do we have only one case until it's solved?" I'm familiar with protocol, but aren't there other things to get to? According to Kierian, we aren't even sure if we can catch the guy.

Preston blinks and then nods. "We move on once we are done with a profile or semi profile. Otherwise, it's too hectic juggling all information at once. Although, if a critical case comes in, we do switch our attention there and pull all our resources."

"How long does it usually take to create one?"

"Depends on the case. It can take months for some cases, as the serial killers don't show up and we have no clues. And then you know how it is with kids. We have to act within twenty-four hours. But we are BAU-2, so we deal with serial killers. We only work with the child department when they need help." Yeah, the golden rule. Most children didn't survive if they were kept for longer.

Like Sarah.

The memory of my little sister singing as she colored in her book, lying on her stomach in my room, enters my mind and I can practically smell her orange juice.

"Ella, look! It's a bird!" She flashes me her gap-toothed smile as I sit next to her and study the drawing.

She used so many vibrant colors it's hard to understand what kind of bird she was aiming for, but since she watches me expectantly and awaits my reaction, I hug her close, and say, "It's beautiful."

"Yay!" And that's when Mom calls us downstairs for dinner.

"Ella?" It takes me a second to realize Preston has been calling my name for some time now and I shake my head, plastering on a smile, because I hate his concerned stare. "You all right?"

"Sorry. Yes. Don't pay me attention."

He drills me with his stare for a moment, but then lets it go. "Kierian should help you out." He clears his throat. "I'm gonna go now." Then he strolls to his office that I've discovered is located in the far corner, down the hall.

This job sure brings up hurtful memories unexpectedly. The case doesn't even remind me of my situation. What will happen if a child is kidnapped or the whole family murdered? Kierian is right; I need to learn to distance myself from the job.

I can't get attached to the case.

My phone vibrates on the desk, and seeing the caller ID, I wonder why she would call me when I'm at work.

I walk to the far corner of the office, not wanting anyone to accidentally hear Chloe on the other end of the line. "Yes?"

"Hello, birthday girl!" she screams into my ear, and it dawns on me.

Today is my freaking birthday; no wonder the nightmares are back. They usually become the strongest around my birthday, when I miss my family the most. With all the excitement over the job and this difficult case, I haven't paid attention to the date.

I roll my eyes, even though a smile pulls on my lips. "As always, I wish you all the greatest things in the word. Except new friends." She pauses. "You already have that covered."

"Well I'm glad to at least be succeeding somewhere," I say while she laughs.

"Seriously, girl. Appreciate what you have. How are you?"

"Good. At work." I hear David, her husband, muttering something to her in the background as baby Travis whimpers, and glancing at the clock, I suspect it's the food.

"Already?"

"We have a difficult case." And tons of folders to read through, so I say, "If that's it—"

Another voice joins us and cuts me off. "You won't get rid of us so easily. We're going to party tonight." Simone greets me; she's probably already e-mailed me a birthday message. For some reason, the girl always does it through e-mail.

"Correct. We are going to the best club in the fucking city. Simone got us in. Peter was kind enough."

Peter and Simone met on a cruise two years ago, and it was love at first sight, or at least that's what they both claim. They married shortly after in a beach ceremony, and only then did she find out that he was heir to an apartment dynasty. Long story short, he was rich as hell and spoiled her all the time. Not that she quit teaching school though; she loved her students to pieces.

"I've been up since three o'clock and still have tons of work to do. And it's Wednesday. Can we reschedule it for the weekend?" The wine already stood in my fridge so I could celebrate with my family's picture on the table; everything else was just for my friends.

Collective groans and moans erupt, and I sigh in exasperation. "I gather that's a no." Amusement laces my voice, because they are such dorks. Both of them get so bored with all the family stuff; they want to go out, and my birthday gives them the perfect excuse to leave their kids with their husbands.

"We bought dresses. And already promised great sex to the guys. We have to go," Chloe pleads.

Simone adds, "And you will unwind a little bit."

Crooking my neck to the side, I wince at the stiffness. Maybe it's not a bad idea to go out tonight.

Dancing always helps me relax, and God knows, after all the images, I need that.

"Okay. So do we meet there or—"

I pull the phone away as they squeal loudly, and then Simone says, "We'll pick you up. Be ready by nine." They hang up, and I just shake my head.

Crazy girls, but the best kind. I wouldn't have survived in this world without them.

I sit back at my desk and open the first file, when a shadow looms over me. "You on reading duty too?" Kierian's voice sends shivers down my spine, and I want to smack myself.

I'm acting like a hormonal teenager around this guy!

"Yeah."

His brow lifts at this curt reply, but he shrugs and grabs a nearby chair. "Let's divide them," he offers, and I nod.

"Just half and half or by victims?"

"Half and half is better, because then both of us can study different messages. Get the feel of both victims."

Yeah, it does sound good.

I expect him to talk about yesterday or give another innuendo, but he doesn't. Instead, he is completely engrossed in the process, and in a while, I relax and concentrate fully on the work.

Nothing much comes up beyond the usual stuff.

Meetings, sales notifications, some random texts.

I pick up the red marker and circle a few words that seem to repeat whenever both of them messaged their wives. Leaning back, I quickly scan other files and, sure enough, I have the same picture greeting me.

"No affection," Kierian says. He must have come to the same conclusion as I did.

Before we can brainstorm on it, Noah and Preston join us. "Anything?" our boss asks grimly, and Kierian looks at me.

Okay then.

"As much as those guys claimed to have perfect marriages, nothing in their texts indicates that. All messages are short, to the point, and usually include an order. Cook this. Clean that. Pick up the kids. You can't go outside." I give him the file with a few marked words and he scans it. "So far, that's the only thing that connects them. The coach is the same way with his kids."

"Maybe the victims weren't into texting," Noah points out, and while that might be the case, I'm not convinced.

"Still though. Not one kind word? It's unusual."

"I agree with Ella. These men seem like assholes." Kierian sips his drink. "But being an asshole doesn't mean they deserved to die, and it doesn't give us any more clues." He then addresses Preston. "Did you check on dog breeds?"

Preston nods and places a piece of paper in front of us. "I called everyone in the city who could have sold that breed of dog. I'm running the names they've given me through the system, but so far, everyone turns out legit. So for now, it's a dead end."

"He could have bought it in another city." Drumming my fingers, I add, "Or it's another breed similar to a Tamaskan?"

Noah stays silent, just frowning, and then exhales. "Preston, continue the search for names. It's our only clue. If he doesn't strike again, the case will be unsolved. The police have nothing as well. The unsub either knows our system or is extremely smart. No DNA, no traces on the victims' bodies to indicate where he might have held them." He gives us a curt nod and leaves.

"I hope we find him," I mutter, and that's when Kierian laughs.

My brows furrow in confusion. What is so funny?

"This is not a TV show, Ella. We work with local law enforcement and help them to see the traits or give them clues to who it might be. But we don't go catch them per se. We don't do field work and surely do not barge inside houses with guns. Most of the time, our job is studying victimology."

"I'm aware of what our job is, thank you very much." Annoyance laces my tone, but he ignores it.

"I don't think you are. We create profiles, and then it's the police's job to get them. So you are not here to *catch* serial killers." He makes air quotes in a mocking gesture when he says *catch*. "But you are here to create a profile that *might* help catch him. Remember the difference."

What am I? A fifth grader who he explains the logistics of BAU work to?

"I really appreciate the explanation, Kierian. I don't know what I'd do without you," I reply, sarcasm coating my every word. "BAU needs more people like you."

He winks at me, cocky jerk!

"Good." Then he grabs my arm, bringing me closer, and I look around to make sure no one sees us.

"What the hell are you doing?"

He ignores my hiss; instead, he leans to me, and whispers, "Happy Birthday, Ella." I blink, surprised. "I'd have gotten you a gift, but I suspect you don't like them."

That's true. They hold very little meaning to me, and the only gifts I do accept are from my best friends, because they don't know any other way.

"The kiss last night—"

"Was out-of-this-fucking-world good?" he supplies. I punch him in the stomach, but he merely grunts softly. "Too light? Should have gone in stronger?"

"Should have never done it!"

"You didn't say no."

"Really low."

He chuckles, removing the lock of my hair that fell to my forehead, and I immediately look around, afraid someone might have seen him. "Just the truth. Outside work, we date. Here though? Focus on the work, Ella." He winks at me and gets up, heading toward the conference room while I sit dumbfounded.

Date?

*P*sychopath

She gathers her stuff into her bag, rushing outside to escape Kierian.

She doesn't appreciate his advance the way the guy would have probably liked.

That pleases me, but it doesn't change the fact that I want to choke her and kill him for their kiss last night.

I heard her phone call with her friends; they want to celebrate her birthday somewhere fancy and think it will help her to heal and chill.

Only one broken soul can recognize the other.

But for her to stroll into the bar unaccompanied?

No fucking way.

Spinning around to face the guys who give me questioning glances, I say, "How about a drink?"

Surprise crosses their faces as they share a look but nod anyway.

Perfect.

I wish I could grab her and drag her to my basement, but the time isn't right yet.

I'm tempted to break my rules for her, very tempted.

But where would be the fun in that?

CHAPTER EIGHT

New York, New York

Ella, 24 years old
*Loud cheers erupt as I hop on stage and wave at everyone while
the chief of the New York Police Department holds the diploma for me, a bright
smile on his face. "You deserve it, kid."*

Fuck yes, I do!

*"Thank you," I reply, and quickly get down while Chloe and Simone clap
like proud moms whose kid has finally graduated.*

"Relax, girls."

*They hug me instantly, and then Chloe whispers into my ear, "You are
almost there." Pleasure spreads through me as I squeeze her tighter and look up,
hoping my parents are proud of me.*

*Through all the sleepless nights working at the local coffee shop while
busting my ass for my master's degree and then attending the police academy
with no one on my side, the only thing that's kept me going is the knowledge that
I'll do something good for the community.*

That I'll be able to stop those monsters who so carelessly destroy all those lives that deserve better.

"*Now we need to get you out of the dump you've been living in.*" Simone scrunches her nose, a horrified expression crossing her face as she imagines my studio on the outskirts of the city with the most affordable rent.

"*I can't now. I need to finish my internship with the FBI, and only then can I find a job to afford a decent place.*" I heard from a girl who worked there that it would play in my favor later on if I interned with them, so that's my intention.

Chloe and Simone shake their heads in disbelief. "*Do you have any savings?*" I nod, not wanting to elaborate on my secret.

Mainly, I help a private investigator with his cases when he needs to figure out if the spouse is cheating or who is stealing. Not much psychology is used, but hey, at least it gives me experience in the investigative work and pays the bills nicely.

In addition, I mostly take pictures when following people, and there is an unmistakable thrill about holding a professional camera in your hands and allowing the beauty to come out of it.

Sometimes at night, what-if thoughts come to me, like imagining what would have been if I'd chosen photojournalism as my profession the way I always dreamed of. But those moments are rare, and it's enough for me to glance at my family photo to remind myself that now my career has a purpose.

"*Okay. Then let's go to my place, order pizza, and have some wine.*" They hook their arms with mine, while dragging me in the direction of the exit, probably thinking they can hide their intentions. It's the moment all families start taking pictures, enjoying their time, and my friends want to spare me any poignant emotions.

A sad smile tugs on my lips as I tighten my hold on them and thank God that at least with everything else fucked up, he gave me my friends and my career.

Somehow, this will have to be enough for the rest of my life.

O ne Year Later
       "*I'm sorry, but you can't be an agent.*" The words are like cold water splashed over me.

Swallowing down the resentment in my throat, I ask, "Why?"

The man sitting behind the desk watches me carefully as if weighing his next words. But then he exhales heavily. "Truth be told, Ella, you'd be perfect. You have a degree, police academy experience, internship, recommendations, and you are smart. Not to mention, you were one of the best in your class."

"But?" I don't need his long-ass speech about me being good. I already know that anyway. But why has this man allowed other students to get their badges and then kicks me out of the academy.

Does he even realize he just crushed the future I have so desperately worked for?

"You are mentally not suitable for this job. Your past—" He takes a deep breath, his voice becoming gentle. "It will make you emotional on the job. It could trigger memories. With you, there is always a risk. You didn't pass the test."

Yeah, I failed just one fucking question when they asked me how I felt about what happened to me.

Maybe I got a little bit emotional, but how can they turn it against me?

"Your decision is final?"

He nods, and I grab my file. "Thanks for nothing, then. Goodbye."

I open the door to get the hell out of this place before tears threaten to spill, when his voice stops me. "For what's it worth, I think you would have been a great agent." A beat passes. "No one can outrun their past."

Yeah, well, fucking watch me.

*E*lla

    "Is this really necessarily?" I wonder aloud as the cab stops at the famous club in town that has a line as long as the Grand Canyon. Simone bursts out laughing while Chloe glares at her.

"Don't encourage her behavior." She fishes for a twenty for the cab driver, and we all get out, our heels clicking on the concrete while the barely audible music can be heard behind the club doors.

Several bouncers stand scanning the crowd before letting them inside. I don't miss how the majority of them are turned away and some of them even cry.

I raise my brow at this, hiding my smile, because the idea of being sad over such a minor thing is truly hilarious to me.

While I have nothing against clubbing—sometimes I even seek it out—I don't feel like doing it on my birthday. Turning twenty-nine is special and all, no regrets there, but my birthday always reminds me of my family. So Chloe always insists we do some shit on it, like coming to this establishment, for that very reason. I know this one was created by Damian Scott a few years ago, but that guy disappeared, never to be seen again.

I have no clue who is in charge now, but clearly the rules haven't changed.

Chloe bounces to the guys, flashing them a grin as she hooks her arms into Simone's and mine. "We are here to party, boys." One of them opens his mouth to say something, but then his eyes run down our figures.

He nods as if finding us good-enough looking, and then he opens the rope for us to enter. I want to knock him upside the head for doing that, and Chloe must have guessed my mood, as she quickly drags me to the hallway.

Well, the club is something else; I'll give the owner that.

Gold wallpaper covers the walls while the floor is made of black, shiny stone, which allows women to walk freely in their high heels. Dancers move with grace on stage, probably arousing every male in proximity; waitresses wear provocative gold shorts, black corsets, and black stockings with stilettos. The light is dim, and the air is oddly fresh. Pearls dangle from the completely mirrored ceiling, decorate the corner booths that are upholstered in gold velvet, and add a touch to the exquisite diamond chandelier, which somehow manages to give the club a mysterious allure. There are couches and VIP lounges, and apparently a VIP corner on the second floor with a mirrored-glass balcony offering a view to the whole club... and several bouncers. I have a feeling there are cameras too, but they aren't visible. People look as though they've stepped out of a *Vogue* magazine, and they spend time trying to be sophisticated as they drink and dance, and now I understand the crowd outside.

The people who are here received a private invitation and are the elite, the high society of Manhattan. So all the folks outside waiting in line are meant to be playthings for the invited elite. The bouncer first had to be sure the people had good assets and would sell well. Sex could be bought. Especially in a society like theirs.

Simone marrying a rich magnate surely opens the doors for us we never expect, but then Chloe loves it.

I'm neutral. I can't say I mind coming to nice places, because honestly, who would? But it's not as if I make it my mission to attend every fabulous place in this city.

Simone points at the booth in the middle of the club and screams over the music. "Let's get a table and then order something. I'm starving." Even though clubs are generally places to drink, this expensive establishment has one of the best cuisines in the world, and it's worth every penny. It's a crime to come here and not eat.

I'm about to trail behind them when I notice Tim waving at me frantically from the bar, and a smile spreads across my face. "Be right back," I say, pointing at Tim, and Chloe winks as I dart toward him. In a second, I hug him over the counter as he squeezes me tightly.

"Hey, girl!" He leans back and whistles. "Come here for a kill tonight?"

I laugh while pushing my hair over my shoulder, glancing down at my tight, black dress that emphasizes my petite form. The red lipstick is the only color I've used in my attire.

"Not at all."

Tim wiggles his brows. "No shame in wanting to score, babe." Tim and I met in our last year of high school. He dreamed about becoming a musician. He would play his new songs to me in the basement of his parents' house and dream about forming a band, although he never clicked with anyone.

He still plays occasionally, but most of the time, he prefers bartending. I know his parents are extremely rich, so I don't understand why he never did anything with his life.

I don't feel like asking either. We catch up from time to time in a bar or some common parties, but that's about it. He once tried to hook up with me, but I refused. Friends are off-limits for one-night stands, just one of my rules.

"Today is my birthday."

His jaw drops. "Well, shit." But then he quickly grabs the silver shaker from behind him and gets all the ingredients for a manhattan. "It'll be done in no time and on the house." The drink is usually stirred, but I've learned a long time ago that Tim has his own ways.

"What will the boss say?" I question, not wanting him to get in trouble over this stupid birthday stuff.

"He has no objections, trust me." He agitates the shaker, and then continues, "So I heard you finally found a way to work as a criminal psychologist. Digging serial killers now, huh? I always said you crave the dark side, wild girl of mine."

Plastering my palms on the counter, I whisper, "You have no idea." He stops his movement as if unsure what to think about my words, but then he must have noticed my mischievous smile, because he grins. Then he whistles to a nearby waiter. "Hey, J! Ask the DJ to change the song to 'Serial Killer' by Lana Del Rey. Fits the mood." And then he continues to amuse me while I wait for my drink so I can return to my friends and celebrate my birthday.

If I'm in the club, I might as well use the opportunity to have fun and let loose.

I'll have time for grief and work tomorrow.

𝒫 sychopath

She bursts out laughing again, running her hand through her silky black hair as she enjoys the company of the skinny blond, who efficiently creates drinks for all the demanding people. Her perky ass is visible through the dress as she leans forward, and my hands twitch to spank her, so she'll know not to flirt with anyone else.

Wanting her has nothing to do with sex; in fact, it's the last thing on my mind. I crave to hurt her, so her mind will be filled with only me and the fear of what I might do to her. With her, I won't have to hide, and just imagining it makes me harder than I've ever been in my life.

But the fact that her attention belongs to another man displeases me to the point of the glass cracking in my hand, cutting slightly into my skin, but I don't give a fuck.

I'm the most important man in the world for her to be with, and she shouldn't look at mere individuals like that guy.

People like me don't feel remorse, so she should be very careful. For the idea of a sexual high with her, I can eliminate anyone standing in my path without thinking twice.

When mine strolls around the city, easy prey for men, would I do nothing about it?

No fucking way.

"Is that Ella?" one of my colleagues asks.

I can't call them friends if most of the time they act like idiots and can't even catch me. But then again, for that, you'd have to be smarter than me, and that's impossible for them.

"Yeah," I reply, and then she spins around with her red drink in hand, sucking on the straw. She scans the place, probably for her friends, but then her gaze lands on us, and her eyes widen as her breath hitches for a second.

And I hate it.

Because who she wants is not me.

*E*lla

I can't believe this! The one night I decide to go out, and my coworkers are out too.

Granted, it's not forbidden, but I didn't plan to wear a short dress and heavy makeup in front of my boss!

Talk about him not taking me seriously.

Right in front of me, I see Noah, Preston, and Kierian occupying a booth with whiskey and nuts on their table, while women nearby trail their fingers on their glasses and bite their lips, eating up the attention Kierian gives them when he only chuckles and winks.

Noah frowns at him, gulping his whiskey, and Preston just quietly sits there, uncomfortable about the whole thing. I have no idea why he is even here, considering he barely leaves the lab.

Clubbing doesn't seem to suit him much, as harsh as it sounds.

I try to blend between the bodies, but I have no such luck, when Noah calls, "Ella!" I pause and then plaster a smile on my face, turning around and facing them once again, but now their whole attention is on me.

They rise from their seats as I come closer, tugging my hair behind my ear. "Hi, guys. I didn't see you."

"Right," Kierian says, and I barely restrain myself from snapping at him, because no one on this planet confuses me more than this guy.

He is hot and cold, a whore, and a mastermind who knows his job. He is sweet one moment and then gruff the next; his constant mood changes give me whiplash.

And most importantly, I don't understand why it bothers me so much and why I think about him all the freaking time. It's not like I don't have more serious matters to attend to. Or that it was me who pushed him away.

One-night stand, Ella. He was a one-night stand.

But somehow repeating those words in my head doesn't help me, and I want to scratch the women's eyes out for admiring him too much.

I sip a bit more of my drink, hoping it will ease my stupid emotions, and flash them a grin. "Well then, have fun. I'm here with friends, so—" The words barely leave my mouth, when Chloe wraps her arm around my shoulders.

"Well, hello there. Are you here to celebrate this girl's birthday as well?"

I groan inwardly, because the minute she says that, Preston and Noah blink and quickly congratulate me.

"Happy birthday, Ella," Noah says, and Preston just grunts.
Great.

"Would you like to—" Chloe starts, but I quickly cut her off, not wanting to spend this evening with them. It's one thing to see them, another to drink with them.

I prefer to have my own personal space and not be worried what I might do drunk while my boss watches me.

"Well we don't want to bother you. Have fun tonight, guys." They raise their glasses and I spin around, but not before I see Kierian's eyes flash and hear some girl calling his name from the back.

Whatever.

Even though my fury has no logic, it rushes through me in waves, demanding to crush something.

I'm losing my mind with this job.

Once we reach the booth, I sit on the side that doesn't allow them to see me, and the assault from my friend starts.

"Wasn't that—"

"Yes."

"And that night, you guys—"

"Yep."

"And now you two work together?"

Huffing in annoyance, I reply, "What's with the questions?"

Chloe grins and Simone whistles. "Someone is touchy about the subject, it seems."

"I don't see the point in this conversation, that's all."

Simone motions for the waiter, and says, "Can we have a few tequila shots?" The guy nods and she returns her attention to me, tipping her head to the side, and I shift uncomfortably under her stare. "You like him," she states, and I almost choke on my drink.

"No, I don't. He is just annoying." My cheeks heat up from the lie, but really, they'll blow this out of proportion and—

"Oh my God, she so does." Chloe nudges Simone in the side. "The last time we saw her this riled up over a guy was in high school, when Colton kissed her." Simone nods as they share a laugh, and I give them a nasty look that probably says I want to kill them both.

"Ha, ha. Now can we please move to another subject?" The waiter places our shots on the table along with some nuts, and we salute him. "It's my birthday, so shouldn't I be the center of attention?" Normally, I hate it, but anything is better than them drilling me about Kierian.

"You're right, of course," Chloe says, and I exhale in relief, but then she continues. "But it's this guy or your job. And no offense, babe, but we are tired of hearing about your job." Considering nothing else happens in my life, it doesn't surprise me much. "So... is he into you or not? Because it sure looked like it from my corner."

Finishing my drink, I lean back in the chair, cocking my head. "He is and would like more, but I don't think it's a good idea."

"Why not?"

"Because we work together, and if it goes south, it'll be an uncomfortable situation."

"You don't know that." Chloe seems bothered by my words,
shifting uncomfortably.

"Yeah, I do. It's me. None of my relationships work out, so it's a
pretty good guess."

They stay silent, all humor gone from them, and my brows furrow.

"You are not broken." Simone grabs my hand, squeezing it. "You
can have a relationship if you want."

"This seriously is not the time—"

"I think it is," Chloe interrupts me, anger flashing in her eyes. "If
you like this guy, then try. Even if doesn't work out, what do you have
to lose?"

"Honestly, you guys are making a much bigger deal of this—"

"I love you, you know?" Chloe says, taking my hand in hers and
squeezing it lightly. "But I don't think you ever truly moved on." They
both grow silent.

So much for my fucking birthday celebration.

"I love you too, and I promise if I really want to go after him,
I will."

It takes a while, but they nod and we lift our drinks. "To the
birthday girl—may she celebrate next year with the love of her life."

Rolling my eyes, I decide to ignore their words.

We toss back our shots quickly and then munch on a few nuts,
because we rarely drink anything stronger than wine.

The music is blasting through the speakers, and as the fiery liquid
slowly transfers from my stomach to my brain, I begin to move the
upper part of my body to the beat. "All this heavy talk has no place
today. How about dancing?"

They eagerly nod, and within a few minutes, we are dancing it off
on the dance floor to some club track, when it stops abruptly.

Everyone shares confused looks, until the DJ shouts, "This one is
for Ella Gadot, who has a birthday today." People whistle while my
cheeks heat up.

I glance at the girls. "It's Tim. He requested 'Serial Killer' by Lana
Del Rey for me."

"Nice." Simone moves her arms, because it's her favorite song too, but the song that starts to play is not that.

It's by the same singer, but it's called "Gods and Monsters."

A giggle erupts from the girls. "So fitting though."

Giving them the bird, which only makes them laugh, I close my eyes and give myself completely to the music, swaying from side to side as we scream with the lyrics to the song.

Someone pushes me from behind, and I end up in strong arms that immediately spin me around, bringing me face to face with Kierian.

"Caught you," he whispers while I laugh and grip his shirt.

"You won't give up, will you?"

He shakes his head, removing strands of hair from my forehead and nuzzling my neck, breathing me in.

The music changes to a slow dance as he presses us against each other, and we gently move to the beat of the song. With each movement, I feel his rigid muscles and hold tight to him.

We haven't even done anything, and my head is already dizzy, craving more. "This is a bad idea." He gives me a half smile as he bites my earlobe and then soothes it with his tongue, sending sparks directly to my core.

"Those are usually the best kind." He captures my mouth with his, slowly nipping my lips as if asking permission for entrance before biting lightly, earning himself a gasp.

I open under his assault, and his tongue seeks mine, kissing me intensely while his hand slides into my hair, not allowing me to move away from him.

It's a kiss that for the first time in my life stakes a claim on me; it lets me know this man wants to be the only one who has access to my lips from now on. My knees buckle, but he catches me, not leaving even an inch between us, and when he finally lets go, I breathe deeply, inhaling his scent, which only enhances my desires.

"I have to have tonight, Ella, or I'll go insane."

"We can wait."

He growls against my lips, nipping my chin. "Can you? You don't want me to fuck you so deep and hard that you'll feel me for days afterward?"

His words instantly send a thrill through me and my core clenches. I realize I won't be able to wait at freaking all.

Giving him one more kiss, I say, "I'm here with the girls who planned all this for my birthday. I won't leave them. But you can come home with me after."

With one last peck, I go back to the girls, and the next hour is spent with us dancing and drinking and having fun, all the while looking forward to the continuation of the night.

The time has come to be daring and, for once, to do something for myself.

A Few Hours Later

*E*lla
        The cab stops in front of my building, and Simone says rather loudly, "We are here." Chloe snickers while the cabbie just sighs. He has protective grandpa written all over him.

"You are drunk," I say, and fish for the money, because in their comatose states, I highly doubt they'll manage to pay the guy. He already knows the address.

I kiss them each goodbye on the cheek and get out, and quickly dial David.

"Hello?"

"They should be home in about ten minutes, so I'd advise you to wait for them outside." David usually hangs out with Peter, so he'll be there to pick up his wife as well.

He barks a laugh. "Sure thing, Ella. Happy birthday. Love you!"

"Yeah, me too." Hanging up, I quickly climb the stairs, only to see a man leaning on the brick wall, and I almost scream before I recognize Kierian.

"Could you be more subtle?" I ask, and he grins.

"Why waste time, right" Electricity prickles between us, but I pass him by and quickly run to the elevator, where he joins me in three quick strides.

It feels like an eternity while we wait for the elevator, neither of us saying anything, and when we get inside, being in close proximity to him in a small space doesn't really help the matter.

Finally, we reach my floor and I end up by the door.

Sliding in the key, I barely have time to enter my apartment before Kierian presses me against the door, his mouth seeking mine. I toe off my shoes, and I think he does the same, because as we sway to the side, I step on his bare feet and tingles rush through me from the contact with his skin.

While he drags us to my room, I unbutton his shirt and slide it off his shoulders, and then I move to his belt buckle, desperately needing to feel him in my hands.

We do all this while kissing, and finally the back of my calves touch the bed as he locks his arm around me while whispering my name and leaning into my neck for his hungry assault. "I've been going crazy with need to fuck you since our last time." His words send a shock directly to my clit as he rubs against me. I still feel him despite our clothed state. My whimper doesn't go unnoticed as he drags me closer. "Missed me, Ella?" I nod eagerly. "Is this pussy wet for me? Ready for the one cock that can bring it satisfaction?"

I don't have a chance to reply, as he rips my dress in two, the buttons flying in different directions as he leaves me standing in my lacy thong. The dress didn't allow a bra. "Fuck. Mine was walking around like that in front of other men?" he growls.

He pushes me to the bed, and I fall onto it, breathing heavily. My body is buzzing with need as he slowly removes the belt from the loops. It drops to the floor along with everything else, leaving him gloriously naked for me to admire every muscle, dip, and a noticeable scar that he most likely got on the job.

He sinks to his knees, rubbing his hands against the sensitive skin of my thighs, and I hiss as he bites one down, inhaling my scent. "You are soaked," he mutters, moving my panties to the side, and without warning, he enters me with his tongue, darting along the inside of my core and spreading the wetness around it. His thumb flicks my clit, as he tightly grips my leg, which is thrown over his shoulder, not letting me escape him... as if I would try.

"Kierian," I moan, and he surges deeper, completely owning me with his mouth. His tongue travels over my folds, laving them with the attention and hunger they've been denied for so long.

He cups my ass cheeks and laps at my core with his full mouth, making sure to play with my clit with his upper lip. I bite my fist, muffling a groan while my other leg bends on the bed, giving him wider access to work in.

"You. Are. Mine," he growls against me, digging his fingers into my skin as a hint of pain touches me. "Don't ever deny me again."

In this moment, I'm ready to agree to anything as long as he continues doing it.

"I won't." My voice is coated in lust and desire. My vision blurs the more he licks and sucks as though he is a starved man who has been denied his favorite treat.

Lacing my hands in his hair, I grind on his mouth, adding friction, and with each suck, I go higher and higher. And then he pushes a finger inside me, and my breathing becomes raspy.

"Don't stop," I cry out, and he doesn't. He adds one more finger and it feels like he is everywhere.

Then he lifts my ass higher and concentrates all his attention on my clit, massaging it with his thumb while pushing his tongue in and out, finding that magical spot inside me.

My body tenses, awareness rushing through me as my orgasm hits me hard, and I tremble, jerking my body from him.

Instead of it calming me though, I need more.

He slowly kisses up my stomach to my breasts, where he fondles them and sucks gently on the taut peaks. He licks them with the tip of his tongue while squeezing both at the same time, and I groan, palming his face and raising it up for a kiss.

I can taste myself on him, but I don't care. His kiss is possessive, aggressive, greedy. I think if he had a plan to make me come with just his kisses alone, he would have accomplished it.

As his hard-on digs into my stomach, my hands slide lower, enveloping it in a tight grip. He groans above me while I admire his thick length that pulses with need. I fist it back and forth, and my mouth waters to taste him, but he must read it in my eyes, as he mutters, "Not today, Ella. Tomorrow or any other fucking day, you can play with it all you want and give me the heaven of your hot mouth, but not today. I'm barely holding on to my control as it is." And for a second, he lets me go as he fishes for his jeans and then throws them back on the floor.

I notice the foil packet in his hand as he opens it then quickly rolls the condom on. He opens my legs wider and drags the tip of his cock against my wetness, rubbing and entering me with the tip, teasing me.

"Kierian, don't tease."

He bites on my neck harshly as he growls. "No teasing?"

I shake my head, but reply anyway, "No."

"You want hard fucking only, Ella?"

"Yes!" That's all I want in this freaking moment. So can he get on with the program already, and—

With one swift motion, he surges inside me, tearing a scream from me that he immediately covers with his mouth. He thrusts deep, deep, then deeper into me, shaking the bed with his force. I wrap my legs around him as he entwines our fingers above my head.

He is slow, steady, and hard. He waits until each thrust shakes my entire system before giving me another one, and each time, the pleasure rises in me higher and higher, my skin flushing, heat spreading through me and reminding me this man is all male.

"Mine," he says, pounding harder, and I arch my back, completely lost in everything he makes me feel.

Then he stuffs his finger between us, pressing on my clit while he digs into my core with his cock, harder and harder, and this is when it reaches me.

With a loud cry, I come, seeing fucking stars as he continues to move inside me, not slowing down even for a second. I actually enjoy and savor the feel of him inside me without the added rush of chasing the high that drives me out of my mind.

In and out, faster and faster, deeper and deeper, and finally, he groans, tightening his hold on my hips and probably bruising them for days to come.

He finishes while above me and then sinks onto me, yet very careful of his weight while I hug him closer, rubbing his sweat-coated back up and down, needing to feel this connection after the sex.

I'm completely satisfied and don't feel like I can lift a freaking muscle even if I try, so he rolls to the side and lies on his back. I rest on his shoulder while we both pant for breath. "Why haven't we done it sooner?" I ask.

No, truly, why?

"Because your head is full of crap."

"Don't pay attention to it anymore."

His laughter echoes around the walls, and it hits me that it's the first time it's this genuine or carefree. "Noted." A beat then. "You won't freak out in the morning?"

"No. If I do, you're allowed to kiss me stupid."

He drags me closer and gives me a soft yet passionate kiss that ends too soon, but I seriously don't have the strength left for anything else.

After several seconds, he disposes of the condom, comes back to bed, and we fall asleep in complete peace.

CHAPTER NINE

New York, New York

Ella, 25 years old
"*Your previous apartment was the size of a freaking fruit. Why do you have so many boxes?*" *Chloe bitches while shifting the box in her hands up, making the contents rattle.*

"*Be careful, those are my plates!*" *I inform her. She rolls her eyes and leans against the wall while I grapple with the key, trying to open the door as quickly as possible.*

"*Whatever. Simone, are you coming?*" *she shouts, and slowly, Simone comes from the elevator, breathing heavily as she drops the heavy book box on the floor and places her hands on her knees, gasping for breath.*

"*Girl, your love for books will end you. Mark my word!*" *The situation is truly hilarious considering they had way more shit to move when they chose different places, but I don't say anything.*

Finally getting inside, I smile brightly as I admire my first decent apartment in my entire life. I still can't believe I got so lucky with the landlord.

Kurt Smith, one of our clients at the investigation firm, claimed his wife cheated on him, but he didn't have any proof. Based on our reports, he was a computer genius who became a millionaire when young and always tripled his investment, no matter what he did.

His wife, Matilda, had a long list of lovers before him and loved the party life. Since she didn't stay home with him and claimed to be with friends, he was suspicious.

After my first day on the job, I quickly understood that Matilda wasn't cheating on her husband, but instead, she was meeting with her brother and that train tickets were involved. Most probably she was helping him to run somewhere. Based on the report I had on him, he mingled with the wrong crowd.

I didn't mention this to Kurt but gave him a full report that it was her brother and not another man. He was so happy that he offered me one of his apartments in his building when he heard I was looking for a place to call home. He gave me a cheap price for a fully furnished, one-bedroom apartment in a prime location. Under normal circumstances, I'd refuse, but honestly, I had nowhere else to go and certainly didn't want to stay in my old place.

Plus, I agreed to the rent for just the first few months, and then I'd pay the actual price. I just needed to get on my feet, since the FBI threw my plans out the fucking window. Life's taught me that sometimes you have to swallow your pride in order to survive.

I've applied at several places to work but have yet to hear back from them. As interesting as private investigating is, I don't want to have it as my permanent job.

"Wow!" Chloe whistles, looking around. "I think we'll hang out at your place from now on." She high-fives with Simone, and they plop on the couch, putting their feet on the coffee table and moaning in pleasure. "Finally, rest!"

"Not to be a downer, but we have three more boxes to bring from downstairs."

They groan while muttering something under their breath, but I don't pay attention to them.

Instead, I admire the beautiful kitchen counter, couch, a chair, and a fluffy rug. A huge-ass window opens onto a view of the park from the eleventh floor, the perfect place for my morning workout. The bedroom has a bed and a closet, along with a bathroom.

Everything is decorated in brown and soft beige, but I hope to add color to it with my various pillows and blankets.

"Geez, Ella, you don't even look at doughnuts like this, and you love those!" Simone jokes, and then passes me with Chloe in tow. "We are going to grab the boxes and be back. Let's order something. I'm starving." They go out and I pick up the phone to do just that, when someone behind me clears his throat.

Spinning around, I see Kurt, who grins at me. "Welcome to the building, Ella." He gives me a large basket of chocolate, and my brows furrow.

"Thanks. You shouldn't have."

He waves his hand in the "don't mention it" gesture. "Standard procedure. Anyway, everything good?"

I nod, placing the basket on the counter. Honestly, this is a bit freaking weird. We discussed everything before, when he gave me the keys. Why is he here now?

I instantly admonish myself inwardly, because my suspicions present on the job sometimes transfer to real life. Nothing wrong with being friendly.

"Anyway, I'll be in the apartment down the hall." With a curt nod, he heads out but not before I ask.

"How is your wife?"

For a second, I think fury crosses his face, but it's gone so quickly I must have imagined it. "She is gone. Left me."

"What?" But he doesn't elaborate, just shrugs and leaves, while I stand there confused.

Matilda never would have left her husband based on the report I'd gathered. She loved the life he provided too much. Those tickets couldn't have been for her!

But if she did, then what could he possibly have done to drive her away?

Chloe and Simone choose this moment to enter the apartment, doing a happy dance as they throw the last boxes inside.

"Now it's party time!" Chloe pumps her fist in the air while Simone rolls her eyes.

"Movie, food, and wine hardly count as party." Slowly, I turn my attention to them; we'll spend an amazing evening where they'll help me put my stuff in place while we watch a movie and laugh.

Everything is right in the world, and all the nagging thoughts about Kurt fly from my mind.

But they come back one year later, when the police find Matilda at the bottom of a lake, killed in rage by her husband who couldn't stand her leaving him.

Which proves to me one more time that if I have a feeling about someone, I should listen.

I'll always recognize the evil lying underneath the perfect exterior.

Ella

Something disturbs my sleep, and I move my head to the side to avoid the annoying touch, but it just follows me.

Burrowing into the pillow, I wave my hand, hoping the thing will go away. It's probably some fly who flew in because I forgot to close the window. The breeze is softly caressing my skin, bringing much needed coolness to the otherwise warm environment.

Then it hits me.

Open window.

I've never left a window open during the night, not after the tragedy with my family. Who knows who and what can get inside?

My eyes snap open, and that's when I see Kierian in all his handsome glory looming over me with his palms caging my head on both sides.

Droplets of water coming from his wet hair hit my face, and the smell of my shampoo penetrates my nostrils.

A chuckle slips through my lips. "Never expected you to smell like exotic flowers." He doesn't share the joke though, his silver eyes drilling me with their intensity instead, and I rise a bit, not really knowing what to do with such attention.

I've truly never met a man like him.

My body aches, reminding me that he took me yesterday in all the right and hot ways.

"Don't look at me like that," he warns, our lips a breath away from each other. Not being able to resist, I slide my hand into his hair, scooting closer as my breasts press against his bare chest, and I can't help but moan at the contact. "Like you want me to fuck you so hard you'll feel me for days," he mutters, before covering my mouth with his, giving me a hot kiss that makes my head spin.

I rise more and circle his neck, demanding better entrance. I feel his erection digging into my thigh and my hand travels down, wanting to close around it, when he groans against me.

To my surprise, instead of placing me on top of him and continuing, he removes my arms and gets up, breathing heavily.

"You are a vixen." He chuckles, and then runs his fingers through his hair that I've managed to tangle. "We have no time, beautiful. No time." My brows furrow, and I glance at the clock. It's barely seven, and Noah said we have to be at work by eight. "We have to be in the office in an hour. Go shower and stuff, while I grab some breakfast from the bakery."

"I don't eat breakfast, and it takes me around twenty minutes to get ready. You woke me up for nothing!" My voice sounds grumpy and childish, but I don't care.

"But I do, and if you had woken up without me, you would have thought I'd left." I blink, trying to process this, when he adds, "Maybe getting revenge for last time." Yeah, my head would have totally gone there. He laughs when he hears my grumble, and I throw a pillow at him, but he dips his head and it misses him. "Come on, get ready."

I get up and ignore his nakedness, although all I want to do is run my tongue all over his tanned skin and enjoy his pecs under my hands; so, I speed up my walk to the bathroom, but not before shouting, "I like bagels." His laughter is the last thing I hear before shutting the door.

God, when was the last time I had so much fun?

This day sure looks promising.

*P*sychopath

I rest against the brick wall where I have a clear view of Ella through her open window. Since her apartment is on the eighth floor, I have to use binoculars.

She stretches her arms, and then places her hands on the windowsill, lifting her face to greet the sun. Her face is filled with happiness and a calmness I haven't seen in months.

A night with Kierian did this to her. The way she looked at him in the club, responded to him, pissed me off to no measure.

She is mine to do with whatever the fuck I please, so any man who touches her has to think twice. But how can she know that if I haven't given her a hint of how special she is for this investigation?

My hands tighten around the binoculars, almost breaking them, but I exhale a heavy breath.

Control.

That's the most important thing for me.

Since she is home alone, I push back from the wall and move forward, pressing the box in my arms to my chest.

I got a gift for her, and I hope she'll appreciate it.

Not that it will make her suffering any less once she falls into my trap.

*E*lla

"I bought Broadway shows for the Fourth of July for everyone. Don't forget," Chloe reminds me on the phone, while I hold it between my shoulder and ear, trying to pour coffee into my cup.

I hope Kierian likes it as well, because the other drinking option is water.

"I'll do my best." The minute the words slip through my lips, I regret them as a rant erupts at the other end of the line.

"It's important, Ella! No way in hell are you spending it alone in your apartment." I love my friends to pieces, but sometimes they make it their mission to surround me with as much attention as possible during holidays and special occasions.

No one cares most of the time. I prefer to stay home, because holidays are too difficult to bear, but for the sake of their friendship, I always suck it up.

So instead of arguing, I reply cheerily, "Okay. I'll be there." She doesn't believe me by the way she huffs into the phone, but then the doorbell rings, and I quickly add, "Someone is at the door. Gotta go." I don't give her the chance to comment on that and hang up, placing my phone on the counter.

Shaking my head in amusement at Chloe's perseverance, I open the door, ready for Kierian. My bright smile transforms to a frown when no one is there. "Umm, hello?" I call, and then hear the elevator ding echoing in the background. Maybe they thought I wasn't home. "So weird," I mutter, and I'm about to spin around when my gaze lands on my doormat and I blink. A white box lies on it with a black ribbon wrapped tightly around it.

I pick it up, searching for a note attached and don't find any. I shake it, but it makes no sound, and although I know better based on the training in Quantico, I bring it inside.

Unwrapping the knot, I remove the lid, only to find a book. "*The Iliad* by Homer," I read aloud. The title reminds me of something from school, but I don't remember the information. It's a Greek classic. And then it clicks.

The history of the Trojan War. How the prince of Troy fell in love with a married Greek queen and got her away from her husband, who declared a war. It lasted for ten long years, with the Greeks finally winning and Helen going back to her husband.

Glancing at my huge collection of books on the bookshelf in my living room, I chuckle at the girls' joke. They kept telling me they are on the hunt for a book that would bore even me, and since *The Iliad* is several thousand years old, it holds a strong possibility.

I suspect I'll love it anyway; I'll just never get time with work to properly enjoy Greek history.

Sliding my phone open, I scroll down my contacts to write in the group chat, when a different message appears.

<**Anonymous**> Did you like the gift?

Rolling my eyes at their sense of humor and desire to prolong the secrecy, I write back.

<**Me**> Sure. I'll read it.

<**Anonymous**> Consider it a hint.

<**Me**> Hardly can be a hint. You've been up my ass about a boring book my whole life.

They don't answer. In fact, I blink in shock as my phone rapidly closes all programs, and a second later, it turns off. "What the hell?" I rise up swiftly, and then a note falls to the carpet. I snatch it up, only to freeze on the spot.

The key you are so desperately seeking... lies within this story.
Unsub

A rush of adrenaline flashes through me as I hold my breath, my mind going in a spiral with the knowledge that he knows where I live and has sent me a personal gift. I place my hand on the gun under the table and calm down a bit, desperately needing to call someone to figure it out.

What should an agent do in this situation?

Sweat slides down my back as I walk to the window and open it up, gulping as much air as possible while willing myself to move forward.

He knows we are investigating him. He knows we have no clues and how much that frustrates me. But why did he choose me for this? Obsession?

Words from many years ago enter my mind, and although I wish to block them away, I fail to do so.

But there is something about you, Ella... it brings more pleasure to watch you suffer than to kill you.

Tightening my hold on the windowsill to the point my knuckles turn white, I count to ten in my mind, a trick I learned back in college.

No matter where my mind went, the countdown always brought me back to the present.

He probably hacked my phone too. Why do serial killers in most cases have to be so fucking smart?

A doorbell ring snaps me out of my thoughts and my heart speeds up, beating painfully in my ribcage. I swallow and at once take out my gun, releasing the safety. Since my phone is off, I can't call for help, and although the idea of facing him scares me, it's better to be outside than inside with him.

I tiptoe to the door, making minimal sounds, and rise on my toes to look through the peephole. I exhale in relief as Kierian's face greets me.

Unlocking the door, he meets me with a frown as he scans my appearances. "Ella?" I immediately fist his shirt and pull him inside, shutting the door and locking it with all the locks possible. Tangling my fingers through my hair, I dwell on the thought that with one stupid message, the unsub took me back to the little girl who didn't understand what to do.

I won't survive on the job if I become neurotic with it.

Instantly, he grabs me by the shoulders as he spins me around and presses me against the door. He throws the bagel bag on the couch, and it lands perfectly without the contents spilling out.

The gun in my hands digs into my hip, but I ignore it, still trying to catch my breath.

"Ella, start talking."

Licking my dry lips, I manage to get out "He knows where I live."

"Who?"

"The unsub. He knows."

Coldness crosses his face, and his voice dips low as he fires yet another question. "What did he do?"

Swaying to the side, I point to the box and the book, my finger slightly shaking. "I think I'm overreacting."

"You are not," he snaps at me, and I'm taken aback by the anger coming from him. "There is nothing to be ashamed of. It shouldn't have happened. I'm calling Noah." He is about to make a phone call that has the power to end my career before it even starts!

"No!" I scream at him, and he stops while I elaborate, hoping like hell he'll listen to me. "Noah will take me off the case and you know that. I'll be in the 'possible victim' section, and everyone will guard me." Based on his raised brow, my convincing game isn't really working.

"Are you insane? He is a serial killer. I'm supposed to just leave your life to chance?"

"Kieran, if he wanted to kill me, he would have done it. It's about the game for him."

"A dangerous game, Ella."

"Please," I whisper, not really understanding myself in this situation either. Shouldn't my safety come first?

Why am I insisting on it?

"I have no words for how stupid that is!" I stay silent as he runs his hand over his hair, sighing in frustration. "I won't tell Noah, but if it gets dangerous, all bets are off."

Relief washes over me, and before I can even think about my

action, I wrap my hands around his waist and hug him with all my might, breathing in his scent. Although I said all those brave things, inside, the little girl still trembles in fear, and I have no one else to calm me down but him.

And dominance and protection always comes in spades from Kierian.

His arms tighten around me as he pats my head, murmuring, "Shhh, everything is okay. But I don't like this, Ella." He rocks me from side to side, while I take a deep breath.

He might not like it, but even he knows it will help us find him. This unsub is so arrogant he thinks my world should revolve around him.

"He wants me to do it. It's better not to anger him." If he watched us, it means he'll know when I tell them the truth. Who knows how he will react? I didn't want another victim on my head.

An experienced agent would have probably reacted differently, but I couldn't.

"I will catch this son of a bitch."

Kierian says nothing, just hugs me closer.

So much for an amazing day.

CHAPTER TEN

New York, New York

Ella, 26 years old
    Kicking the rock lying on the ground, I huff so loudly in frustration that the woman walking next to me jumps, but I don't care.

Rejection, once again.

I barely restrain myself from bursting into tears as the realization sinks into me and my knees buckle, but Chloe's strong hands catch me in time. "Shhh, babe. Let's sit down." She guides me toward the bench at the side of the New York Police Department building, where we sit down as people pass with curious glances, probably at my mascara-smeared red face.

I don't even try to stop my tears as I press the heels of my palms on my eyes. "It's over," I murmur, desperation and resignation lacing my voice.

Although it probably was over a few years ago when Dean Holt warned me no one would ever approve of me getting into criminal psychology.

It seems everyone has made it their mission to make it impossible for me. And I finally accept my defeat, having no strength left to fight an entire system.

Chloe pats my back, while saying, "It's all right, babe. You can always look in other cities."

"No one will give me a job in any type of field work, and without that, it's impossible to get into BAU, and you know that." Even though the FBI refused me, I still hoped after I had a few years of experience, they'd let me work for them.

She stays silent, not having anything to say to that.

No matter how much I've studied, no matter that I've read all the books on criminal psychology and took them as general electives, all my knowledge doesn't count for shit for those people. They just look at my past and assume this work is not for me, that I'm on some kind of revenge path.

I'm not. I just want to give other families out there a fighting chance.

Is that so wrong?

"I thought you love working with—"

I don't let her finish. "Yes, I work with abused women and kids in shelters and at the centers, because I want to help them. But if I worked in BAU, I would actually have the chance to prevent the rapes and abuses from happening. Don't you understand? Sometimes it's too late to fix the problem once the monster inflicts his evil. Those kids and women have to live with it forever," I yell in her face, while she stoically listens. She takes a sip of her tea, exhales a heavy breath, and then raises my chin so she can have my whole attention.

"But it doesn't mean your work doesn't bring any value. Those people have no one but you to let them know it's okay to move on, and they shouldn't be stuck with their scars. It's worth a lot too, girl. If you don't see it, then maybe your two degrees in psychology mean shit." Then she stands up and gives me a glance over her shoulder. "Once this self-pity party is done, call me. We are in need of shopping." With those parting words, she leaves me alone, strolling down the street, her blonde hair swaying from side to side.

As much as I hate it, she is right. I've spent all this time trying to get into that kind of work while devaluing everything else in my life.

Is it worth it, though? Smiles and grateful words from the kids at the shelter flash through my mind, reminding me that I make a difference in their lives. That they know they matter and no one is allowed to treat them that way.

I give them something important. I teach them no one has the right to bring them pain. How can I view it as nothing, simply because I don't get to work for the FBI?

My attitude is disrespectful to all of them and to me. I've worked my ass off for the position I have now. Even if criminal psychology's door is forever closed for me, the rest welcome me with open arms. I attend every convention, have connections in many places, and make sure to write a daily column for one of the female blogs.

This counts for something, a hell of a fucking lot.

Wiping away the wetness from my cheeks, I get up, put on my sunglasses, and grin widely, hoping I will find peace in knowing I'm doing something valuable.

Even if catching serial killers is not one of those things.

*E*lla

Silence echoes through the space as the soft light showcases the office in a mysterious way, with not another soul around. No one's stuck around after hours; most of them have a family. All the desks are neat and tidy, as the janitor lady has cleaned already and left, but not before warning me to make sure not to mess the place up or she will remember my name.

I sure as hell won't leave a mess.

I've spent the whole day going over the case in between a few different ones too. Mostly it was paperwork, and we didn't have much to do on them.

Kierian stayed true to his word and even dropped me a few blocks away so no one would see us driving in together. He acted so distant and professional that no one could have guessed what we'd shared.

He wanted to take me home, but I refused, because I need to concentrate on the case. Or that was the excuse I gave him.

Truthfully, I'm surprised he let it go so easily, and relieved at the same time. He respects my boundaries and doesn't try to push this thing on me, now that I've stopped denying there is one.

I can totally work with that.

But deep down, I can admit to myself I'm a little bit scared to go back home alone when the unsub knows where I live. And I don't want to bring all those bad pictures and details home anyway; it's supposed to be my sanctuary.

No blood or murder belongs in my house.

I try to unscramble all the wounds the unsub has left on the victims, racking my brain for a clue why he would let his dog do the rest. What was the whole point of kidnapping those poor men? To torture and kill them in the vilest ways? Why is he so easily satisfied and doesn't feel attached to his victims?

Pouring myself a cup of freshly made coffee, I groan inwardly as spasms of pain travel from my nape to my lower back, reminding me of the stiff chairs in the office that drive me crazy. The idea of spending one more minute in it kills me, but I have no other choice, considering I plan to figure it all out tonight.

"You know, ancient Greeks believed all our pain comes from our mind."

I jump at the soft voice behind me and swirl around on the chair to face Preston holding his bottle of water and smiling at me.

The guy can actually freaking smile!

Blinking a few times, I finally speak. "You don't say."

He nods, sitting on my desk while continuing his thought. "Healthy mind in a healthy body. I think they couldn't name it back then, but they meant psychology. One of the reasons I got interested in this art so many years ago."

"It's science," I correct, but he brushes me off.

"No, it's the art of learning a mind. What can be greater than that?"

I don't think I've heard the guy talk so much in the span of one minute. "That's because you love it. I suppose it's like that for everyone who loves their profession."

"Maybe the pain in your back will ease once the problem in your head resolves."

A light laugh escapes me. "And here I was, Preston, hoping it would go away with a nice bath. Seems like I'll have to live with the pain till the case is closed."

He doesn't comment on that, just stares, but then his eyes land on the book, as he exclaims, *"The Iliad!"* Picking it up, he flips it open while searching for a certain page, and then points his finger to the quote. "My favorite part."

Everything inside me freezes. I swallow the coffee that all of a sudden becomes bitter in my mouth. My mind registers the words in the quote; my palms get sweaty while my breath hitches.

"It is entirely seemly for a young man killed in battle to lie mangled by the bronze spear. In his death all things appear fair."

How many people are out there these days who love this book and have a favorite part memorized?

"I see." My survival instinct screams for me to scoot back and run away from him as he actively studies me and then exhales heavily while adjusting his glasses firmly on his nose.

"Now you think I'm a freak or something. Noah and Kierian love it too. Actually, we had to do it for work."

Slowly I resume breathing, cursing my stupidity, because honestly, did I seriously think he could be a serial killer? They don't hang out with us!

"Interesting case?" Why didn't Kierian mention that to me earlier, then? He could have helped with the research, but he didn't even offer.

Preston nodded while elaborating. "There was a weird case of a dude who was obsessed with Greek mythology and stuff. He had different quotes scattered around his place, and we sort of had to read a lot of stuff. To understand him, we had to read this book, because he associated himself with King Agamemnon." He rolls his eyes as if he finds the notion alone stupid. "But we did like the masterpiece."

"Why?" Maybe if he explains to me his love for it, I can connect all the clues that the unsub desperately wants me to find. And although I realize it's a dangerous game I'm playing with him, I don't intend to give up until I find him.

"It shows what war does with mankind in the span of a decade, when people had different lives and values. Of course, some historians claim it's nothing but a myth, but it was discovered that Troy indeed existed." He pauses as if gathering his thoughts while I make some notes on my pad. "But also, it's the characters... it's very character driven, you know? I think we can all find ourselves there if we try." His cheeks are flushed and he avoids my stare.

Character driven.

That must be it! He found his character and associates himself with him. "Who was your favorite?" I ask, but he stands abruptly, his water spilling onto his pants as he curses under his breath.

"I won't tell you now. You have to read it first. I think then you will guess." With that odd statement, he walks away while I'm left confused.

Even though he didn't say anything major, a feeling of doom around him doesn't escape me, and I always trust my instinct. I just can't name what I find odd about Preston.

Shaking my head from the complicated scenarios, I bring all my attention back to the case while munching on the cookies I was smart enough to bring.

It's taken me almost eight hours, but I've finally figured it out.

And in a way, the truth breaks me.

The profile is done.

*P*sychopath

The honk of the car snaps my attention to the right as I wave at Christian, our coworker who recently got married, and he motions for me to call him sometime.

Cracking my neck from side to side, enjoying the pleasure it provides me, I think about bringing an iPad next time while waiting for Ella. Nothing but excellent planning has gotten me to this level, the small fact of preparation most serial killers skip.

And that's why they are caught.

She decided to stay inside last night, working on catching me, and I couldn't leave her alone without security.

I have every intention to hurt her slightly, but no one else has this right, and with life, you never know. I didn't work so hard to get her here to have an accident happen and ruin my plans, especially with the anniversary so close.

The idea of spending every night in the car waiting for her doesn't bother me much. I've learned to operate on minimal sleep.

You never know when a monster will decide to disturb your sleep.

Running my fingers through my hair, I get out of the car and walk to the building while checking the current news report. I don't find anything interesting.

"Good morning," security greets me, while I press my badge to the gate.

"Hey, Karl. Everything good?"

He nods, sipping his tea while several doughnuts lie nearby. "Yes. Only, Ella Gadot stayed the night." He frowns at that, probably not understanding why a young woman would be this dedicated to the new case.

I don't understand it either, but a thrill of pleasure spreads into my veins when I think how much my actions attract her mind. She should be careful with her attention, or I'll bring her a new body.

Once inside the BAU, I stop in my tracks as my eyes drink in the beauty Ella presents asleep at her desk, her body bending while her cheek rests against the plastic table. Her shirt is wrinkled and light puffs of air slip through her lips, emphasizing the fullness of them that I long to bite to see how quickly I can draw blood.

A silky black lock falls across her nose, and she winces a little, not liking it, so I can't resist removing it. Immediately, she calms down. She looks so innocent right now, so young, so pure that the idea of bringing her to my basement for a second feels wrong.

My darkness shouldn't touch a person who has already suffered enough nightmares.

But then the smell of her perfume penetrates my nostrils, and it pulls me out of the haze created in my mind by her.

She is mine.

And I will take good care of her once she proves she can stay around... no matter what.

Unfortunately for her, it means being kidnapped and tortured until—

The screams from the past assault me, and I slap my head, grabbing onto the desk while the anger and pain shake my body.

I count to ten as I concentrate only on the numbers and how they look in my head, so no images of the past will enter it again.

In seconds, everything passes, but it once again reminds me that remorse and the greater good hold no meaning for me.

Selfishly, I need Ella to numb the past, and it has to happen sooner rather than later.

Otherwise, I will go insane.

*E*lla

"Ella, wake up." A deep voice penetrates through the haze of sleep and my eyes flutter open.

A groan of pain leaves me as I sit up straight, disoriented, while wincing at the stiffness in my back. I should really invest in massages with this job, no joke.

Finally, I register where I am and raise my eyes to the three men standing at my side, each one of them with a different expression. I blink, not used to such attention.

Noah, well put together in his suit as always, has surprise crossing his face as he glances at my spread notes. Avoiding my gaze, Preston sips his coffee and holds one out for me, which I gladly take, and I'm not even surprised it's my favorite flavor. This guy is full of secrets!

Kierian chuckles in amusement, and once again, my body reacts to that smile, but I shake my head, hoping to escape that. "Hey, sleeping beauty. Rough night?"

Noah rolls his eyes, shooting him a warning, "Kierian." But then adds, "When I said think about the case, I didn't mean to stay at the office twenty-four seven."

That's when it hits me.

The case!

"I know who he is." They freeze, zeroing their whole attention on me. Licking my dry lips, I get up, waving a file in front of them. "Well, I mean, I know why he does what he does."

"Let's hear it then, because so far we have nothing. In the conference room in five," Noah orders and goes to his office, leaving me alone with the guys.

"I need to prepare my laptop," Preston says out of the blue and runs into the computer room.

"It's not healthy." Kierian leans closer, removing the strands of hair from my forehead, and this barely noticeable touch surges a rush of energy around us, creating an unfamiliar cocoon, and I swallow. Before I can even blink, he gives me three light pecks on the lips, burning me up with each touch.

This job will be the end of me.

I step back, looking around, hoping that no one saw it. "Kierian."

He ignores my hiss, as he picks up my books and notes. "We have no restrictions about dating coworkers."

I almost choke on my drink, wincing as it burns my lips. "You're sure?"

He shrugs. "No one ever informed me otherwise."

"Relationships don't work for me most of the time." I feel the need to warn him, because if we truly decide to make it a thing, maybe we shouldn't inform anyone. Who knows how long it will last? "So hold your horses, Kierian."

"Why not?" Curiosity and boredom, if that's possible, lace his voice as he moves slowly in the direction of the conference room, where I can see through the glass door to the rest of the team occupying their chairs and laughing at something Jacob shows them on his phone.

"They just don't." I've tried relationships twice, and both times, I failed.

"Do you know what my most prominent character trait is?" he asks, right before pushing the door wide open.

"What?"

"Stubbornness. And when I want something, I get it. You are mine, Ella. Just accept it," he whispers against my ear and then steps inside, while I sigh heavily, praying for patience and resistance, because God knows I'll need it with him.

Unsub, I remind myself. *Think about the unsub, Ella.*

Noah raises his brow. "You said you've got something?" Nodding, I quickly turn around the board that shows us all the victims spread horizontally with the detailed description of their wounds along with some hypotheses about our unsub.

"Okay, so remember how I said it's odd that the victim's wife acted so weird?"

Andrea nodded. "Yeah, she wasn't crying."

"Right." I grab the black marker as I go to the white board and quickly write all the wounds. "So first, he goes for the kidneys. Then he moves slowly to the gut. Then it's the back. And finally the throat and face."

"We know that," Jacob's voice is filled with boredom, and I grit my teeth and continue. A little bit of patience wouldn't hurt! "Also, once he is done with them, he leaves them for his dog to tear apart. He doesn't bother to inflict more pain on them than those three main wounds. The last victim was an exception."

"Ella, I hope you are going somewhere with this, because so far this is all in the file." Noah drums his pen on the table, although his assertive eyes focus on my writing as if he is trying to figure out my train of thought.

"I've spent the last few years working with abused women. Do you know where they were usually hurt? Kidneys/ribs"—with each word, I point at the board, the sound echoing through the space emphasizing it even more—"Stomach. Arms. Back. Throat. And finally face." You can kick at a kidney and there will be no bruises left.

Kierian crosses his arms and leans on the table while rubbing his chin.

Preston, however, clicks with his fingers, and says, "The wife of the first victim. She was covered from head to toe and got nervous whenever we asked her about family pictures."

"Connecting all this, I can only make one conclusion."

"Her husband abused her," Andrea says, but then straightens. "So our unsub hurts men who abuse their women."

Noah raises his brow, while scrolling through his file. "That would be the missing piece that connects them all. That's his victimology."

"I'll check out the other victims' families. Their medical records, absence at work or school, everything." Preston's fingers immediately click on the laptop, his focus sharp, and I hope he can find helpful information.

No matter what the unsub does, his killings are wrong. Those men don't deserve kindness, but he shouldn't be the judge, jury, and executioner.

"Call in Mary Parker. We need to ask her a few more questions," Noah says to Andrea, and then his attention is back on me. "Anything else to add?" The book in my bag weighs heavily on my shoulder and conscience, but I don't tell him about it. I know it holds the key to figuring out where he is, but if they find out he's targeted me specifically, they might put me off the case.

The unsub threw me a challenge and I intend to win. People like him are the reason my family died. I'll put him behind bars, no matter the cost. I can't give up on my first case.

I shake my head and clear my throat. "I think we will have a profile once we confirm it with Mary. Then we can move on." And although that's usually the extent of our job, I hope like hell he makes one more wrong move so we'll be closer to catching him.

One Hour Later

Ella

"Ella," Noah calls, and I spin around to face him. "Mary Parker is here. She's waiting in the office." Nodding, I quickly grab the file and dart toward the office while searching for the appropriate words in my head.

She's sitting on the chair, this time alone, while fumbling with her fingers. She shifts uncomfortably as I walk in. "Agent Gadot. Your call surprised me." She shakes my hand, but at the same time, worry crosses her face.

"There are a few new details regarding your case."

She freezes, barely breathing. "What details? Is he alive?"

My expression remains neutral, but with this statement, she confirms our profile is correct. Usually a family will demand to see the body, but in this case, she wants to forget him like a bad dream.

"No, of course not. But we have a few questions for you." She exhales in relief and nods. "I need you to be honest with me please. Everything you say stays in this room, but it will be very important for the case."

"Yes, okay."

Pausing for a second, I ask gently, "Mrs. Parker, did he abuse you?" She swallows and casts her eyes down. Working for so long with such women, I know what she is feeling right now. Shame for staying with such a man. But she shouldn't. "It's very important for us to know."

She takes a deep breath and speaks up. "He wasn't at first." She licks her lips, while cracking her knuckles. "He was so gentle, so attentive. It felt like I was the only girl in the world for him." She gulps from the water bottle then continues. "Everything changed once we got married. He became quiet, nervous, and every little thing would piss him off. It started with screaming and gradually transformed into punches."

My heart aches for her, imagining how scary it must be to have the one person you trust the most turn their back on you and transform into a monster. People often ask how all those women could not see the signs, that it must be obvious. The truth is that the abusers are the best at hiding it.

Deception is their favorite mask, because that's how they lure in their victims.

My brows furrow, my mind lingering on that information, but I shake my head, pushing it back to dwell on later. I concentrate on Mary, who now bites her thumb, nervously tapping her foot, and by the glazed look in her eyes, I realize she is not here anymore, but back in time with her husband.

"He apologized at first. He would bring me gifts and beg me to take him back. I wasn't weak because I didn't say anything," she assures me, her cheeks flushing.

"Of course not. You were in a bad situation."

She laughs bitterly. "I should have run away from him the minute he became abusive, but I hoped and hoped. Then I got pregnant and I had no choice," she finishes on a whisper.

While all this confirms our theory, it doesn't really help us much in the investigation, so I probe softly. "Do you remember anyone new in your circle? Someone who might have known about his abusive ways?"

"No, it's impossible. He was loving in public, and besides, we just recently moved."

Except the unsub must have spied on them. Otherwise, what explains his obsession with the victims?

Noah raises his chin in question through the glass door, and I shake my head, because this information doesn't move us forward. How does the unsub find these men?

"Although—" she starts, and my ears perk up. She straightens in her seat, frowning. "One day, after he disappeared, there was this man who stopped by the door asking if I, by any chance, had lost a bike. It stood on the road, but I told him it wasn't mine. I thought he was just a neighbor. He apologized and was about to leave, but then he murmured that my nightmare had ended. He also glanced at my baby, but I got scared and shut the door in his face."

The baby. He didn't come to check on the mother.

Oh my God.

"Do you remember what he looked like?"

"He wore a hoodie and sunglasses, and had a beard. I wouldn't recognize him." She gasps in shock. "Was he the killer?" Knowledge that it may have been the killer who stopped by her house might fill her with fear, and since I'm sure he won't attack her, I try my best to reassure her.

"Not likely. But this information helps us. Thank you, Mary." She nods and I pause for a second, contemplating my next action but do it nevertheless. I place the card of the center where I used to work in her hand. "If you ever feel like talking, it's a good place to share your pain."

She holds it in her hand for a few seconds, then whispers, "He is dead."

I smile sadly. "Unfortunately, the scars they leave behind stay."

She doesn't say anything else, but puts it into her bag, and with a pat on her shoulder, she exits the office while I huff in frustration.

We made a mistake in the profile, a small detail that changes everything.

What did you have to live through, unsub?

. . .

*P*sychopath

Pressing the elevator button, I curse the thing for taking so long when I feel a presence next to me.

Glancing to my side, I recognize the woman, the wife of one of my previous victims as she thinks about something, absently gazing at the doors.

The elevator dings and she gets inside along with me. I study her features. She's gained some weight, which is probably normal considering she just recently had a child, but there is also an aura of calmness around her.

And most importantly, no fresh bruises.

I don't know what a sane person should feel in this moment, but the only thing running through my mind is the fact that her child will be free of all the nightmares his mother experienced.

A minute later, the door slides open. I'm about to leave, when her murmured voice stops me in my tracks.

"Thank you." A pause as her breath hitches. "I recognize the tattoo. It was you."

I do not react to her statement and continue to walk toward the printing center.

My job here is done.

*E*lla

"Where is Noah?" I fire the question at Andrea, who munches on her doughnut.

"Have no clue. The guys are scattered all over the place. Why, do you have new information on the unsub? The wife remembered something?" She wipes her hands clean, her whole focus on me.

"The unsub went to the house to check on her."

"What?"

"Yes. But that's not what makes it so interesting, if that word can be applied here."

"Then what?" She truly looks confused, while studying the pictures in front of her from the crime scenes. "He is a serial killer! And you are not concerned he was at the house?" She hustles through the notes. "We need to check surveillance cameras. Maybe they managed to catch his face."

"He is punishing the abuser."

"To protect the wives because he surrogates them for his mother. I know." But that's the thing though—she doesn't understand.

Noah and Kierian walk in, and I spin to face them. "It's the kids." Their brows rise, so I elaborate. "The unsub is saving the kids from having to live the life he went through. It's not about the mothers."

"Meaning he surrogates himself with kids?" Andrea slaps her forehead. "This is even worse."

"How is this worse?" I mean, it does change the variables, but not the outcome. It just means we need to look at family men, because those will be his victims. And this profile allows us to search through databases for him.

Noah speaks up. "He kills the fathers, because he knows no one will protect the kids. His mother, in his mind, failed him. So he is doing the dirty job, so to speak."

"But why is it dangerous?"

Everyone stays silent and only Andrea speaks. "One day, he will meet a woman he wants. And he will punish her for it, because in his mind, love is a fleeting emotion that needs to be punished."

As in, he can fall in love with a woman?

It's scary to think what his love entails.

* * *

*T*he police officers stand in front of us, ready to listen, although I can see they huff in annoyance, clearly not expecting to hear much.

A detective claps his hands. "Okay, everybody, listen up."

Quiet falls in the room as Noah clears his throat. "We are ready to present the profile." He nods at Andrea, and she steps forward, firing information like bullets while officers write it on their notepads, their pens scratching against the paper and reminding me that I've missed something.

The book. I still haven't found the connection to the book. Why did he send it to me if it's not related to the case?

"Our unsub is a man around twenty-five to thirty-five years old. He needs to be in good shape to carry the bodies and fight them when they resist. All his victims have one thing in common: they abused their wives, and probably their kids. That's why all the pain he inflicts has to do with domestic abuse." She continues, "He grew up most likely with a violent father and psychologically absent mother."

"Child molestation?" one of the officers asks, but I shake my head.

"No, at least not to him. He only hurts men, but he doesn't touch their genitals, which implies that he wasn't raped as a child. His mission is to bring as much pain to the victim as possible. In other words, he puts them in a helpless position. Like all their victims were."

"He is confident, controlled, and meticulous in choosing his victims. He is extremely smart and manipulative. He is educated and charming, so it's easy for him to be part of society. Considering that anyone rarely knows what happens behind closed doors, he spies on his victims and never picks someone randomly," Jacob pitches in. "In other words, we are dealing with a psychopath with years of experience. He probably started back in his teens."

"You mentioned psychologically absent mother. What do you mean by that? Will his next victim be the wives?"

We share a look, and I decide to answer that. "His mother probably took all of it without fighting back, allowing the husband to grow more violent. In most cases, statistically, such women either die of their injuries or commit suicide." My heart hurts for the small child and woman who lived through hell, because no one deserves that, but at the same time, it doesn't excuse what he does.

"In most such cases, child has a chance, but our unsub..." Andrea pauses, then remorse fills her voice. "... had no chance."

"He will never stop, because in his mind, he doesn't do anything wrong." Jacob shares the most important information, as it's crucial. Our unsub doesn't feel remorse of any kind.

In his eyes, he is the savior.

"All those men are surrogates for his father. Each time he kills one of them, he kills his father all over again," I say, and they blink in surprise.

"You think his first victim was his father?"

"One of the victims. Usually the person hates the father so much they want to inflict the most torture on them. And it takes training."

"So how do we catch this guy?" asks a police officer, and isn't that a good freaking question?

Noah steps in. "The profile gives you more or less an idea of him. If he shows up again, you will know, as he likes the attention. Catching serial killers like him takes months, if not years. He needs to make a mistake."

The conversation continues as they make plans and adjustments, and that's when I catch Kierian's gaze, as he gives me a harsh stare I can't quite understand.

But maybe it's about the book. In such circumstances, can I really hide it? The team deserves to know.

It won't change much, since the case is now in the police's hands unless something crucial comes up, but what if I put my team at risk?

*P*sychopath

I squeeze the plastic cup in my hand so tight it buckles, splashing hot coffee on my wrist. A policewoman close to me gasps and quickly gives me a tissue. "Thanks," I mutter, hating every word uttered by the team as they present the profile to the police officers, because it feels like she is justifying my life, but doing it coldly and making me sound insane.

When in fact, I'm the sanest person of them all! What do they know about my life anyway? Sociopaths, psychopaths, serial killers. Who sees our side of things, truly? Criminal psychology teaches you how to catch them.

It doesn't teach you to truly understand them.

But she is wrong. About my motives and my end game. She will know soon though.

The action needs to speed up, because I can't control my anger anymore and can barely contain myself during sex. It doesn't bring me the pleasure or clarity of the mind it used to.

But getting Ella will, because it seems she is the only one who truly understands me.

Mine.

CHAPTER ELEVEN

New York, New York

Ella, One month ago
    Falling on the mat, I laugh uncontrollably while Simone glares at me from above. "You, bitch, did not just give up."

    "Ella, get your ass up. We aren't giving you a free pass," Chloe says, while whirling the Twister spinner again, and then ordering, "Right foot on red." I groan into the glossy mat but lift myself up to comply, holding one hand in front of me while the other hand is on the side.

    I'm not flexible, so I feel the strain in my muscles from that. Leave it to Chloe to remember our childhood game and insist on playing it so we can cheer up.

    I know she's worried sick about me after the whole train incident, so I agreed to this, along with a few bottles of wine and a girls' night. Simone baked some delicious goodies, so in my book it is a win-win situation.

    "You are buying us all massages after that, just saying," Simone informs her while glancing at the spinner to figure out where to put her left hand.

    "Me? You are the one with the rich husband!" Chloe sounds outraged and

nudges her on the shoulder, and they both lose balance and end up tumbling to the floor.

A beat and then loud giggles erupt, and I just shake my head. "Now who did that on purpose?" Before they can reply, my landline rings loudly, the screeching sound loud enough to make my ears bleed, and the girls cover theirs.

"Fuck, Ella, make it stop." A morning hangover apparently is a bitch to everyone, so to ease my pain and theirs, I hurry to the phone and pick it up quickly.

"Hello," I say breathlessly, and there is a pause on the other end of the line before the masculine voice speaks, sending shivers, and not the best kind, through me.

"Ella Gadot?" he asks, and I nod, only then realizing how stupid it is, considering he can't see me.

"The one and only."

"My name is Noah Davis. I'm from the FBI." All humor leaves me, and I motion for the girls to shut up with my index finger on my lips, and instantly they listen. We rarely use this signal, so they know it's important.

"Is everything all right? I gave my statements two days ago." Although the police let me go before the feds arrived, but then there was nothing else to say.

"The case is closed." His voice is laced with authority, as if he finds it offensive I've interrupted him. "Would you like to work with the FBI?" Everything inside me freezes, and I pull the phone back from my ear, gaping at it in shock, because I never expected to hear those words.

And at the same time, they are everything to me.

"Well, yes—"

"Terrific. Please come to the New York office tomorrow. We need to interview you first. Have all your paperwork with you." With that, he hangs up on me while I still stand there, blinking a few times and trying to calm my rapidly beating heart.

Will my dream come true after all?

*E*lla

Taking a deep breath, I knock on the office door three times, and when I hear the harsh "Come in," I step inside to find Noah behind the desk writing, probably the report on the unsub before closing the case for us.

His jacket is thrown over his chair, his sleeves are rolled up, and a steaming cup of coffee is wrapped tightly in his left hand as he writes furiously with his right. All in all, the boss seems tired as hell and probably dreams about going home, when I'm about to bring him more problems than he expects.

He frowns at me, but then resumes his work as if I'm not even around. "Ella, why are you still here?"

Fumbling with my fingers, I try to search for the words, still afraid of his reaction. My mouth opens of its own accord, but the words spilling from it surprise even me. "Why did you hire me?"

Noah pauses his writing and raises his eyes to me with an unreadable expression. "What do you mean?"

"The FBI didn't want me due to my past. But then you showed up and they hired me despite not having three years of experience in the field."

He leans back in his chair, his hands clasped in front of him as he studies me, and I shift uncomfortably, because his drilling stare has the ability to see past the façade.

Past the lie I'm harboring, but I came to confess anyway. The man trusted me when he picked me, and by hiding the book, I showed exactly what all the professors and professionals predicted.

A personal attachment and obsession over finding a suspect.

Was I not cut out for the job after all? All those years spent in training, and hoping, only to what? Find out I wasn't meant to be an agent?

"You showed great skills with the Smith case. Plus, your work experience spoke for itself. Sometimes it's not about experience in the field. I believed you'd be a good asset to the team, and I wasn't wrong. You just helped to figure out his profile, Ella." He picks up the folder with the case and shakes it. "This case is closed because of you."

"We still haven't found him."

He shrugs. "That is not our job." He pauses. "Ella, we are profilers. We investigate the mind of a serial killer and help the police figure him out. It might help the police catch them. Sometimes they can do it even without our help. We are needed on other cases too. I know it's hard to let go, but you have to learn," he finishes, and I glance down.

He is right, of course. Profilers cannot spend their time waiting to catch a criminal when thousands of cases await them, but I'm not sure we can let go of this one.

So with no further delay, I say, "He sent me a book." Noah freezes, straightening up at once. "After that, he messaged me saying it holds the key to the investigation."

"When did this happen?" His voice is low and harsh; his hands fist while his face is filled with barely contained fury.

"Two days ago."

The table shakes as he punches it hard, the sound reverberating through the space as he stands up, shouting at me. "And you are just telling me this now?" My shoulders sag while he continues to scold me. "You should have told me the minute it happened. Do you realize how dangerous that is?"

"I thought—"

"What? You thought what? We need to inform the police. You are his target, Ella."

My brows furrow while my mouth opens and closes, desperately searching for words. "He just plays with me to see if I can figure out who he is." We've studied cases like him. They feel so invincible they usually pick one of the team members to elevate themselves in their eyes.

Hollow laughter erupts while he shakes his head in disbelief. "Ella, he is not playing with you. He hunts you."

I croak, "What?" Surely he is mistaken, why would he want to hunt me down?

He presses the intercom, and in a second, Jacob's voice responds, "Noah."

"Get everyone back in the office as soon as possible."

"Why?"

Noah's harsh reply freezes me to my bones while a loud *oh shit* echoes in my mind. "He found a woman."

An hour later

*E*lla

Everyone throws me accusatory glances, but no one comments on the fact that I placed all of us in a dangerous situation.

"We can stop the 'drilling Ella' contest and focus on the case, shall we?" Andrea suggests, and Preston snickers.

Jacob claps his hands fast as he rises from his seat, goes to the board with all the killings, and starts talking. "So far, there is no indication of female bodies. Which means that killing Ella is not his MO, and serial killers rarely change them." My brows lift in surprise that he actually tries to solve the puzzle instead of screaming at me. The guy doesn't like me much, but it turns out he was always on his team's side.

Well there is that at least.

"But he sent her the book with a note about hints. It's like he wants her to find him," Noah says, while studying the board with a frown.

"She's new. What is so interesting about her that he wants her?"

With that question Jacob addressed to me, I shrug. "I'm boring. I have no clue."

"Any boyfriends that didn't take rejection well?"

The bile rises in my throat just from someone assuming my ex could be, well, this.

"No. My last boyfriend was a lawyer in a firm who has an amazing father. He married two years ago." My cheeks flush, because honestly, who wants to discuss this aspect of their life?

I catch Kierian's gaze as he sips his drink, a wistful expression crossing his face when he speaks up for the first time during this meeting. "Maybe we need to take a step back."

Andrea rests her cheek on her arm. "Meaning?"

"We know for sure this guy is the victim of family abuse. If Ella is the surrogate for his mother, then something in her past makes her similar to his mother." He pauses. "He is a control freak. If he knows where she lives, he can easily hack the system and get her file. Or get to know something that's already public knowledge."

Everything inside me freezes when I understand his meaning, and my breath hitches, betrayal running through my veins at him outing me like that to all of them.

I shared my pain with him, and that's how he proves his trust? "You son of a bitch!" I exclaim, my chair hitting the wall, and he follows suit, plastering his hands on the table.

"I'm saving your life here. You don't want to look in the past, then don't. But we have to."

Everyone moves their heads from me to him, confusion written all over them... except for one person.

Noah sighs heavily. "He is right, Ella. That's probably why you are so interesting to him."

"What the fuck is going on?" Jacob finally roars, clearly fed up with all this.

By the stubbornness flashing in their eyes, I know they will tell my story if I don't. So with a trembling voice, I answer his question. "Twelve years ago, I came home from a party. My parents were very strict about that stuff, constantly having boundary after boundary. They never explained why, but I suspected it had to do with my mother's crazy-wealthy family who were against her marriage to my dad." I open a bottle of water and take a generous gulp, my throat suddenly dry. "Long story short, when I came home, my father had his throat sliced open, Mom was shot, and my sister taken. A few hours later, they found her dead in our basement, raped and battered. I didn't know back then who it was, but a year later, we found out it was our neighbor, the father of my best friend," I finish, and wrap my hand around my neck, wincing at how sharp those words feel even after all these years.

No matter how much time passes, my wound will never heal.

Is it the same for him?

I blink at the sudden thought and shake my head. Each serial killer is screwed up in their own way, and most of them have had hard childhoods. But it's not an excuse to do what they do.

I chose differently. Why couldn't he?

Silence falls over the room as they stare at me, some with pity, some with horror despite their profession. I'm used to all this, and this is one of the reasons I so wished to avoid them knowing.

It's one thing when something happens to abstract people, but quite another if it's a friend or a coworker.

Andrea opens her mouth and then closes it, lost for words, while Jacob shifts uncomfortably.

The only one who doesn't have a reaction is Preston who continues to type on his laptop, searching for clues on the case. A humorless laugh begs to slip past my lips as realization hits me. He probably knew all along; he is a hacker, after all.

"So if this gives you a clue why he might have set his hunting ways on me, be my guest. Because I don't get it." Sarcasm laces my voice as I sit back, digging my pen into the paper, imagining Kierian's face as my target.

And people wonder why I have trust issues and don't do relationships.

"Your suffering." Preston clears his throat as all our attention shifts to him. "Out of all of us, you are the only one with a messed-up childhood. You don't have a husband or kids or serious relationships."

"So?"

"In his mind, you are in pain over what happened to you. And he wants to ease it."

Say what now? This couldn't be it. Before I can comment, Noah clicks his fingers.

"And if he set his eyes on you, he is not going to stop."

"This is not his MO. Why me? He is a controlled serial killer who hunts his victims. And all of a sudden, he decides to save me? It makes no sense." Why am I the only one who sees reason here? He sent me the book, because he probably considers me the weak link in the circle since I'm new.

"Unless he waited for the specific day for us to find the remains. The call came from an anonymous number, Ella."

Kierian hits the table with his fist. "You were his target all along. And those bodies? Were for you to admire his work."

"This is insane," I whisper, and that's when Jacob finally speaks again.

"No, Ella. This is our work."

Andrea's voice is laced with defeat. "You are our only way to find him."

"What does it mean?"

"The case won't be solved until he wants it to be. Whenever he decides to strike next will depend on how much he wants to impress you." Noah curses, but then continues, "Preston, run more research on the kids who might have fit the profile, but beyond that, we will leave the case open and proceed as usual. The police are informed, but I highly doubt he will do anything in the next few months. He probably gets a thrill out of you being scared."

This is it then.

I have to be the prey for the unsub, and it will be on his terms. I want to scream in frustration, but what good will it do?

Instead, I get up and dash toward the elevator, pressing the button feverishly, willing the damn thing to come faster so I won't have to face the rest of the team for the time being.

"If you break the thing, it won't come faster either," a husky voice speaks next to me, but I ignore it. Finally, the doors slide open and we get inside.

All the way down, we stay quiet while I barely restrain myself from punching him in the face. I don't want to lose my shit in the building though, or they'll think the stress of the job is too much for me to handle.

Once outside, he grabs my arm, spinning me around to face him while I grit my teeth. "Not here, Kierian. Can you at least honor *this* request?"

His mouth transforms into a thin line as determination and fury crosses his face. "Someone had to be the voice of reason."

"Well then, thank you." With that, I hop into my car and drive in the direction of my house, not caring in the least for his side of the story.

How can you find someone's weak point and then press on it before that person is ready? It's just not done!

The drive is done in a haze, and once in the parking lot, I rest my head against the seat back, exhaling a heavy breath. Three days on the new job, and I'm wondering why I ever wanted it to begin with. My first case sucks, a serial killer is obsessed with me, and I didn't come closer to easing anyone's suffering. At least in the center, when we spent time with the victims, they got better. I felt like I made a difference in the world.

In this job though? I feel like a constant failure.

A swift knock on my window startles me, and I frown the moment I recognize Kierian. Grabbing my bag, I get out while huffing in annoyance. "If you don't mind, I'd like to rest after an eventful day. And for your information, this is private parking."

My words don't fly with him as he motions for me to go inside the building. "You want to scream or be stubborn, fine. But you can't run around unprotected."

I laugh in his face, which he doesn't appreciate if his barely audible curse is anything to go by.

He has a lot of nerve ordering me around.

"I'm an agent, trained as well as you. So you can take your worry and shove it down your thro—" The rest of my words are muffled as he picks me up over his shoulder, and I'm upside down watching the concrete move. "Put me down, Kierian!" He doesn't listen, just walks speedily to the building and presses the elevator call button while I punch his muscles and, yes, his fucking sexy ass—not that it matters to him.

What is he? Made out of stone?

I push up on his shoulder, but as he enters the elevator, I have to drop low again and growl in frustration.

"Stay put, Ella. Or you'll hurt yourself." This man has to be seen to be believed!

"I won't hurt myself if you put me down!"

He slaps my ass, and I'm so shocked, it takes me a moment to react.

He slapped my freaking ass?

"You—" He exits the elevator and places me on the floor, and I push him away—not that he moves. "You know it's called stalking, right?" He shrugs, leans against the wall, and waits for me to unlock the door. "You are not invited."

He rolls his eyes and gives me a patronizing smile that pisses me off.

Finally, I open it and step inside, and he trails after me, inserting his foot so I won't be able to close it in his face. "Ella, you don't know if he is around. Let me stay for a while so I can be sure nothing disturbs you. All things aside." All humor leaves him as he gazes at me with a serious expression, and the situation settles on me.

The unsub knows where I live. What will it take for him to enter the house or ring the doorbell so he'll have easy access to me?

Fucking men!

Exhaling heavily, I let him in, then collapse on the couch, resting my head on the pillow and covering my eyes with my arm.

"You are such a great hostess, just... wow. No words," he says, and I flip him off, to which he just laughs.

I hear the water running in the sink, and then my refrigerator makes a sound. Peeking through my fingers, I see him frown as he studies my very empty cupboards.

"You've got nothing."

Oddly, this brings me satisfaction, as he looks like a kicked puppy.

"I told you I don't cook."

"You told me you don't eat breakfast."

"Hence the not cooking part. Duh."

"I'm starving, so I'm going to order something. What are you in the mood for?"

At this point, I just give up and deal with his presence, because my head will explode from all his jerkish ways. "Pizza."

He nods, dials the phone, and orders it, while I play back the conversation at the office and fury rushes back in.

And I don't want to keep it inside.

"You betrayed me!"

He walks to me on the couch, lifts my legs, and sits under them so my feet are resting in his lap.

What in the world? I honestly don't know how to act around this guy. None of my previous men were... well... him.

"No, I protected you. They needed to know." He wraps his hands around my foot and gently squeezes it, applying pressure on the sole, and I moan as pleasure travels all over me. "Spending the night in the office is not healthy," he mutters, massaging up and down, and relaxing me more and more. I lie more comfortably on the pillow and groan as my back finally finds a horizontal position.

"Just don't stop, and you are forgiven," I mutter, and he laughs. Rationally, I understand that if not him, then it would have been Noah who spilled the beans.

Slowly, I drift to sleep, in heaven with the soft couch and Kierian's magic touch. And that's when the doorbell rings, pulling me out of my nirvana.

Groaning into the pillow, I grumble, "You and your pizza."

But then my stomach rumbles, and he says, "Apparently not only mine." He pays for it and places it on the counter, then opens my cupboard for two glasses for the wine he pours from the open cask he took out of the fridge earlier.

"Forgot to tell you, yeah. Make yourself at home." Sarcasm laces my tone, but he just winks and motions for me to come closer.

Sighing, I do and sleepily munch on pizza, and only then realize how starved I am. "You are forgiven."

He chuckles. "Since I'll be staying around, we'll need to invest in food. Takeout's not healthy."

His words fall on deaf ears, considering the delicious taste still has me in a happy place.

"What are we doing?" I ask, leaning my arm on the counter in a half-lying position as he sits next to me.

"What do you mean?"

"Well, wine and food and you here. It's weird."

He doesn't say anything at first, just eats his pizza and then washes it down with wine.

"That's called a relationship. You've told me you had two of them."

I snort, taking a sip. "Yeah, and we rarely did this. Mostly we just went out or had sex." His hold on the napkin tightens, and I can't help but tease. "You know, kissing under the stars while they wrote poems for me." I sound dreamy, but it transforms into a yelp as he pulls me closer and captures my mouth with his, sliding his hand in my hair as we forget ourselves in a passionate kiss that makes the outside world disappear.

Slowly, he lets me go so I can breathe as he tugs on my lower lip and then bites on my chin. "For my sanity, don't mention your exes, Ella."

A giggle escapes me. "Why? You don't have any?"

"I had my first and last so-called serious relationship back in high school." He picks up his wine and goes to the couch, kicking his legs up on the table, and my jaw drops open.

I lounge on the chair in front of him, and ask, "How old are you?"

His brows furrow. "What does that have to do with anything? Thirty-one."

"Are you nursing a broken heart or what?" The idea doesn't sit well with me. Is there a girl who holds his heart and everyone is just a passing-the-time thing for him?

Look at you now, Ella. Welcome to the insane club!

"No. I just like sex, and I've had plenty of it without the emotional attachment."

Is that explanation supposed to make me feel better?

"But you want one with me? Why?" I truly feel like a freaking teenager on her first date.

Something crosses his face, but it's so quickly gone I can't read it. "We had an instant connection; that's never happened before. We fit in bed. And to add to it, we work in the same field. You are perfect."

The way he says the last words sends goose bumps through me, and I don't know how to react to them. "Just remember I told you they never work out for me."

"Duly noted, but here it will work." He places his arm on the back of the couch and wiggles his finger at me. "Come here, you are exhausted."

Without complaining, I join him and rest my head on his shoulder. "What will happen now?"

He exhales heavily, running his fingers over my hair in soothing motions and kissing me on the head. "We will move on, and if he shows up, the police will investigate. Meanwhile, try not to think about him much. It could have been anyone. Maybe he just thought he would scare you more because you are new."

I don't believe that, but I don't want to argue about work anymore.

He turns on the TV and puts on some action movie, while I listen to his heartbeat and think how tired I am, yet I don't want to leave the cocoon of safety he's created around me.

Slowly, I fall asleep, completely secure in his arms.

And that's a first for me.

*P*sychopath

Patience is a virtue.

Too bad I've never had one.

Just a little longer... and she will be mine.

CHAPTER TWELVE

*E*lla

    Pushing through the sweaty bodies on the dance floor, I aim toward the bathroom while the club music blasting from the speakers creates euphoric emotions inside me.

    I got the job! I got the freaking job!

    Stepping inside the bathroom, I quickly wash my hands of the spilled beer and go out, ready to continue my celebration, knowing full well once the work starts I won't have nights out. As I step out of the bathroom, I bump into someone.

    His back is as solid as a rock, and I can't help a giggle escaping me, as I mumble, "Sorry." He swiftly turns around, and I blink several times as I drink in his handsomeness.

    Holy hell, hello there!

    My breath hitches as my hands slide to his shoulders, steadying myself, because these fucking shoes are killing me, even though Chloe insisted they look pretty on me.

    An unfamiliar surge of energy sparks between us, creating an awareness that swamps me in a wave that awakens every little hair on my body. I've never felt anything like it, the instant attraction that people talk about.

    Everything in me screams to step back and run in a different direction, because if someone has the power to have such an effect on me in the first minute of meeting, what would he be capable of in the future?

But I don't move. Instead, he introduces himself to me. "Kierian." His voice is husky, disturbing me in the most teasing way.

I nod, while replying, "Ella." But then blab, "What an unusual name." My cheeks heat up when I realize what I said to a stranger, but he just chuckles next to my ear, and it sends shivers down my spine.

Control yourself, Ella!

"It's an Irish name."

"Meaning?"

A sinister smile graces his face. "The dark one."

I'm slightly taken aback by his explanation, or implication for that matter, but then it registers as I touch the silky strands of his black hair. "Because of your hair, huh?"

Something flashes in his smile while his hold on me tightens. Usually, it would send alarms going off in my system big time, but this time, I can't look away from him.

"Would you care to have a drink?" he asks without answering my question, shifting us a little to the side so people can pass by without bumping our shoulders.

As a result, I end up pressed between his muscled chest and the wall, because we can't take our eyes from each other.

"I'm here with friends." As much as I'd love to say yes to him, this night is not about hot guys, but friendship. So even though every nerve in my body protests the action, I step back, freeing myself from his arms, and wink. "Thanks though." With that, I quickly dart back onto the dance floor where Chloe and Simone jump to the beat of the music.

"That trip was long," Simone says, but then glances behind me and smirks. "Hot stuff!"

Chloe follows suit, and her eyes widen while she winks. "Got yourself a hunk for the night."

"Who talks like that, Chloe?"

She punches her chest with a fist lightly. "Me." But then she whispers, which is still loud as she tries to do it over the music, "If you want to leave with him, we don't mind. You need to get laid, girl." Simone nods eagerly, and I barely contain myself from rolling my eyes at their suggestion.

Why does everyone care about my sex life? It's not like having sex on a daily basis is a must.

And besides, ten months is hardly long. I just haven't met anyone interesting to share the night with.

"Let's vote," Simone offers, and then adds quickly, "Okay, voted. You stay with the hot stuff while we head home."

My brows furrow. "Already?"

Regret washes over their faces. "The guys are feeling a bit restless with our boys. So it's better we go."

Loneliness hits me hard, reminding me that my friends have moved on with their lives and have families of their own.

It shouldn't hurt, but it does.

Maybe because I won't ever allow myself to have it, so what is left for me in this life, then?

"Sure." They kiss me goodbye as I stand in the middle of the dance floor, contemplating my next action.

Placing my hand on my chest, I hate the emotion that threatens to raise old nightmares, so I spin around, and thankfully Kierian is leaning on the bar, his entire focus on me.

Fire is blazing from his eyes as I come closer, and my breath hitches at the intensity of his gaze.

We can have a drink, chat, and dance around the inevitable ending of this night.

But why would I waste this opportunity if he has the ability to erase this loneliness, if only for one night?

So with a determination I've never felt before, I stroll to him and bump into his chest as he catches me swiftly, circling his arm around me while I fist his shirt and lift my head for a kiss.

He immediately complies, covering my mouth with his, and gives me the best kiss of my life.

I don't know what the future holds for us, but for sure, he is perfect for the night.

. . .

*E*lla

A finger traces down my spine, tickling me as a soft giggle slips through me, and I bury my face deeper into the pillow, not wanting to wake up.

"Wake up, sleeping beauty," Kierian murmurs next to my ear, his body pressed flush to mine, but I shake my head and try to cover myself with a blanket.

"It's too early." He laughs behind me, the sounds vibrating on me as he sucks on the skin in the crook between my neck and shoulder, and I angle my head, so he'll have better access.

"It's almost noon." His hand slides down my hip as he squeezes it, sending jolts through me, but I don't budge.

With a growl, he flips me onto my back, covering me with his body, and tugs on my hair so I have no choice but to gasp, and that's when he goes for my mouth.

The kiss is wet and deep, as he devours me as if he hasn't had it for days instead of several hours, like he is reclaiming me all over again.

Although I could kiss him for hours, I push him back as my lungs demand air, but it doesn't sway him from his intentions.

He licks around my collarbone, traveling down to my breasts and lavishing each of them with attention, enveloping them in his hot mouth and pulling with little bites. My hands slide down his back as I make a place for him between my thighs, but he stops and blows on my nipples softly, which brings more awareness to them, transforming them into hardened peaks that could set me off any minute.

He slips his tongue lower, biting my stomach and leaving hickeys on his way to my core, where I feel wetness coating my skin. I pulse with desire to feel him inside me.

Each time with him only makes me more addicted to his brand of torture, more desperate for his every touch and lovemaking.

Kierian is always so hungry for me, being able to go at it for hours and demand complete submission. In these moments, he is not a compatible boyfriend who understands me; he is a raging beast who wants to own his woman.

"Mine," he growls right before placing my legs on his shoulders and grazing the walls of my pussy with the tip of his tongue, barely touching me, but it's enough to send electricity through me and my moan fills the space.

He rubs his five o'clock shadow on the skin of my inner thigh, scraping it lightly, and sucking because he knows it's my sensitive spot. "You are so beautiful." His voice is filled with lust, as he grabs my ass cheeks and scoots me closer, his breath fanning my core and finally giving it his whole attention.

He ravages me with his tongue, licking me and biting on the flesh, scraping with his teeth against my sensitive skin.

A sob escapes me as I grab the pillow nearby and muffle my moans with it, not wanting the neighbors to hear me. They've already complained once, and Kierian hated it because they heard my moans.

I was just mortified.

He continues to lap at me, enveloping my clit between his lips and sucking on it, and an electric charge bolts through me. I keep repeating his name and gasping for breath, needing more, but at the same being afraid of what comes next.

He pushes his tongue deep, sweeping at my walls and tasting me as deep as he can.

He is hungry, domineering. I lock my legs around his neck, my pussy clenching, but it's not enough.

Kierian needs to get on with the fucking program before I lose my mind!

My hips jerk, lifting to his seeking tongue, as I pull at his hair, shamelessly rubbing myself on his mouth, and he welcomes it.

His fingers push inside me as he holds me down, his arm thrown over my stomach—not that I'll go anywhere.

It feels as if fire flickers over my skin, the release coming closer and closer, needing just a little friction that he denies me.

He rises as a whimper of protest leaves me, but he just murmurs, "I told you not to tease me. Now you get your punishment."

My brows furrow, my body still hungry for his touch. I'll go insane without him finishing what he started. "If you don't want to help me —" I warn, and yelp as he flips me to my stomach and grips my hips, sitting me on my calves as he makes a wider space between my legs.

And then a loud whack echoes as he slaps my bruised flesh, making me hiss in pain, and pleasure too, as it sends awareness through my entire body, alerting every nerve. He ignites my skin with each touch.

I bite the pillow, enjoying the game as he slowly slides a hand up my back to my hair, fisting it and bringing me up while his other moves to my core, seeking entrance to the wet heat he created.

Kierian dips his head to give me a hot kiss, practically eating my mouth as we share each other's taste. His fingers sink into me and we both groan, as I take my mouth away and rest my head on his shoulder, needing more.

He lets go of me again. I huff in frustration but return to my stomach as he trails kisses down my back, licking and sucking on the way, leaving his marks everywhere.

Whoever sees me naked will know I'm taken.

He bites on one ass cheek and then the other, but before it can sting, he dusts kisses on them, soothing the skin and driving me freaking crazy.

He even manages to give me a lick from behind, and my core clenches around his tongue, but it's not enough anymore.

My ragged breath is a warning that I'm close, so close, but I don't want to come like this.

I need him.

"Kierian," I cry out, and this time he complies, probably having enough teasing himself.

Smoothing his hands along my ass, he grips my hips as he thrusts deep, pushing me forward on the bed, and I fist the sheets for a source of steadiness.

For a second, he doesn't move as he adjusts himself inside me, and I gasp, wiggling a little, because I can't take it anymore.

Kierian's nails dig in my skin as he pulls back and then thrusts forward. The bed moves right along with him as he repeats the action again and again, causing my pussy to pulse around him. My breasts heave and my stomach sinks as fire spreads through me, awakening every nerve in me and sending me into a pool of sensations that makes the outside world disappear.

Yanking my head up, he gives me a harder push while he thumbs my clit, pressing it lightly, and it's enough to end me.

The fire burns and burns within me, demanding an outlet, and finally everything explodes, and with a loud cry tearing from my lungs, I clamp around him. He groans above me, still moving back and forth while I breathe heavily, trying to snap back to reality.

He spills inside me with a loud roar. He settles me on my back gently, and we both gaze at the ceiling, our bodies coated in sweat as the morning sun slips through the window.

"I've changed my mind. I'm so awake."

He laughs and slaps me on the ass, and I glare at him, rubbing it since the skin is still sensitive.

"I'm here for your pleasure, Ella." It warms my heart that he doesn't use stupid nicknames on me, since he knows I don't like it. Nothing is better than your man saying your name; at least you don't have to wonder how many other women he's called by the same name.

Giving me a light peck on the lips, which seems so chaste after what just happened, he rises, grabs his sweatpants, and goes to the kitchen.

Sighing in pleasure, I stretch my arms wide as a smile permanently settles on my mouth.

I get up and quickly go to the bathroom to wash off all the sticky and sweaty mess, even if I love his smell on me.

Stepping inside the shower, I turn it on and groan as hot water touches every sore muscle.

We've had three very eventful, intensive days at work, where a child was kidnapped and all the BAU analytics had to come in and help. Hopefully the child has survived the fifty-hour mark. We managed to locate a prostitution ring that operated in a different state. They collected kids all over the country and sold them to the highest bidder.

A shudder runs through me just at the thought of what could have happened if the police didn't manage to get to the ship on time.

Shampooing my hair, I think back on all the things that have happened in the last month and wonder how my life has managed to change so drastically in such a short time.

We've had many different cases to work, including a serial killer who murdered beautiful blonde women, and one man who liked to torture his victims then release them after cutting off their ear as his trophy. We assisted the police as much as we could and rarely made any mistakes in profiling, although our profiles weren't always the major factor in catching the killers.

Police even solved the Blake case; turned out his so-called secretary killed his wife in jealous rage. It felt good to know that my first impression of the man was correct and he wasn't a killer.

The team has finally accepted me, and we usually hang in the bar after work. Jacob held a barbecue at his house a week ago, where he and Andrea announced their engagement.

That came out of the blue, considering I had no clue they were even dating.

Kierian and I have given this thing between us a shot, so he practically lives here. He goes home only for clothes or when his family visits.

I haven't met them, and I'm not ready for it either. We go on dates and normally have interesting conversations. I had no idea there could be such harmony between partners. He understands me and my passion for this job, and slowly, with each day, he convinces me more and more that this thing between us can work.

Chloe and Simone like him too. We've even had a night out where we went together with the guys to a bar and danced the night away.

This is all so surreal to me, and sometimes I wonder what the catch is... although it quickly passes.

The problem is, nothing in my life ever goes according to plan, and if good things happen, inevitably someone or something bad comes along to snatch it right out from under me.

After getting out of the shower, I quickly blow dry my hair and put on a white fluffy robe. A smile pulls on my lips from the smell of freshly made coffee and toast.

I pad to the kitchen, where Kierian flips the eggs in the skillet and then places them on plates while grabbing the toast on the way to the kitchen island. "You're never going to accept the fact that I don't eat breakfast, are you?" I ask, and jump on a barstool, moaning as the first taste of coffee hits my tongue.

"We both know you're lying. You're just too lazy to cook it," he replies cockily, and I burst out laughing, because it's so true. Since most of our mornings are spent together, he's made me a fan of break-fast. Now I look forward to those special moments in the morning when it's just us.

"So we have an entire two days for us!" The last case was brutal, so the team got two days off to get some sleep and regroup before going back to work. "You have any plans?"

He occupies the seat next to me, munching on toast. "I have to meet my family for dinner; there's some news they want to share." He doesn't sound happy about it, but I don't dig for details.

His family is a sore subject for him, and although it's hard for me to understand, I don't push him. I'd give anything to have my family back and enjoy time with them. Each one of us has our own story, so there it is.

"Cool."

He tugs on my robe, giving me a soft kiss on the nose. "I can stay if you want."

Shaking my head, I palm his face and rub his cheek. "I'm fine. We saved those kids, and that's the most important thing."

He nods, but then his eyes narrow and he sways to the side, and I curse inwardly.

Why did I leave it on the coffee table?

"You have to be kidding me," he mutters, and then gives me a harsh stare. "This fucking book again?"

"There is nothing wrong with reading it. You did!"

"Yeah, because I had to. Not because I was obsessed with a serial killer!"

"I'm not obsessed with him, Kierian." But he was my first case, and we failed. Plus, the killer sent me that book! Surely it meant some-thing. Even if he killed the abusive jerks, it didn't make his crimes any less bad. "I just want to find the clue he spoke about."

He gets up, his food half eaten. He grabs the counter and leans on it, and I wait for the fury to blow, because we're going to have the same argument all over again that we've been having for weeks now.

"Let go of this case, Ella." Crossing my arms, I shake my head and he growls.

Too freaking bad for him. "I can't."

"Why?"

I blink, surprised by his question.

Because there is something bothering me about this, like I'm missing an important piece of information.

I constantly feel like there is doom looming over me, and I don't know when it will hit the target, aka me.

I can't say all those things out loud though, so I settle for, "It's important to me, because it's my first case." He exhales heavily, but then hugs me close, kissing me on the head.

"Then if it gives you peace, continue, but I don't think it's healthy." And then he asks again, "Are you sure you don't want me to stay here with you tonight?"

Why does he keep on insisting?

"No, I don't." He must read the conviction in my voice, because for the rest of the day, he doesn't push; he jokes around and packs his stuff for the weekend with his fam.

Once Kierian leaves the house, I message Preston.

<**Me**> Did you find anything?

<**Preston**> Yep. E-mailing it to you now. FYI, it's so fucked up. Not sure if it's him, but it's the only case that matches.

A second later, my phone dings with a new e-mail and I read the information there.

And all the blood drains from my face once I discover what he had to live through as a child. Not that it gives me a clue what name he operates under now, but it gives me a better understanding of what drives him.

A conversation from a week ago with Preston plays in my mind.

"Andrea, have you seen Preston?" I ask, and she points at his office. With a thankful nod, I rush inside to see him humming a song while he types information from some files. Clearing my throat, I wait for him to spin around in his chair. His brows lift in surprise as I rest my back against his table.

"Ella? Something happened?"

Biting my lip, I contemplate my thoughts before speaking up. "I need a favor." *If it's possible, his brows rise even higher.*

"From me?"

"Yes."

He frowns. "Why me?"

"You are the only computer wizard I know."

He grins at that and puts his hands behind his head. "That's true. What do you need?"

Okay, here comes the hardest part. Technically, I shouldn't go around digging for information, but it might help the case, so here goes nothing.

"I've been thinking about our Hudson River unsub lately. The violence and stuff. If he kills his father all over again, what if he was his first victim?"

Preston blinks a few times. "That's a possibility, but it's vague."

Grabbing the chair nearby, I place the file in front of him. "I narrowed it down. He should be in his thirties now. We can search any crimes that involved father and son. Maybe they are still searching for him."

"I don't have unlimited access to various databases, just saying." *His sarcasm is not welcomed much.*

"It won't be secret information, just the police report."

"In what state?"

"Southern states, because both Greece and Troy are located in the south." *Even though it sounds insane, he shrugs and types that in.*

"What else?"

"Suburbs, no big cities. Most probably an only child." *He runs his fingers through his hair and gives me the look.* "It sounds vague again, but listen further. Highly intelligent kid. Maybe weird bruises. Along those lines."

"Hundreds of cases will come up, just so you know."

There is one more thing that I think will help narrow it down as much as possible without any key factors. "His mother either committed suicide or died at home, before he became a teenager." *Something must have triggered his tendencies.*

"Fine, once I have more info, I'll let you know."

Preston is the freaking sweetest!

I hug him closer and give him a light peck on the check while he groans, not liking the contact much.

Well, I have the name. But to learn the rest, I need to find out about him.

Good thing I have an entire weekend for that.

*P*sychopath
It ends tonight.

*E*lla
Placing the book on the table, I get up and a groan slips through my lips as I stretch my back. It's stiff from constantly bending my head over the book, searching for any trace that can help me catch the unsub.

Why did Homer have to use such a hard language? Half the stuff I had to google to figure out.

Turning on the coffee pot, I rest my back on the counter and think back over all the information I've found so far.

The Trojan War lasted for ten years and the Greeks won. Logically speaking, the unsub is a narcissist who would associate himself with a winning side.

Using this train of thought, I gather all the information possible on Achilles, as he seems to be the only logical person on the winning side, but nothing in his life or book or wars connect to anything with this case.

Pulling my hair in frustration, I'm about to pour coffee in my cup when three swift knocks at my door grab my attention.

"Open up, Ella. I know you're home." Chuckling, I do just that, only to see Chloe in all her glory holding wine and chocolate in her hands, along with a copy of *The Iliad*. "Since you are so busy with work, I decided to help you out." My brow rises and she rolls her eyes. "No need to be so surprised. It was one of my favorite books in high school."

"Right," I mutter as she enters, removing her shoes and placing her gifts on the table. She plops on the couch, kicking her feet over an armrest. "You forgot we went to high school together. And who helped you pass English literature?"

She laughs, and I pick up two glasses while sitting down on the carpet opposite her.

"True, but then again, I had a crush on Billy Jenkins."

I choke on my drink, and she giggles again. "What? The nerd from second period?" Not that I judged or anything, but the guy always said some weird shit and considered everyone stupid because they didn't know the periodic table of elements by memory. It's hard to like a guy like that, hence why he never had friends. So in time, his parents transferred him to another school.

"Hey, he had beautiful eyes. But that's beside the point. He was obsessed with the whole Troy war and I wanted to impress him, so I read those two books."

My brows furrow. "Two?"

She nods eagerly. "Yep. *The Iliad* and *The Odyssey*. You know what happens with Odysseus after the war."

Right, the king of Ithaca, who loved his wife Penelope a lot. For twenty years, she kept her vow to him and never married, despite other men approaching her. It took him another ten years to get back home, but the two lovers reunited at last.

"What do you have so far?" Chloe asks, popping a chocolate in her mouth, and I exhale heavily, scrambling through my notes scattered all over the place.

"Not much. There must be some connection, since he sent me the book. But it escapes my notice, you know?"

"Maybe it's not about the character." She grabs the maps of the wars mentioned in the book. "Maybe it's about a victory that someone accomplished? He is a psychopath, right? This can be his driving force." After her father was outed all those years ago, she learned as much as she could about them. It brought her peace, as she explained it. So whenever I had exams at the university, she'd study with me just to learn more. Maybe I shouldn't have shared my case with her, but I'm drowning in this stuff.

I need to find answers soon, and my best friend is trained enough to help me, at least in the researching process.

"Like something he would admire?"

"Yep." Nibbling on the pen in my hand, I rack my brain, scanning all the information I've found so far, but come up blank. "The only event mentioned in *The Iliad*, and I have to concentrate on this book because he sent it, is the Trojan War." Pointing at three thick piles of books on the floor next to her, I say, "And trust me, my mind knows everything on the subject at this point."

Chloe goes "Hmm" and then clicks her fingers. "Then themes." One of the reasons I love Chloe so much is that, due to her artistic brain, she has the ability to look at every situation from different angles and never gives up.

"Themes?" I repeat, and she puts a blank ledger-size piece of paper in front of us while removing everything else from the table.

"Yes. You didn't go into details of the case, since it's work and shit, but let's break down the story into themes and see which one could be the most applicable to him. It might hold the hint you are desperately seeking."

I deposit a few different markers next to us, and say, "Great idea. So red is the theme, blue is an explanation, and green is the likelihood of it happening."

"You and your notes obsession," she mutters, but writes love, family, friendship, war, victory, and deception. "Let's do illumination, shall we?"

And although I'm tired as hell and know that this probably won't bring many results, I can't resist sitting next to her and hugging her close. "Thanks, babe. Great to have you on my side." She winks at me and squeezes me too. Although I love Simone to pieces, Chloe and I always shared a special bond that nothing, even our history, could break.

"Anytime. Then you can tell me about the new relationship developing between Kierian and you," she adds mischievously, and my laughter is a nice break to the silence I had before she came along.

· · ·

*P*sychopath

Placing the blanket on the mattress, I step back to admire the carefully created place for Ella for the last time before I end our game once and for all.

After putting on a hoodie and gloves, making sure not to leave any traces, I leave my secret house. I inhale deeply, filling my lungs with much-needed air.

I've given her all the fucking time in the world, but she still hasn't figured it out. And although playing with her mind has become one of my favorite hobbies, it's not enough anymore.

This needs to end tonight so we can finally start the final chapter in this challenge we've thrust upon each other.

All my devices are clean and ready for her beautiful skin. I'll break her spirit piece by piece until she gives up.

Her giving up will be her ultimate downfall.

Unfortunately for her, it's inevitable, as none of them stuck for long.

And although the unfamiliar emotions in my chest nag my mind, reminding me she is innocent and doesn't deserve what I'm about to do, it doesn't stop me.

I lost my soul a long fucking time ago.

*E*lla

Shifting on the bed one more time, I give up on sleep altogether, and with a loud huff, I move the blankets to the side and get up. My toes curl in the fluffy white carpet, welcoming the warmth it gives me.

I turn off the AC as a shiver runs through me and pad softly to the kitchen. Grabbing the carafe, I place it on the coffee machine and turn it on.

I resist the urge to message Kierian and distract him from his family reunion. Considering I practically pushed him to go, calling him now would be a stupid move. The last thing I need is for him to worry about my safety.

When the machine dings at its completion, I pour myself a coffee while my mind instantly wanders back to the conversation I had with Chloe about the book. We drank all the wine and ordered Chinese, but it didn't help us in searching for the truth.

We discussed the themes and book to hell and back, but nothing suited the unsub. We even studied the moments leading up to the war and after, but came up blank. She left only a few hours ago, when David came to pick her up.

Something is not adding up for me. The connection between the unsub and the book is clear, because he sent it to me. But how can it hold a hint to his identity?

He uses surrogates for his father, but the Trojan War is not about a family relation. It's a love story gone wrong. Why is he so fascinated with it?

Then Chloe's words echo in my ears.

I mean, the Trojan War was no joke, but I truly feel bad for Odysseus. He came up with this plan for the horse, but it took him the longest to get back home to his wife. Kind of ironic if you ask me.

The cup pauses midway to my mouth as all the memories assault me at once and realization hits me like a ton of bricks.

This is a great book.

We all read it.

We all have this tattoo.

I did my research for Achilles and Hector, the two most important warriors in this story. They were strong characters, loved by people, and arrogant in their nature. Psychopath admires only people who he can associate himself with, no one else.

Among all this mess, I've never considered Odysseus, the one man who came up with the Trojan horse that won the war.

A deceit, something that looked like a god's gift when in fact it was a weapon to kill.

The cup falls on the marble floor, shattering into tiny little pieces as the wet pool circles around my feet.

The man we try so desperately to catch is one of us, the greatest deception of all.

Oh my God.

I turn around quickly to get to my phone, but I halt my movements when I see the man sitting on my chair, playing with a silver blade that glitters in the light of the full moon shining through the large window in my living room. The only other light in the apartment comes from the kitchen.

"I knew you'd figure it out eventually," he says, his voice void of any emotion as he plays with the blade, shifting it through his fingers. "That's why I chose you."

I swallow. Taking a step back, I wonder how long it will take me to get to my gun located under the table a few feet away from me. I open the drawer next to me and take out a knife; at least I won't meet my enemy empty-handed.

"You fooled all of us." Oddly enough, I stay calm, not letting my fear get the better of me. The woman in me weeps at the cruelty of the situation, at the monster I haven't seen even though he has always been so close.

Maybe that's my destiny, to be forever fooled by them. God, all those people who claimed criminal psychology was not for me clearly were right.

"One trait of a serial killer is high intelligence, and another is manipulation. But then again, you know that." He rubs his chin as something flashes through his eyes. "But the game is over, the time has come." Knowing full well I won't get another chance, I dart to my room to activate the alarm and grab my gun, but he is next to me like lightning, knocking me to the floor where I land painfully.

I cry out in pain, but kick him hard in the stomach, crawling from under him to scoot forward, but his strong hands holding my hips prisoner don't let me. I try to stab his arm with the knife, and he grunts but pushes me onto my back as we both breathe heavily. His hand rises, and I shut my eyes, expecting a harsh blow, but instead his fingers gently trace my cheek and our gazes clash.

And that's all I remember before he plunges a needle in my neck that slowly drains my energy and everything goes blank.

CHAPTER THIRTEEN

Evil is not born. Evil is made.

*P*sychopath, 7 years old

Snapping my eyes open, I hear something crashing on the floor downstairs as loud screams echo through the house. Digging my fingers into the blanket, I cover myself from head to toe, hoping the darkness will swallow me whole and I won't have to be part of it anymore.

The rain is pouring outside, the tress swaying from side to side, and the wind slips inside the room through the cracks in the windows inside the old house, which scares me so deeply.

I count to ten, hoping it will keep the monster away from me. My teeth chatter in fear as I hear heavy footsteps rush up the stairs, closer and closer to my room. Tears form, but I quickly wipe them away.

It will only anger him more.

The door bursts open and the harsh light blinds me for a moment as he removes the blanket and harshly grabs me by my hand. "Come on, boy." Ignoring my cry of pain, he drags me downstairs where my mother sits on the carpet, holding her busted lip. He throws me at her feet, where I land painfully on my stomach. I bite my lips so he won't see it.

"Now your bastard is here," Father hisses, the smell of alcohol strong in the air as he gulps from the bottle. "You think I didn't notice how you smiled at that

new neighbor? Did you fuck him too?" he asks, and even though I'm small, I know what it means.

Father always asks Mother this whenever we go out, which rarely happens, because he doesn't trust her to "stay put," as he calls it.

"I didn't even raise my eyes," she replies softly, glancing down at her hands while I scoot closer to her, hoping to feel her warmth, but she shifts back as if my touch pains her. Even though she does it because of him, it still hurts me.

"You think I'm stupid?" And with that, I hear the whoosh of the belt as he removes it from his pants. He plays with the leather, the smell penetrating my nostrils and sending fear through me, because I know what will come next. "Decide, you or the boy? I don't care who." He smirks, leaning in to her and tracing the belt over her cheek.

She swallows and then turns to me, palming my face. "Hide, darling," she whispers, and then points at her bruised face. "No matter how much I scream, do not come out of the closet," she begs, hugging me closer and rocking me from side to side. I close my eyes and count to ten, imagining my favorite song playing in the background.

Our embrace doesn't last long. He snatches me from her and pushes me harshly in the direction of the small closet near the TV, which is blasting a loud football game.

"Know your place, bastard." I've tried to find this word in the dictionary, but I can never do it, and asking people is out of the question. He is all perfect and smiley with them, which I never understand, because he transforms into a monster at home.

Everyone on the outside loves him; he is always there to help his friends and family, teaching kids to ride bikes and having the best barbecue in town.

But when the night comes and drinks are out, he is the only father I have.

Closing the door behind me, I sit on the floor and watch through the small holes, as he orders Mommy, "Get up, you whore. Let this be a lesson to you and your bastard."

Mom listens, and the minute she is up, he strikes her with the belt on the side. She doubles over and he hits her back, one, two more times, and then she falls to her knees. He kicks her in the stomach and she coughs, then spits blood from her mouth. Probably because she bites her lips rather than scream a lot, so no one will come to the rescue.

"Fucking whore, you were always one. Should have never married you. You will know not to smile at all those men." Hit, hit, hit.

My hands clench, and I want to rush outside to help her somehow, but then I catch her gaze as she looks straight at me—I don't ever know how she guesses where my gaze is—and she shakes her head.

She doesn't want me to be part of this.

Then I hear the most hateful sound in the entire universe, the zipper being lowered, as Father spits out, "Since you were so eager to open your legs for him, do it for me now."

"Please, not in front of him," she begs, edging away, even though she can barely stand from his blows. His laughter fills the space as he sips his whiskey again.

"Let it be a lesson to the boy that women are nothing but whores who'll turn their back on you the minute someone else wanders around." I spin around and put on headphones attached to a small music device. I press the On button, and the classical music fills my ears, overshadowing what is going on in the living room.

I've promised Mommy to be a good boy and do it in case Father does this again.

She always told me to count to a thousand, and I do.

At some point, she opens the door and fiercely hugs me close to her while sobs rack her body, and I do everything I can to soothe her.

While the monster sleeps on the couch, lullabied by the sound of a football game that I've learned to hate.

*E*lla

An annoying smell penetrates my nose, and I move my head to the side, trying to avoid it, but it's no use as it trails after me. Water drips on my cheeks, forehead, and lips, and finally my eyes snap open.

Piercing pain assaults me from every corner as if tiny needles dig into my scalp, scratching it. I wince and groan wondering how much wine I consumed last night with Chloe to have such a hangover.

"I thought you were a light sleeper." A deep and slightly husky voice fills the space, and I freeze as the memories come back, playing like a vivid movie in front of me.

Immediately, I glance down to see myself lying on a mattress. With an effort, I sit up only to hear the rattling of a dangling chain wrapped around my right ankle, long enough to walk freely if the pile of metal nearby is any indication, but tight enough to dig into my skin and cause unbearable pain if I ever try to free myself.

One, constantly shining light bulb above my head is the only source of light that allows me to study the place, and with each new detail, my stomach sinks, creating tight knots of desperation.

I'm in a wide-spaced cage that has metal bars surrounding me on all sides. A mattress and one table with two chairs are the only furniture items on the concrete floor. Nearby is a sink with dripping water that grates on my nerves and a small door with a tight space to the side, probably a bathroom.

At least it's locked, I think, barely containing the hysterical laughter that threatens to spill out.

The place reeks of chlorine and antiseptic. I hear a barely audible humming echoing through the space. Behind the cage's bars, I see a wide metal table, shelves with different kinds of weapons, and stairs that lead up, up, up, and only then, I gasp in surprise.

No.

"Underground, Ella," he speaks, and I finally shift my attention to the man, the unsub, as he grabs a chair, reverses and straddles it, zeroing his assertive and cold silver eyes on me. He wears nothing but black jeans and boots, with which he kicks the legs of the chair.

I open and close my mouth, unable to find the words, even though fury washes over me in strong waves. I want to scratch his eyes out, painfully.

At the same time, the deep realization that I was a fool comes too, and pain.

Unbearable pain from trusting a person who proved me wrong yet again.

"Congratulations," I finally whisper, and he raises his brow. "You won your prey." In my situation, most likely everyone would demand answers, scream for help, or beg. Or try to talk reason to the psychopath, hoping he would make an exception just for them and free them from the nightmare.

That's the normal reaction, but there is nothing normal in this situation between us, because I already have all the answers.

He will never willingly let me go, so it's my job to get myself out of here. Even if it seems hopeless at the moment.

"Why?" I finally ask, wondering if this was his plan all along, or if he just decided to keep me in a spur of the moment thing.

"You're strong." His statement takes me aback as I frown. "You don't give up." His knuckles turn white; that's how hard he squeezes the top of the chair. "You love me." The way he says it, as if he's glad and sorry at the same time.

My love pleases him?

Kierian throws those words in my face, words I've spoken to him, opening my heart for the first time in my life.

"I thought you loved me too," I whisper before I can stop myself, and he freezes but then chuckles, although it lacks any humor.

"I'm incapable of it." Images of our time together, all the tender moments, movie nights, and making love, dance in my mind, and I wonder how it could have been a lie. Is he that good at hiding his emotions? He managed to deceive me.

Me!

And I thought I knew everything about serial killers.

"Am I like her?"

"Like my mother? No. She was blonde. Young. Haunted," he mutters while zoning out. "You are the exact opposite of her." He chuckles again. "Most of the things you wrote in the profile were correct, but not about my mom. I do not see the resemblance; it would have been too sick and weird, even for me." At least there is that, although in the current situation it gives me little comfort.

"Then why?" Like all those years ago with Benjamin, I need to know the reason he was obsessed with me.

He stays silent for a second, studying me, and then gets up quickly. "You have to eat. You've been out for about five hours."

I blink at this change of subject, clearly understanding he has no intention of answering my questions. "Wow! Thank you for being so thoughtful. I wish you'd thought about it before kidnapping me just to kill me."

He freezes but then resumes his walk, although not before telling me over his shoulder, "I've never said that's my goal."

I watch him go to what I assume is his torture table, pick up a wood tray, and come back inside. Seeing him now, I wonder why I ever thought he was easygoing and not possessive?

He just knows how to hide his tendencies better.

Kierian places the tray of food on the table inside the cage, and by the smell, I recognize pizza and chicken parmesan, my favorites. He pours water, and then orders, "Get up." I don't move or listen, staring into space over his shoulder, knowing how much it pisses him off.

Serial killers deem themselves kings of their world; they either like attention on them or none at all. Maybe I should be wiser and not antagonize him, but I can't.

I'm not just a victim; I'm a woman whose heart he broke. And it's even worse, because I'll never be able to completely escape him, even if I manage to get the hell out of this place.

He growls in frustration and dashes toward me, and I scoot back, but it's useless against him. He grabs my arm and pushes me toward the table, the chain dangling from my ankle scratching loudly against the floor, reminding me of my prisoner status.

As if bruises weren't enough.

I stop at the chair, and he presses into my shoulder. I have no choice but to collapse onto it with a loud thud. I ignore the pain traveling from my lower back to my shoulder, which is stiff from being in the same position for hours.

"You need to eat."

Hollow laughter erupts from me. "Why? You prefer your victims fully fed?" He doesn't appreciate my sarcasm, if his frown and growl are anything to go by, but I don't give a fuck.

He won't leave me alive anyway, so what's the point of listening to him? I prefer to die with dignity.

"Eat."

I pick up the fork next to me, and while staring right into his eyes, drop it to the floor where it dings loudly in the otherwise silent space.

Fury flashes in his silver pools as he fists his hand. "Ella, don't make me—"

"Do what? Kidnap me? Torture me? Rape me?" I supply all the options, and part of me feels awful for throwing all those words at him when he never once tried to do any of it, but I honest to God don't understand his intentions.

He hunted me down and won, but instead of proceeding with his plan, whatever that might be, he gives me food and has conversations with me. Anytime now and we'll be playing chess!

With one swift move, he gets up, taking me with him, and presses me roughly against the wall. I groan in pain. "You don't know what torture is," he says harshly against me, and shakes me hard enough for my teeth to clack against each other. Some unrecognizable emotion crosses his eyes as he leans forward, and whispers into my ear, "And this body?" He squeezes my hips even though I try to pull from this hold. "It loves only my touch. You go up in flames whenever I touch you, and nothing will change that." His confidence has to be seen to be believed.

"No! It doesn't want you. I used to want Kierian. You have no power anymore."

"Don't make me prove you wrong, Ella. You won't like it."

"Do your worst, unsub. We both know it's a failing task." Truth be told, I needed to shut up like yesterday, because I don't know this man.

I still act as if my boyfriend is in front of me, and I need to separate the two in my mind as soon as possible.

Not that he gives me much time though.

The minute the challenge slips past my lips, he picks me up and throws me on the mattress. Before I can even blink, he's by my side.

I struggle, kicking him blindly while he doesn't even budge under my assault, and instead, he covers me from head to toe, wrapping a leather belt—God only knows where he got that—around my wrists and securing them tightly above my head.

Then he takes something out of his pocket and wraps it around my eyes, securing it behind my head. Only then does the soft cloth register as a blindfold.

"Let me go!" I pant.

His breathing is the only indication of where he is.

I'm completely at his mercy, and even though this man has seen my body from every angle possible, I've never been more vulnerable to him than I am now.

"Everything went away just like that?" He snaps his fingers next to my ear, reminding me of my earlier words, while I just huff in annoyance.

Should I be scared?

I'm more disgusted.

"Yes! The man I wanted was Kierian, not you!" I shout right into his face.

His chuckle, echoing in the space, lacks humor, and he tenses above me, clearly displeased with my reply. "Unfortunately for you, it's one and the same man. And your body wants me." His weight is gone in a flash, and I feel him hike my flannel dress up until it dangles on my arms, creating an even bigger cocoon around my hands.

A light breeze touches my bare skin. I hiss, thrashing on the mattress, needing to escape, especially when his hands slide down my waist to my hips and ass then go back up.

As insane as it sounds, goose bumps rush over me and the hair on my skin prickles, awakening sensations only he is capable of evoking.

Apparently, my body didn't get the memo that our lover turned out to be a serial killer!

"I hate you!" He doesn't listen but instead clucks his tongue.

"You might, but your body knows who it belongs to." With that, his hot mouth envelops my hardened nipple.

My back arches up as he sucks firmly on it as if trying to pull it from me, feasting on the flesh that sends shivers directly to my clit, and I bite my lips, because I don't want him to hear me moan and give him satisfaction.

He doesn't let me escape it though as he thumbs the other one lightly, nipping on the tip of the nipple aching with need, and then swoops down again, lightly biting the flesh.

"Kierian." My voice is full of hatred and desire at the same time, but I'm not sure if it's directed at him or me.

How can I submit to his desires?

"Who do you belong to, Ella?" he asks, and I almost snort, because if he thinks I will admit it's him, he has another think coming.

Growling, he shifts to the other breast and repeats the action, driving me mad. I fist my hands and my nails dig painfully into my palms.

Wetness is coating my thighs, as humiliating as it sounds, and he slides his tongue down my stomach, circling my belly button then dipping his tongue inside, making my hips jerk. "All in good time, Ella," he mutters, slapping my ass and earning himself a yelp. "There won't be relief until you admit it."

"In your dreams." Shouldn't I be acting differently after finding out the truth? Aside from this moment, I can think rationally, but now?

Now it's as if my being doesn't see the difference between Kierian and Psychopath, and it should.

It so freaking should!

Gripping my ass cheeks tightly—and probably leaving bruises, the fucking caveman—he shoulders my thighs and must've lain between them, because his breath fans my core. I try to lock my legs, but he doesn't let me.

I expect him to aim for my heated flesh, but instead, something cold slides along the inside of my thigh and my heart stops for a second, my stomach flipping.

My adrenaline spikes and I gulp for breath as fear rushes through me, intensified by the pleasure I previously felt.

"Ah, you're scared," he murmurs against my skin, licking me, and my body jerks. He holds me down, not letting me move. "Do you know what's been driving me for months now?"

I rasp through my dry lips quietly, afraid to even blink. "What?"

"To see how your pale skin looks coated in blood, just droplets. When your body knows exactly who owns it. When you don't have illusions about Kierian." He speaks about himself as if they are not the same person. "When I don't have to share you with anyone, even my alter ego." That's when the blade scratches me and a scream tears from my throat as I feel warm blood sliding down my skin, as the annoying sting assaults me.

He repeats the action on other side, giving me light touches here and there so I won't have deep scars in the future, but will sting and leave a mark.

His permanent fucking mark!

Tears stream down my hair and temples, the salty taste registering in my mind, when he whispers, "Shh, I'll make it better." And his hot mouth covers my flesh, latching onto my clit while his fingers press against the wounds, creating unfamiliar pleasure enveloped with pain.

He swipes his tongue inside me, probing deeper as if French kissing me, but then moves away, the tip of his tongue only lightly touching my lower lips, giving me a minute to breathe while desperation and desire fill my every pore.

He dives in again, but this time he is more dominant, more demanding, asking for my complete submission. He pushes a finger inside me, and my breath hitches, the pain almost gone from my mind as he lifts my ass up, sucking on me harder while my toes curl and fire spreads through me.

I pull at my restraints, trying to escape this confusing encounter, but he doesn't let me; instead, he continues to feast on me, growling into my pussy, and the vibration adds to my pleasure.

Then it's too much; everything he has done culminates in a single moment of ecstasy exploding inside me and I cry out.

He continues to lick my wetness for a moment before moving up to my navel and likely leaving a hickey there. He continues to lick, suck, and kiss until I can feel his mouth an inch away from mine.

"Who do you belong to, Ella?" The desire slowly fades away and reality slips back in, leaving me mortified by what I've allowed to happen with the man who kidnapped me.

Even if he is a man I loved first.

"To Kierian," I reply, and he tenses, and I know it will piss him off.

I expect him to shout and hurt me, maybe even wish for it, because then it will give me an excuse to never succumb to him again.

But instead, he leaves my side, and I hear his heavy footsteps as the cage opens and closes. I swallow down the tears that threaten, and wince in pain from the small cuts he left on me.

In a minute, he's back, pressing something warm and cold against me. My skin itches, like someone rubbed salt into it. I yelp.

"Stay still. I need to put antiseptic on the wounds."

Now he cares about it? I stay silent, because he took everything I had to give.

Once he is done, he removes the blindfold and I slowly adjust my vision, and then he rips the bindings away.

I instantly pull my dress down, scooting to the corner and covering myself with a blanket. I don't pay attention to my legs or the way he watches me.

How could I have done this with him?

So I lie on my side and pray for a solution to come to me, because this situation will slowly kill me inside.

Unless he does it first.

CHAPTER FOURTEEN

Psychopath, 9 years old

"*Seriously, Matt, what do you put in this meat? It's fucking delicious!*" *Uncle Bill moans around his bite of the burger, while Aunt Hetty scolds him.*

"*No swearing in front of the kids.*" *She sends an apologetic smile to my mom, who pours more iced tea for the guests.* "*Sorry, Margaret. He is a brute.*"

My mom wears one of her best pink dresses that causes her green eyes that stay dead most of the time to flash brightly, not that anyone notices.

After all, he has personally chosen it for her.

"*It's okay,*" *she reassures her, but quickly glances at Father, who flips the meat on the grill a few feet away from us. She must be satisfied with whatever she has seen, because she shifts her focus to me as she slides a plate full of french fries my way.* "*Here you go, honey. Have fun with your friends.*" *She runs her finger softly through my hair and nudges me in the direction of the pool, where all the neighbor kids are playing. Gideon and Alp are already there, waving frantically at me from the water as they jump on the float.*

This get-together has been organized by my father, who invited the neighbors to celebrate the first day of summer together, sort of a tradition to keep. Since no one cooks better than my dad, everyone eagerly agreed.

He has a façade to maintain, after all; he likes to tell my mom that no one

will ever believe her if she goes to the cops or friends. He'll take her to the psychi-
atric clinic with a mental disorder and he will be given custody of her "bastard."
We don't interact with them much anyway unless it's under Father's watchful
eye. Everyone just thinks Mom prefers to stay at home and do nothing. I've
heard some women whisper that mom thinks she is too damn good for their
friendship.

Shaking my head from the bad memory, I practically bounce on my way
as I think about diving into the water. I munch on the fries and pleasure
spreads through me, as I haven't had anything but soup and rice in over a
month after Mom's last punishment. Suddenly, Uncle's Bill voice freezes me to
the spot.

"Matt, Alp says your son doesn't know how to swim or hold his breath
under water?"

Dad halts his movements, his lips thinning, but he keeps his smile intact as
he raises his brow. "Really?"

Uncle Bill nods, comes closer, and lightly punches him on the shoulder. "What
kind of father are you that your son doesn't know how to do that? You've been
slacking." Everyone collectively laughs, and I relax a bit.

Father is not angry, which is always a good thing, but with his mood swings,
Mom and I don't really know what will set him off.

With relief, I join my friends, who talk about PlayStation and Disney trips
while I eagerly listen, since I have nothing but books to occupy my time.

Even cartoons are strictly forbidden, because they'd take away Dad's time
from the sports channels.

"We're going camping this weekend with Dad," Alp suddenly says, while
Gideon adds, "Me too." Then he splashes water at me and I dip down, grateful it
doesn't stain my favorite shirt. "Come with us?" he asks hopefully, but I just
shake my head.

"I don't like to go out." That's the excuse I always give to everyone, that
nothing but school interests me, and it's not hard to believe with my nose
constantly in a book. On the bad days, I wonder why they even stay friends with
me and buy me ice cream if I can't.

And I can't most of the time, because there is no money to spare.

The rest of the day passes by with tasty food, good times, and warm water,
while Uncle Bill teaches me how to swim and dive.

Once Dad closes the door after his last guest leaves, he places his palm, splayed open, on the door, and my mom's breath hitches as we see him shake with barely contained fury.

She pushes me in the direction of my room, but he turns around rapidly, grabbing me by the nape. I stifle a groan of pain in my throat because he doesn't like them, and he screams in my face, "You like to insult me, bastard, just like your whore of a mother, huh?"

He's dragging me through the living room when Mom hits his back, begging, "Let go of him, Matt." He doesn't listen and throws her on the floor with his beefy arm as he continues to walk.

"Mom?" I call, not knowing what to do as fear rushes through my veins. I've never had his anger directed at me before. She was always there to intervene. One of the reasons he always started with me was because he knew she would always protect me and never let him hurt me.

"Uncle Bill is your favorite person now, huh? Well let's see what he has taught you." With that, we end up in the downstairs bathroom. He turns on the water in the bathtub and picks me up, only for me to land painfully on my back as the water splashes around me. It's ice-cold, soaking my clothes instantly, and I try to sit up, but he presses on my chest, keeping me on the bottom, while muttering, "Let's see how long you can stay under." And slowly the water covers my entire face and ears. It's too high to breathe, so I hold my breath, but it's hard, so hard that I move frantically, desperate to find an escape from his hold but not succeeding. He pulls me up then, and I gulp in as much air as possible, but then he pushes me right back under. I choke beneath the water, my lungs burning from lack of oxygen. He repeats the action, lifting me up and pushing me under five more times before he stands up, wiping his hands with a towel while I grab the edges of the tub, breathing frantically and finally managing to turn off the water.

My body is almost paralyzed from the cold, running on adrenaline alone, but I have to get out of here before he comes back.

Tears mixed with water stream down my cheeks, and I hide my face from him, not wanting to give him the satisfaction, but he laughs as he leaves the bathroom. "Let it be a lesson, boy."

A lesson.

Everything is a lesson with my father.

Mom rushes inside, pale as a ghost, and I notice a red mark on her forehead; she must have hit the table with her head. That's his favorite thing to do. She sways a little as she comes to me, probably still dizzy from her wound. She wraps me in a towel and rocks me from side to side.

She murmurs softly into my ear, "My baby, my poor, poor baby." As I inhale her scent, I think that everything is okay, because she is here to protect me from the monster.

*P*sychopath

Ella rolls back from me, lying on her side, and covers herself with a blanket from head to toe. She breathes evenly, although she's probably dying inside.

After all, despite her claims, her body surrendered to me; even if her mind can never accept me, her body knows who has owned it for the last month.

All this time, when I've imagined kidnapping her and introducing her to all my sick wants and desires, that for some reason I desperately want to inflict on her, I never thought that once she was here all I'd want to do was take her the fuck away.

My darkness demanded to be seen by her, because she claimed she loved me. But for the first time in my life, my darkness didn't need to hurt; it needed to possess.

The damage I've done to her beautiful skin is minimal. Sure, it'll sting, so she'll remember her challenge, but that's about it. I could never bring her more hurt, and that pisses some part of me off.

Faking a relationship with her was part of the game, and certainly entertained me. I needed to learn her weaknesses, make her fall in love with me first so I could fully enjoy all of this. It was hard some days to act like a lovesick fool, but if it brought me victory? I didn't mind.

Right now though, I don't feel all that good about my victory, because although her body was in it, mentally, Ella was not.

Who the fuck have I become?

Disgust washes over me as I get up, putting on jeans and pulling at my hair, unpleasant memories entering my mind.

The beast inside me roars to get out, and I need to be far away from her to get a hold on these confusing emotions that are so foreign for me.

Grabbing another blanket from the chair, I cover her with it; although her eyes are closed, I know she's awake.

With one final glance, I close the cage behind me and go back to the house, where the raging inferno inside me can calm down.

Although I have a suspicion that nothing will be ever the same.

*E*lla
              Waking up groggy once again, I sit up swiftly, only to be reminded how much my body is sore after Kierian had his way with me, and disgust at my willing body sets in.

How could I have allowed it?

I remove the blanket and see myself dressed in a white flannel dress that reaches my ankles. The chain lies nearby; I'm free of it. A buzzing sound comes from above me, and the sink slowly drips water, which is getting on my nerves, so I do everything I can to block the sound from my ears.

I get up, looking around but not seeing Kierian anywhere.

He left me alone in his basement! I come closer to the cage and pull at the bars, but they don't budge. I kneel in front of the lock, studying the small opening all around.

Searching through my small prison, I try to find anything that will help get me the hell out of here, but I find nothing. If I had a bra, I could have used the metal from there, but he had to kidnap me in the middle of the night.

Screaming in frustration, I kick the bars, only to have pain travel to my knee, and I mutter, "Ouch." I touch the wall, hoping there is an opening in it, but come up blank there too.

Same with the floor, so much fucking stone that it would be impossible to dig.

My fingers are red and swollen from constantly searching for a means of escape, and my throat feels dry, although I ignore the food and water he left for me on the table.

Eating and drinking will mean agreeing to his methods or taking his generosity, and I won't do that.

I try a few more times to squeeze between the bars, to scream for help, to find a way out, when it finally sinks in there is no escape from here.

With a silent cry, I kneel in front of the bars, clutching them tightly as my body shakes with sobs.

"Think, Ella, think," I murmur to myself, desperately needing to hear my voice so I won't go insane. "How can you get the hell out of here?"

Slowly, I go back to the mattress and sit there, rocking back and forth, until realization hits me.

And with that, I fall asleep.

CHAPTER FIFTEEN

Psychopath, 9 years old

"Mommy, he is so beautiful," I whisper, clapping my hands as a tiny puppy searches for the source of the pat I'm giving, and the lady laughs softly.

"I think he already likes you."

Tearing my gaze away from the Labrador, I raise my eyes to her hopefully. "You really think so?"

She nods, grinning widely, but then she winces and a light sneeze escapes her. "Sorry," she apologizes, but I just shrug.

Christmas lights brighten up the neighborhood, as everyone has gone out of their way to decorate their houses, some with Santas, others with sleighs and reindeer, and some with both.

People are laughing all around us, engaging in snowball fights while running toward the end of town, where the biggest Christmas tree is located.

My mom catches my longing stare toward the kids who are inexplicably happy and hugs me closer, running her fingers through my hair, as I exhale heavily. "Do you like the puppy, honey? How about we give it a home?" she asks cheerfully, and I blink in surprise, because I know the rules as well as she does.

No one is allowed inside the house without Dad's permission.

The lady's face brightens as she extends the puppy to me while he leans and licks my nose, barking softly, and a giggle slips through me. "Here, take him for free. Merry Christmas." She sounds relieved, since it's the last puppy she needs to find a home for. Her dog recently had a huge litter, and since she had no way to keep them all, she just gave the puppies to anyone who wanted one.

We probably wouldn't have even encountered her if it weren't for Dad's order to go out a few times this week to stroll around the neighborhood and wish everyone happy holidays so no one would be suspicious. He mostly spoke to my mom, and I didn't understand half the stuff he said.

"Thank you," I whisper, bringing it closer to my chest and hiding my face in the soft fur, happiness unlike any other spreading through me when images of how we can play together dance in my mind.

A companion and friend who'll be with me all the time, even when Mom cries in the bathroom or when she sleeps the whole day because she took magic pills.

At least that's what she calls them.

Mom pushes me in the direction of the house just before a car pulls up. She freezes, and I tighten my hold on the puppy as Dad gets out of the car, waving at the lady and smiling at us warmly.

Oh no. This usually means bad things.

"Darling," he greets Mother, placing a grocery bag in her arms, and then ruffles my hair, tangling his fingers in it and pulling painfully, but I don't show it.

No emotions in front of people. His list of orders is always never ending. "It's cold out here." The puffs of air leave his mouth as he points at the door. "Let's get inside." We go in, and with each step, my heart beats faster and faster, and I feel it in my throat, as I don't know what to expect next from him.

Once we are in the hallway, the door shuts behind us, and Mom's painful gasp echoes through the house. My shoulders sag and I close my eyes, tears welling up in the corners.

I hear the bag fall to the floor, and I spin around to see him dragging Mom by the hair to the living room, not caring in the least how she hits her hips and knees against the furniture. He throws her on the floor, slapping her cheek harshly, which knocks her head to the side. "What kind of clothes are these?" He fists her small jacket and shirt that barely cover her from the cold since he refused to buy her new stuff for the winter, claiming she would use it to seduce someone. Whenever I asked Mom what it meant, she just told me to forget about it, but how could I? Is there a child who can forget his or her mom's tears?

"You bought it," she croaks, and then sends me a smile as if reassuring me everything is okay.

"I never bought this. You just want attention. Well, I'm here to give you mine." He rips the clothes from her as she tries to hide her naked skin from his gaze, and then he unbuckles his belt. "Get ready."

"Please, Matt. Don't. Not today. Not on Christmas."

Dad laughs sadistically while squeezing her chin so tight her lips come together and she breathes deeply through her nose. "Why would I give a fuck about that?" He's right though. We don't have a tree or toys or gifts. He doesn't even allow Christmas songs. He claims to hate it, and whoever does what he hates... always has to face his wrath.

He removes the belt from the loops with a loud whoosh. Immediately, I scratch my skin, remembering the last time he hit me with it across my back and how the bruises didn't fade for days, even though Mom put ointment on them daily. Dad even excused me from PE in school so no one would know.

The puppy chooses this moment to whimper in distress as he shifts in my arms, eager to get down, but I don't let him. Dad stops what he's doing and narrows his eyes on me. "Just what are you holding there, boy?" I step back, not answering, but that doesn't fly with him. He flings Mom on her back and she groans as he snatches the puppy from me, while I shout, "No!" He dangles it in the air, swaying it from side to side, disbelief written all over him, then drops it, but thankfully the puppy lands on his paws although a little unsteady.

"You have to be fucking kidding me," he mutters, and then grabs me by the nape, squeezing so hard I choke. "Who allowed you to bring this here?"

Mom covers her face, ready for his blow once he knows the truth, but I lie, wanting to protect her.

"I did. Mom didn't see it."

His brow rises as he leans closer, his breath fanning my face, as he asks, venom lacing his voice, "So you are brave enough to make your own decisions, huh?" He pats my cheek, delivering a hard blow with each touch. "Then get the fuck out of my house." Then he kicks the stumbling puppy and it hits the wall, whimpers spreading through the room. I run to him and pick him up; the frightened and injured puppy trembles and whines in my arms.

Dad opens the back door and throws me outside. I land painfully in the snow, but I still hold the dog. Mom begs him, "Please, Matt, please. He didn't mean it."

"Rules are rules. Say goodbye to your bastard."

"Mom!" I call, but all I see is her terrified face as he shuts the door. I rest my back against the steps as my soaking wet clothes become colder with each breath and the puppy's breaths are raspy against my chest. "Sshh." As light snowflakes settle on my skin, I pat him, hoping Dad's blow didn't do much damage.

My body is shaking, my teeth chattering against each other as the frigid air registers in my mind more and more, but I use all the warmth from the jacket on the puppy. "If we live, I'll call you Max," I whisper in his ear, relieved to hear light snoring coming from his muzzle.

However, I can't block the sounds coming from the house as dishes shatter, and Dad roars, "Useless piece of shit!" Then flesh is slapping against flesh, probably him using the belt on her, because that's his favorite torture when she doesn't manage to make good tea for him.

"Matt, please. My baby—" Another slap.

"Your bastard." She screams in agony, and I don't have to see it to know he kicked her in the side while she is probably lying on the floor, soaking in the hot tea spread in our kitchen. "Repeat after me if you want to see him in here. Your bastard." Nothing happens as he obviously waits for her reply, but I can't hear her response before something else crashes, and he yells, "You bitch!" I can hear them better now, which means he's dragged her back into the living room. "Bastard. Say it."

Mom finally gives up, defeat evident in each word. "My bastard."

"Good girl. And now you know what to do to lift my mood before I have to see your bastard, don't you?"

I close my ears, because I can imagine what will follow next.

I start to sing my favorite song and picture a different place, hoping to eliminate everything else, although Mom usually keeps quiet during these moments.

I'm on a beach, reading a book, the ocean caressing my toes, as I enjoy the sun and sand while my mom laughs softly behind me. A place where Dad has no access and I'll never have to be afraid.

A place where I don't have to watch my every word or expect pain every single day.

A place that doesn't exist.

I don't know how many hours pass, but I'm almost numb from the cold as my eyelids close, sleep claiming me by the time my mom opens the door and gets me inside, instantly wrapping her arms and a soft blanket around me.

"Mommy," I say groggily, "Max—"

"Get that dog out of my fucking house, now," Dad orders from the couch, his football game blaring loudly where some man comments on an amazing quarterback... and I hate it.

Hate it with all my heart.

"I'm sorry, baby," Mom says as she takes Max away. I try to stop her, but it's useless and she lets him out. "I will try to do something about it in the morning." But what will change in the morning anyway? She shouldn't have allowed me to have him, then!

She gave me hope! At those thoughts, I snap back to reality as guilt flashes through me for feeling angry at Mom. She is not at fault.

He is.

"No, Mom, please. He'll die." Tears are streaming down my cheeks, but she just shakes her head and takes me up to the bathroom, where she makes me a warm bath all while applying antiseptic on her wounds.

In the morning, the first thing I do is check the backyard for Max, hoping to get him to someone who can love him freely because they don't live with a monster.

But all I find is his dead body lying on the piles of snow.

Let it be your lesson, boy.

Someday, I will teach him a lesson too. That is a vow I intend to keep.

*P*sychopath

As quietly as possible, I unlock the cage and step inside while Ella lies on the mattress, the blanket softly covering her body.

A single bulb shines above with its buzzing adding to her captive experience. I walk to the sink and turn off the water, as the sound starts to grate on even my nerves. I wanted to have her unsettled so all her survival instincts would come into play and I could see how she reacted when danger hit her, but I fucking couldn't do it.

Leaving for an entire day, although I was just upstairs, didn't help me ease my hectic emotions regarding her or the fact that what I'm doing doesn't feel right.

My fists clench at the sight of untouched food and water—fucking stubborn captive.

Her face looks so peaceful as she rests her cheek on her hand, breathing evenly with not a care in the world. She must not have expected me to come back so soon; otherwise, she would have never allowed herself to fall asleep.

Where was her FBI training? I expected more fight from her than this quick surrender.

The search party started the minute I reported her missing, and the team has been crazy ever since but has come to dead ends everywhere they look.

I act like a worried lover, but at the same time hate myself because part of it is true.

I'm a fucking worried lover who is attached to his victim.

Kneeling in front of her, I trace my finger over her face, closing my eyes at the softness of her skin, and breathe in her scent.

I should be using my knives on her to see her break, so she will admit she has nothing to hold on to.

That's all I want.

But I do none of those things. Instead, I silently watch her, hating her worn-out state.

She flips onto her back, exposing more of herself to me, and suddenly her eyes snap open, our gazes clashing. A smile spreads on her face, as she stretches her arms, confusion crossing her face. "Why are you awake?" she asks sleepily, and then rises slightly to fist my shirt. "Come here, sexy guy." She pulls me to her and I fall, our chests pressing against each other as she runs her nose along the crook of my neck as she always does in the mornings.

Sexy guy.

That's what she called me anytime she was in the mood for sex.

Her hands travel up my stomach, lightly grazing the skin under my shirt, but then they slide up to circle my neck. "Relax, Kierian." She nips on my chin, lifting her hips a little, begging me to thrust.

She doesn't realize where she is or that I'm no longer just her "sexy guy." The haze of her sleep consumes her, so she still believes we are back in our apartment, where I made her body crave my touch.

Her mind might reject me, but her body? Her body fucking remembers everything.

A better man would have walked away, but I never claimed to be a saint. Maybe this will help both of us.

I remove my shirt then roll back to her. I smash my mouth on hers and she moans, rather loudly, but a weird emotion slips through me as her hands fumble with my zipper and she seeks my tongue with hers. Her velvety softness sucks on my tongue and my hands grab her hips, bringing my hard-on closer to her pussy, which is probably dripping for me.

Then a stunning thought slams into me like a ton of bricks, halting my movements as I realize I've missed this complete acceptance from her.

Where she welcomes me into her arms instead of fighting me.

Palming her face, I hold her stare as she gasps for breath and I freeze, hating the beast that rages for me to hurt and protect her... at the same time.

Why is torturing her not easy?

She laces her fingers in my hair, begging for my mouth as she brings us closer, and my eyes close while I breathe her in.

But then it happens, and I have no time to react.

She bites painfully on my lip, drawing blood as a piercing pain assaults my side. I huff in surprise, looking down to see she's stabbed me with a knife.

The fucking knife I must have forgotten earlier.

My state allows her to push me to the side as she quickly gets up, the keys for the house dangling in her hands that she must have taken from the loop on my jeans.

Blood coats my hand as I concentrate on a different place so it will help me ignore the pain and move forward.

A field, a green field where I don't have to do anything.

In seconds, I have control back and stand up, running on adrenaline alone, but then I realize she is nowhere in sight.

And that's when the door shuts loudly above me.

My little prey threw a challenge my way.

Big mistake.

*E*lla

My lungs fill with fresh air as I try to study the view in front of me but fail because my vision is still blurry. The massive brick house behind me seems to be located in the middle of a huge field with a forest on the horizon and no other houses or civilization in sight.

Desperation fills me, but I don't give up. Instead, I hold the hem of my dress up and rush forward, seeking either help or a hiding place from the man who without a doubt will chase after me within minutes.

For a minute, guilt penetrates me for what I've done to him, but it quickly disappears the minute the pain in my entire body registers.

He doesn't deserve my pity. My anything for that matter.

The sweat drips down my back as I inhale the smell of lavender and roses, and my legs take me farther and farther into the field. The only sounds are my feet smacking the ground and my gulps for air while I put all my power, or what is left of it, into running. I ignore my blisters and how hunger almost makes it impossible to move, let alone fight.

I can't let him get me; it will mean he wins.

Not noticing the slippery spot in front of me, I fall down on my ass, causing pain to burst through my body. Biting down on my lip, I allow the metallic taste of blood to enter my dry mouth that hasn't had water or anything else to drink for ten or more hours straight now.

Maybe I shouldn't have been that stubborn. But I just couldn't give him the satisfaction of me eating food after he used my body as his personal toy. It responded to him, and I hated myself for it. He knew this would break me, but he did it nevertheless.

And I knew me not eating would alter his plan, so I used it. No matter how much he claims I mean nothing, I don't believe it.

No, I'm not a lovesick fool to think he does it out of love.

He just cannot bear someone or something else bringing me pain besides him; that's how his twisted mind works.

He certainly didn't expect me to take the stand I did, and silent laughter escapes me along with a little whimper.

Did he really think I would accept him and beg him to touch me? I might love him, but no fucking way will I develop Stockholm Syndrome.

He can go fuck himself!

Placing my hand on the grass, I glance down to study the bloody fingers and stubby fingernails I'd bitten off with worry.

I wonder if this escape and whatever the future holds are worth it.

But despite what everyone might think, despite being alone in this world, my life does matter.

And I will fight for it till my last dying breath.

Slowly, black leather boots come into view right under my nose as Kierian's sadistic chuckle echoes over the field. "Little spitfire, aren't you? Quite the fight for your life you gave me." He kneels and grabs my chin while I struggle away from his hold, but it's useless.

My strength is nothing against his.

That's when I notice the blood oozing from his wound, but he doesn't even flinch in pain. In fact, he has a hollow expression, as if he's a different man.

He created a sub-reality in his mind to distract from the pain, smart fucker.

Raising my chin up, our gazes clash, and I can't help but whimper in despair as his unmasked face reminds me once again of the fool I have been.

Because all these weeks chasing the psychopath, I never once anticipated it was him.

And now he has come to collect the most valuable thing I have to offer.

My life.

What I did back in the basement is probably unforgivable in his mind, but I don't care.

I'd rather die trying to escape than because I gave up in a dingy, dark basement.

"You are mine now, Ella. The hunter has won his prey," he mutters, as he leans down and licks the blood from my lips.

His blood.

He throws me over his shoulder, marching in the direction of his sanctuary.

I can't move my muscles, and no matter how much I kick, he doesn't budge under my assault. All my training was shit, because, apparently, I can't take down one single guy.

Part of me feels sorry for everything he's had to endure in his life that led him to this.

Not that it matters.

The end will be the same.

Either I kill him, or he'll kill me.

Till death do us part after all.

𝒫sychopath

Entering the house, my ears are almost deafened by her screaming, but I ignore it, focusing my entire attention on the brown door down the hallway. I use all my strength to continue to my bath as she shivers on my shoulder. She asks, "What are you doing?" Her head shifts slightly as she grabs my waist to look beyond me.

I don't give her much though, as I drop her on the floor. She sways a little and I steady her, but she immediately steps back, fury crossing her face. "What? You brought me here to inflict more damage?"

"Quite a stupid statement for a professional like you." Before she can say anything else, I point at the shower. "Take one and dress in the set of clothes on the counter." Her brows furrow as her eyes widen in surprise. "And then come back to the fucking living room." I close the door behind me, grab the first aid kit on the way, and drop onto the couch with an exhausted huff.

Only then do I allow myself to come back, and the pain follows, hitting me from every corner. I notice she didn't touch any important parts, and I can handle patching myself up.

In other words, the wound isn't dangerous enough to kill me, but it hurts like a motherfucker, alerting my other senses.

The man in me is proud of the skill she possesses, but the serial killer?

The serial killer wants to wrap his hands around her pretty throat and choke her until she regrets her decision.

Clearly my first tactic didn't work.

But I'm nothing if not adaptable.

CHAPTER SIXTEEN

Psychopath, 10 years old

Hopping from the bus onto the street, I wince at the slight pain in my arm, and a second later, my bag lands next to me as the kids laugh behind me.

"Loser," one of the bigger ones shouts, but I ignore it, adjusting my glasses on my nose better before scooting all the books back in my bag while the teacher yells at them to behave.

Maybe she should have paid more attention inside the bus, and then I wouldn't have pain in my stomach from their hits. Adding that to all the other injuries that Dad likes to inflict, I can barely walk most days. But no one asks and no one cares; they even ignore my holey shoes.

Turns out that at some point, popularity becomes more important than friendship, because Gideon and Alp joined the forces who make fun of nerds, and I'm always on the receiving end of their cruelty. Destroyed schoolbooks that we can barely afford, finding soap in my bag, stumbling in the halls and painful landings. I try to fight back, but it only earns me more blows.

Everyone constantly laughs at me, pointing their fingers while I do my best to stand up after each encounter. During class, it isn't any better; teachers scold me for not doing my homework or not studying enough. I'm bad at everything but math. Numbers are my only salvation.

I hate school with all my might, but then it's a safer place than home. Some-
times I look at all those kids in our neighborhood who ride bikes or eat food,
enjoying their time, and I wonder what it is like to be so carefree.

To not be afraid. To not constantly apologize for breathing.

I sit in my room and often try to find what's so wrong with me that no one
loves me.

Even Mom. She always protects me, but there is this stare in her eyes as if
she regrets I'm even there. Maybe because Dad always screams and hits her
when I piss him off, which is almost always.

What do you have to do to be loved?

My stomach growls loudly, the pain inside so bad it halts my movement for a
bit, but I blow out a heavy breath. Eating lunch in the school cafeteria once a
day isn't enough, but I know nothing waits for me at home. Mom gave up
cooking a long time ago when Dad constantly hit her because she messed up
something.

Thankfully, he isn't home now; his broker job called him to go out of town,
and I wanted to use this opportunity to read books in peace.

Entering the house, I call, "Mom?" She doesn't reply, and I remove my shoes,
being careful not to leave any stains, as everything should shine perfectly.

The TV plays loudly in the living room and I frown, surprised she allowed
herself to watch the news, since it's not allowed according to Dad's rules. And
Mom acts as if he's around even when he's not.

I despise her for it on most days, but it's always laced with guilt as she with-
stands everything for me.

But the question that always haunts me is why does she stay? Why can't she
run away from him?

Is that the love that everyone experiences?

"Mom?" I call again, but still no response. She is turned away from me
sitting on the chair; I can see her blonde hair resting against the chair back. I put
my bag on the couch and go around in front of her, only to gasp loudly.

A pool of blood surrounds her from where she's cut both her wrists open. The
blood drips down onto the white carpet that soaks it up. Her eyes are closed, and
I quickly grab the phone, dialing nine-one-one while shaking her, hoping she'll
wake up.

"Nine-one-one, what's your emergency?"

"My mom's hurt." Those are the only words I manage to spill, and immedi-

ately she tells me to stay there, but I barely listen to her, the phone slipping through my fingers to the carpet as my eyes focus on Mom's face.

She smiles, the corners of her mouth lifting for the first time instead of being thin, and she is peaceful. Not one wrinkle mars her face, and I walk closer, touching her cheek softly.

She is not breathing, and I know I should cry and scream for help, but I can't.

For in death, she's found peace, and it can't bring remorse in me. My mom was never more beautiful than in this moment with life gone from her bruised body forever.

It's like she finally found happiness, far away from this awful place.

I kneel next to her, hugging her knees with my arms, resting my cheek on her lap while I stare into nothing, forever picturing her in this moment. I don't even care that I get dirty with blood, because for me it has brought salvation for my mom.

Why didn't she do it to both of us? Then we'd be free forever. Away from the evil that feeds on our misery.

How can I live without her?

After an hour or just minutes, people barge inside the house, their eyes widening in shock as they mutter, "Dear God," and pull me away from Mother, while I desperately try to cling to her.

Paramedics check my vitals while murmuring words to me I don't understand, because I don't even pretend to listen. Instead, I think about the fact that my father will never be able to hurt her again.

But with this realization also comes anger so deep it slices through me as I fist my hands and inhale the putrid air.

Because she has left me alone to live with a monster.

Ella

Getting out of the shower, I step on the soft rug, curling my toes into it, and lean toward the mirror, wiping the fog away from it.

I've spent around fifteen minutes in there, scrubbing myself with a new container of shower gel, wanting to wash away all the dirt I collected back in the cage.

The humid air envelops me in warmth as I gaze at my reflection and study my body as if seeing it for the first time.

My black hair falls down my spine in wet strands as water drips on the floor. Bruises appear on different parts of my body. They are not large, but enough to be seen.

Dark circles under my eyes, a haunted look, and cracked lips create a picture of a woman who suffered a deep loss, yet at the same time I do not resemble a victim held captive.

More like a woman scorned who has gone through heartbreak. In a way, I have though, right? The man I love has turned out to be a monster.

A monster who for some reason doesn't kill me or torture me as he should.

Resting my hands on the sink, I breathe in and out, trying to recognize all the emotions swirling through my system, demanding to be felt.

There is rage for him deceiving me and putting me in this situation, luring me into his trap.

There is pain for him turning out to be someone else and placing me in a position where loving someone cost me something precious.

There is love, because how can I turn it off just like that? Even if it feels wrong.

But the most prominent of them all?

Desire to understand what has driven him to this and why he still keeps me alive.

It's like he wants to kill me but can't even explain to himself why he can't do that. And discovering why and playing it to my advantage might be exactly what I need to escape from this hell.

So I can't be stupid and irrational anymore. I have to use all my knowledge to save myself from the man I've considered the love of my life.

Exhaling heavily, I put on the black hoodie lying nearby and find it reaches my knees. I roll the sleeves up, enjoying the softness of the fabric. It's thick compared to that joke of a dress, so it gives me more protection, at least in my mind.

I wince as I put pressure on my foot, still sensitive after the water, and go out, not really knowing what awaits me.

Kierian sits on the couch, breathing heavily as he concentrates on the needle and thread, as he methodically stitches his wound.

A bottle of whiskey sits nearby, half full, so he probably used some of it as antiseptic and drank some to dull the pain.

The woman in me longs to soothe him and make it all right, and I step in his direction but stop myself quickly.

Rational. You should act rational.

Instead, I focus on my surroundings, assessing the place while being slightly taken aback by the design.

The place consists of a wide, spacious living room that has a couch, two chairs, and a fluffy fur rug right in front of a fireplace, albeit a fake one.

The kitchen counter has an arc-like shape so it's the extension of the room with an assortment of pots and pans on the stove. Why the hell does he have cooking devices here?

Also, from the corner of my eye, I see a hallway that leads to one more room, probably the master. Everything is colored in shades of gray, even the curtains, and all this gives the vibe of a black and white movie.

Especially the silence that echoes around the walls louder than any sound could.

Nothing in this room indicates that its owner tortures and kills his victims in the basement.

"Before you consider running..." Kierian's deep voice snaps my attention back to him. "The security system is activated. No one can get in or out without my permission. I haven't turned it on before, but you aren't very obedient." He clucked with his tongue. "Bad girls get punished."

Not answering his jab, I ask instead, "Does it hurt?"

His brow lifts as he laughs. "Why? Want to come and kiss it better?" I shake my head, and he adds, "Maybe you can distract me enough and then stab me again. That's an option too."

"I won't feel guilty about this. And when an opportunity arises again, I will take it." No need to hide my intentions.

"You need to eat." He points at the plate on the nearby coffee table, right next to him. "And before you open that mouth of yours, this is an order."

Funny, I wasn't about to argue anyway. I have to be strong to escape, so I won't refuse food or hydrating my body ever again. Plus, my mouth is watering at the possibility, so I stroll to him, and my hands are on the plate when his frustrated groan fills the space.

He is trying to attach the bandage to his side, but the thing keeps slipping and he can't angle his body as it probably brings more pain.

Snatching it out of his fingers, I press it to his wound, and he grunts because I'm not gentle. Plastering it firmly on his chest, I make sure it doesn't slip and secure it across his side as well.

A hot breath fans my cheek, and my eyes rise to clash with his as he leans forward. "Thank you." I scoot back, but he fists his hand in my hair, slightly tugging on it and bringing us closer. "Don't do anything stupid."

A humorless chuckle slips through my lips. "Or what?" He doesn't answer but lets me go, and I begin to eat, shoveling bites without tasting much, because it doesn't matter. Eating has only one purpose after all, nutrition. "Why am I here?"

He stays silent for a bit and then slides lower on the couch, resting his head on the back of it, his eyes closed. "I have different plans for the basement."

"Like?"

"Why, you miss it already? Be my guest and sleep there, then."

Gritting my teeth, I bite my tongue, because antagonizing him doesn't play well for me. "So you sent me the book?"

He laughs. "I thought you might like it. Granted, I didn't expect you to become obsessed with it, but it was fun to watch. It's a great masterpiece."

"Noah, Preston, and you all have the tattoos."

"Yeah, and we all read it. Noah likes Hector, which fits him, always the protector. And Preston is into Paris, God knows why."

"So I came to the team, and you chose me?" I don't really know how his victimology works with women, considering I've never encountered a serial killer except Benjamin.

If someone told me I'd breezily be discussing a psychopath's motives, I would have laughed in their face.

He drinks from his whiskey bottle. "You bumped into me on your morning run." He chuckles. "I didn't understand at first why you caught my attention. Women are never in short supply. But I couldn't let go and needed to know everything about you."

I vaguely remember that day in January when some guy in a hoodie bumped into me and said nothing.

So that's when my destiny took a new turn?

"But when I got to know your file, I knew what attracted me to you." He sits closer and catches my chin, even though I try to evade his touch. "The grief flashing in your eyes hidden by indifference. But if one experiences it for years, it's easy to recognize."

Slapping his hand away, I hiss. "What am I? Your toy?"

"Hardly. If you were, I'd already be playing with you." He gets up, wincing, and I concentrate on my food while trying to digest this information.

Everything is a plan and a game. But his explanation doesn't give me anything. Why does he want me?

"Why me? Tell me."

"The more I got to know you, the more I wanted you. To hurt. To possess. To inflict bruises." He clears his throat. "I've never felt this before, so only your past explained it." What he described reminded me more of a guy who fell for a girl at first glance, but due to his fucked upbringing, transformed it into something else in his mind entirely to justify his attraction.

"How many people did you kill?"

"Lots." Right. If he started in his teens, I could imagine what the number is now.

"You worked alone?"

"No. I've had sort of a friend who has taught me all there is to know about torture."

"So you like torture?"

"I used to, in the beginning. It fed my desires. Not so much after that. I grew bored. There was no drive in it anymore, no interest. Until you," he finishes.

"Will you kill me?" He stays silent for a while, and the food I ate lies like a heavy rock inside my stomach. Although I want to smash the plate on the wall, my mind keeps chanting.

Survivor. Survivor. Survivor.

"Will you ever accept life with a serial killer?"

"Never."

"Then you have your answer." With that, he disappears behind the bedroom door while I sit there numbly, not allowing tears to spill from the unfairness of this situation or the desperation or the unbearable pain, not in my body, but my heart.

Sounding and acting dramatic won't help my situation.

But how can I escape him? Or make him give me up?

Without harming him in the process?

*P*sychopath

She falls asleep, shifting her neck to an uncomfortable position, and for sure, it will be sore tomorrow if I don't take her to bed.

Gulping two more painkillers, I shake my head and ignore the sting in my side.

I smile at the idea that my beautiful Ella is a tigress when it comes to fighting. She won't ever allow anything to hurt her without a fight.

A quality not everyone possesses, and although it makes me proud, I should be annoyed.

Nothing is going according to my initial plan, but maybe I shouldn't have started a relationship with her first.

I wouldn't have known her laughter. How her eyes sparkle when she is excited about something, how much she suffers without her family.

What a loyal friend she can be, how dedicated she is to her work.

There is so much about her to admire, and anyone would be lucky to have her. But all those qualities make her a curse for me, because I won't ever let her go, and she won't stay with me under such circumstances.

She might love me, but she won't stay.

So I have two choices: either kill her or break her.

But what do I do when my entire being protests this, not allowing anyone, even me, to harm her?

Sliding my hands under her back and knees, I pick her up and go to the bedroom, where the warm bed is ready for her. I place her on it and tuck her in as she murmurs something, and then she squeezes my hand and brings it to her chest. "Kierian," she murmurs this time, and my heart stills, because up until I met her, I thought the thing only fucking existed to pump blood throughout my body.

She moves restlessly, frowning in her sleep, so I get on the bed, and immediately she rests on my shoulder, sighing deeply.

"Ella," I whisper against her hair. "Why do you have to be so perfect?"

Closing my eyes, I will myself to stop being Kierian to her and be only a serial killer who hunts his prey.

But for the first time in my life, I can't separate the two.

CHAPTER SEVENTEEN

Psychopath, 12 years old

I sit on the couch, waiting for Doctor Anna to finish her report. She sends me a reassuring smile as I study her office and find it boring.

White walls, chairs, desk. A few photos of loved ones, but besides that, she has everything in order as if nothing can throw her for a loop. Her son is in art class with me, and he is as calm as she is.

Always fucking friendly with everyone.

"How are you?" she asks. When will they stop with their never-ending, stupid questions?

I shrug, repeating the same thing all over again. "Good."

Her lips thin in displeasure as she bites on the pen. "The reports from your teachers show that you've upped your grades by sixty percent. That's excellent. And you joined the football team," she reads with surprise.

After much consideration, I figured out that education was my only out, so I focused all my attention on my studies, which with the current situation was a piece of cake.

Turns out Mom's death brought more peace than expected. Everyone, and I do mean everyone, felt sorry for the kid whose mom committed suicide and he had to find her. Neighbors pitched in to bring clothes and food, making sure I was always fed. School didn't nag me about my grades, but instead gave me time

to focus on my answers. Even the kids backed off; they didn't want to be friends
with me, but at least no one touched me. It was as if I almost didn't exist.

Dad still smacked me around on occasion, but other than that, it was almost
bearable to live with him. He was waiting for the attention on us to die down; I
just knew it. He couldn't give me long-lasting bruises, because people would see
them. He spent a lot of time outside town, claiming it was work, but I didn't
believe him. But as long as he didn't bother me, I was good. The neighborhood
moms watched over me. After all, that's what they are "supposed to do," quoting
the words right out of their mouths.

I don't appreciate their help or feel all that grateful. They should have
helped when my mom suffered. Why were they so blind for so many years?
Didn't they hear the screams? Or is it easier to feel like a hero while taking care
of an orphaned kid instead of helping an abused woman?

Though their support means nothing to me, I use it well.

"Sports are a good way to get a scholarship."

Her brows furrow, probably because I'm not supposed to think about college
just yet, but I do. My dad will never pay for it, so being fast on the field is my
only out.

I think all sports are stupid, but if it provides me with a ticket to another
state? I'll do anything to stay on the team.

And chemistry. It became my salvation, learning different chemicals that
can be matched together to create the weirdest combinations. Teachers thought I
was too damn smart for my age, but all this played to my advantage. I chose as
many electives as possible.

"Right. Today is the anniversary of..." She clears her throat, adjusting her
collar. "Your mom's death."

I know well what is expected from me, so even though I don't want to do it,
I manage to squeeze out one single tear from the corner of my eye that slides
down beside my nose to my chin. She takes out a tissue and gives it to me. "I'm
so sorry."

I just nod, hoping it will be enough and she'll let me go. I have homework to
do and she is interfering with my plans.

If she only knew, I don't feel anything; I'm a completely blank state. The
only driving force for me is to get what I want. And with people so willing to
accommodate my desires, I've learned to play with them.

It is funny on good days, and tragic on bad ones.

"It's okay," I manage to get out, as she walks around the table to me and pats me on the back.

"That's it for today. Just remember I'm always here to talk."

I get up quickly and get the hell out of the office while wondering what awaits me at home.

I'm on my way to the bus when I halt, my eyes widening in shock as I see my father standing a few feet away with a woman around Mom's age, who smiles at me brightly as he squeezes her hand.

It's barely visible to anyone else, but I don't miss the wince that mars her face and is quickly replaced with indifference. A small girl with pigtails is jumping around her, as if chasing someone and counting something under her breath.

"Hey there, boy," Dad greets me, his voice gentle. "I have someone I'd like you to meet." He walks closer while continuing to talk. "This is Suzanne; she will be your stepmother. She's agreed to marry me. And that's her daughter, Kim."

The woman extends her free hand to me, but I step back. "Hi, darling."

I don't reply or react as the little girl waves at me happily.

The only things I can focus on are the faint bruises spread on Suzanne's neck along with deep fear settled in her green eyes.

With clarity, I understand that Dad has found a new victim and a perfect excuse for everyone to leave us alone.

The monster is back.

*E*lla

Fluttering my eyes open, I wince in pain as I shift my leg, and my brows furrow. "What in the world?" And then I glance down to see fresh bruises and everything from last night comes back.

Sighing heavily, I rub my forehead while gazing at the ceiling and pondering what to do next.

Yesterday's experience was surreal to say the least, nothing I expected. Although I know he wants to hurt me, I can't figure out why.

He can't do it, and that pisses him off; that much is clear. Not that it gives me an answer to what is really going on.

Or how to handle this situation, for that matter.

I get up and then notice a dip in the other pillow that tells me

Kierian slept next to me. Placing my hand on it, I pat it softly and wince, because the truth doesn't change my love for him.

But it doesn't mean I'm willing to die or to be destroyed for this love.

Padding softly to the living room, I look around, but he is nowhere in sight.

The kitchen table has breakfast ready for me with a note.

"Let me not then die ingloriously and without a struggle, but let me first do some great thing that shall be told among men hereafter." – Homer, **The Iliad**

Well if this doesn't send a message, I don't know what else should.

"Good boy. Catch!" Kierian's voice is coming from outside through the wide-open door, so I go there, and the picture in front of me makes me blink.

A Tamaskan dog runs around the field in the direction of the ball then snatches it into his mouth and brings it back to Kierian, wagging his tail. Kierian takes it from him and repeats the action, while his bare muscles flex with each movement.

Standing on the grass barefoot in his sweatpants with his hair loose, his handsomeness shines brightly under the sun in all his masculine glory.

Because that's what you're supposed to think when a serial killer kidnaps you.

The dog notices me, stops midway, and raises one ear as he cocks his head.

Keeping in mind that this dog bites human flesh, I don't do anything when he slowly strolls to me, circling me and nuzzling my knees, until finally he sits down in front of me, whimpering.

"He doesn't bite."

I chuckle, although it lacks humor and is laced with nervousness instead. Easy for him to say. Gently, I pat the dog's muzzle and he lifts it, his tongue out, clearly enjoying it. "That's your wolf, huh?"

"We are a team."

I can't help but bite at him. "You even turned a poor animal to the darkness."

He comes closer; my hair prickles on the back of my neck as, next to me, he says, "His name is Rex. I found him in the ring for fight dogs. He was barely alive. Trust me. I didn't introduce him to the fucked-up world. We just found each other." He rubs the dog, the bond evident between them.

Of course.

After all, they have pain and a secret that binds them together.

I flip the Post-it note up. "So that's your plan? Kill people until you get caught?"

He shakes his head and grabs a bottle of water from the grass. He gulps it greedily and then adds some to Rex's dish. "There is always a greater purpose in life. I found mine. Yours is catching serial killers, or so you think." He heads back inside and I trail after him, confused even more, if it's possible in the current situation.

"My purpose is to serve the people."

He munches on a pancake, nodding, and then points with his fork. "People, or your family?" I freeze, my mouth hanging open as he continues. "Tell me that each case doesn't bring you back to your parents and sister that you failed... at least in your mind. You didn't come in time. Or early enough. Or didn't die with them. Just who are you saving each time? Aren't all the cases surrogates for your family?" Since I have nothing to say, he cracks a smile. "Right. But because I have different thoughts about justice, *I'm* the bad guy."

"It's incomparable. Just because you think justice failed you—"

He leaves all pretense of eating and focuses his harsh stare on me, and I shut my mouth, stepping back, because the killer is clearly back.

"I do not think justice failed me. I wouldn't work for the FBI if I thought so. People always blame justice or the system, claiming it does nothing for kids, families, or others. But what can justice do if people allow it? How many people do you think ever asked my mom if she was okay? I'll tell you. None!" he bellows, and I swallow, afraid of his next move. "Because it's okay to tell on your neighbor if his fucking grass is too high and he doesn't take care of his yard. But God forbid interfering in their private business, right?"

I have nothing to say to that, because in a way he is right. "Killing people is not the answer. You can put them behind bars to rot in prison and—"

"And you think that helps? They will get out and continue to do this shit with another victim. I cannot help those who do not seek help."

This conversation is leading us nowhere.

"Why am I here, Kierian?" I finally ask about the big freaking elephant in the room. "I was in a cage yesterday, now I'm in the house, and you treat me to breakfast. Why did you kidnap me? It wasn't enough to just have me as your girlfriend?"

"You want to know?" he asks as something dark crosses his face, but I don't bother to read the signs anymore.

I can't walk on eggshells around him.

"Yes! I don't need breakfasts as if everything is normal. Nothing about this situation is!" He doesn't even flinch at my shout; he just grabs me by my elbow and drags me in the direction of the basement. "What are you doing?"

"Showing you exactly what you want." Rex barks at us, but Kierian snaps at him. "Stay." And then we go downstairs, and all the while I pull at my hand, but it's useless.

He throws me inside and places me on the chair located right in the middle. "It's brand new," he tells me, and I blink in surprise.

I hadn't even considered that other people might have died on it. "I should appreciate the small things, I guess," I mutter, while he straps me down and tightens the ropes on my wrists behind me as well as my legs. I have to keep my back straight—there is no other option —as the metal painfully digs into my skin and my bare feet become cold from the concrete under them.

"You are awfully cheery for a person who is about to get tortured," he says, although something is off about his voice.

And then it hits me.

It lacks confidence. Does he hesitate to hurt me?

But he shatters my illusion as he takes the silver knife that glistens in the light, its tip so sharp. He rests his hand on the back of the chair as he traces the skin on my neck, but he doesn't put enough pressure to draw blood. "Do you know what was constantly on my mind through all these months?" He slides the knife lower near my artery. "To see how you'd look here in my hell with blood decorating your skin. How I'd have the chance to fuck you after giving you pain." I force my gaze away from him, hating the words. "And here you are in my basement, alone, helpless, completely at my mercy." The blade travels lower to my breast, my stomach, and finally reaches my thighs as he dips the tip in a few places, deepening the previous wounds. I cry out softly. It hurts as if thousands of ants bite me.

He repeats the action on the other leg and then pulls my hair, angling my head back while I groan in pain, and he holds my stare. "How do you feel about love now, Ella? Is it worth it?" he asks, bringing the blade dangerously close to my cheek, but he doesn't do anything with it. "In my fantasies, after I was done with this, I use other torture arts I've learned." His hands move lower; he reaches my restraints and lightly squeezes the sensitive skin. I close my eyes, and although it doesn't hurt me much, it still stings.

"Are you happy now?" I whisper, needing to know if hurting me soothes his raging desires, but he just growls and pushes back.

"No. Because it doesn't bring me pleasure. I get no satisfaction from it." He voice is laced with self-disgust and loathing, as if he prefers to hurt me than love me.

Than show me his tender side.

To have this excuse behind which he can hide from me.

That's when an epiphany strikes me, and all the puzzle pieces make sense in my head. How could I have not seen it sooner?

"It's not about punishment," I breathe through the pain, as he freezes near his equipment, his hand pausing midair gripping his kitchen knife.

My skin burns from the tight rope wrapped around my wrists digging painfully into my flesh, while the cuts leak blood down my thighs, but I don't pay attention to that.

"It's about love, isn't it?" I ask but don't wait for his reply as the muscles in his back tense, yet he doesn't move to face me. "It's about seeing how far you can hurt me to destroy my love for you." My humorless chuckle fills the space. "That's why you wanted a relationship with me first." Licking my dry lips, I pray for enough strength to survive this. "You are trying to understand how much a woman can love a man to be able to live with all this. Why she lived with it."

He spins around, reaching me in two short strides, and locks his fingers around my chin, squeezing it hard. "Stop talking."

Instead of listening to his warning, I continue to fire at him with my mental blows, barely croaking the words through his hold. "Despite the pain he inflicted on her and you, she stayed. Didn't ask for help. Didn't blame him. You can't forgive her that, so you try to understand. But I'm not her." He lets go of me, breathing heavily. His hands travel to my hair, gripping it painfully, as I wince in pain but do not defer my assault. "I won't love you despite everything, Kierian. If there is a chance to kill you and escape my captivity, I will."

He doesn't reply, but instead presses the blade to my neck, threateningly close to an artery, many expressions crossing his face as if he doesn't know what to feel. "And that kills you, doesn't it? Because compared to your mom, I have nothing to live for. She had you."

He growls and unties my hands, clearly wanting to get rid of me. "Shut. Up!" he screams in my face, deafening me for a second, but I can't stop.

Kierian is a prisoner of his psychological trauma that unfortunately my presence triggered. Why? Because the minute he saw me, he wanted me.

A normal man would have chased me down, and in time, we'd call it an instant attraction that led to a relationship.

But because he can't explain his desire, he transformed the first attraction into this grand plan.

Killing any chance we might have ever had.

"I won't!" Fisting his shirt, I bring him closer as he shakes with the impact of my words. "You will never break me. Never." Licking my dry lips, I add, "It doesn't mean I don't love you, but I can't be with a man who wants to hurt me." I don't see where I put my other hand as I reach out for him and my palm connects with the knife, bringing forth an instant scream. "Ouch, ouch, ouch." The blood pours from the wound, and it hurts so freaking much. The skin prickles around it, and it seems deep. I suspect it will need stitches.

"Fuck!" he roars, and it surprises me so much I close my mouth. He frees me and picks me up, almost running upstairs.

There he places me on the counter in the bathroom as he takes out the first aid kid, then turns on the water and wipes away the blood. I can't help the whimper of agony that slips out of me and the tears that are unstoppable at this point. So much for my stoic front.

"Why did you have to do something so stupid?" he asks gruffly, displeasure written all over him as he focuses on my palm and puts on gloves to clean it up properly. "You're hurt now."

In any other circumstance, that would have been sweet, his worry. But now?

It's quite funny.

"Wasn't it what you wanted? I just sped up the process."

CHAPTER EIGHTEEN

Psychopath, 13 years old
Walking down the hall to the library, I ignore the stares thrown my way and place my headphones back over my ears as the hard rock blasts, eliminating the outside world.

Idiots.

Stepping inside the library, Miss Jane smiles at me widely, and I return it. She is the only person who has always allowed me to take more books, so yeah.

I stroll to the table at the far end, then go hunt for a book.

I shuffle through the shelves, searching; we are supposed to submit a history report about the Civil War. I have to have it done a few weeks ahead, because my chemistry teacher, Mr. David, has promised to show me a special chemical reaction plants have on a toxic mix of certain atoms. Although it's forbidden to show me this kind of information, he seems to live in his own world and drinks up any attention from students who show an interest in his profession. He had dreamed about a big future in science, but he wasn't "smart enough."

His words, not mine.

My eyes land on the strange additions to the pile of used books, and I pause while cracking my neck to the side. They are brought here by people who no longer want them, so they donate them to schools.

"Criminal Psychology," I murmur, the title sparking my interest, and I pick it up. "How to understand the mind of a serial killer."

Serial killer?

My history project long forgotten, I open the book while resting my back on the chair and read.

Because the book gives me the perfect description, play by play, on how to pull off a spotless crime.

*I*t took me a few more months to create a plan to turn my life for the better, but back then, I didn't see it was a sign.

A sign I was just like the people I'd read about, and even though I thought I was doing it to protect myself, truth was I liked it.

That later on I would use it on other people.

Evil is not born after all; it's made.

But if I had to do it all over again?

I would.

*P*sychopath

Her words freeze my movements, but then I raise my troubled eyes to her, only to see her avoiding my gaze, as if she is afraid to look at me.

Stupid, beautiful girl.

She cut herself deep; it will throb like a bitch, and I won't be able to do anything about it.

And I hate it, just like I hate the fact that I can't hurt her.

I don't want to hurt her.

Seeing her pale skin covered in bruises doesn't bring joy or pride or whatever the fuck else I'd hoped for. My lips long to trace them with my tongue and make them all feel better; she deserves better than this.

My Ella.

"Or it's only okay for you to hurt me, but not the other way around?" She still fishes for answers I don't know how to give her.

Despite claiming everything under the moon, she loves me and searches for good. But there is no good in me.

My father killed it.

"No one is allowed to hurt you. No one. Even you," I growl against her as her jaw drops open, and she shakes her head.

But then her brown pools widen as she notices me preparing the injection. "What are you doing with the needle?"

My brows furrow at the fear detected in each word. "It's a pain killer. I will inject it into your palm so you won't feel me stitching it."

"Do you know how to do that?"

My mouth lifts in a smile. "Yeah. Learned at an early age." And then God knows why, I add, "Mom taught me. Someone had to tend to her wounds. Mostly it was me if the places were hard to get to."

She blinks and then casts her eyes down, sighing heavily. "It was hell, huh?"

I administer the injection and she winces, biting on her fist while she kicks the cupboard under her with her heel.

"Shh." I keep her still then apply antiseptic and begin to stitch it. "Won't be great work, so you'll most likely have a scar." Her healthy hand travels up my stomach to my chin and grabs it, to my fucking surprise.

"You didn't answer me."

A humorless chuckle echoes between us, while she grinds her teeth. "If it wasn't hell, would you be here now? But it doesn't matter what I lived through, does it? Nothing justifies what I do in your mind, so this is a moot point." *This fucking wound will sting. Why did she hurt herself?* "We all have our own demons. No need to know mine."

"But I already do," she mumbles, but it's so barely audible I think I've imagined it. She clears her throat. "I'm sorry about your mom. No one deserves that."

My jaw tics, as do my hands, because the thought of an amazing yet not understandable woman always brings hectic emotions inside me.

No woman deserves the hell Mom lived through.

Looking back now, I see I could never have saved her, because I was just a kid. But I wonder how a man could have brainwashed her so much that she thought dying was better than escaping him?

Is it the same as what I'm trying to do with Ella? I don't kill her, because my entire being doesn't allow it, but I keep her here and wait for her to break.

Breaking a woman's spirit... what will be the consequences?

And will that love have meaning?

We stay silent for the next fifteen minutes as I stitch the wound, apply cream, and patch it up with a bandage, securing it tightly around her palm.

Then I clean her thigh scratches, but she doesn't even react to those.

Finally done, I pick her up and place her on the couch, while she mutters, "I can walk."

"And do something stupid again? No thanks."

"I'll die anyway. What difference does it make when?"

Pulling her hair hard, I bring her mouth closer to mine as she breathes heavily. "I'll advise you not to harm what's mine, Ella. Or show me sass."

Now she becomes angry, slapping my hand away. "I have either sass or hysterics. You think any of this is normal? You know how a woman acts in this situation?"

I shake my head. "Not from firsthand experience. I don't kidnap women." Or kids. Or anyone besides abusive fuckers who think they are the kings of the world.

"Well, she'd scream and beg. I can't afford such behavior, as it won't do me any good or help me escape you. So I don't care that you don't want me to hurt myself. You should have thought about it before you kidnapped me. You know I'm a fighter."

"That's why I chose you."

She runs her fingers through her hair, sighing. "You want me to fight for this love?"

"No. I wanted you to fight for yourself."

She rises and sways a little, and I make a move to help her, but she steps back. "Well, you got that in spades. This is a dead end, Kierian. A dead end. We have no chance," she whispers with resignation and collapses back onto her seat with a loud thud.

Her stomach rumble fills the space and her cheeks heat up. "I told you to eat breakfast." I quickly grab the untouched pancake plate and place it on her lap. "Eat." She doesn't object, just like yesterday, and it hits me. "More strength when fed, right?"

"I don't have to justify anything to you."

And she continues to munch on her food while I try to study the unfamiliar emotions inside my chest that make me act and sound like a hormonal teenager instead of a serial killer.

CHAPTER NINETEEN

*P*sychopath, 14 years old

"I told you to fucking clean it yesterday," Dad's voice bellows from downstairs, and I snap my eyes open and turn on the bedside lamp, rubbing my forehead. There is a loud crash and a stifled cry as he raises the volume of the football game louder so it will eliminate all other sounds.

My door opens, a crack of light from the hallway visible as Kim slips in and quickly jumps on my bed, hiding under the covers as she plasters her small body against me. She trembles all over, whispering something under her breath, probably a song.

That's what she usually does.

I roll my eyes; the kid is annoying. No matter how many times I've told her not to come in here, she won't listen.

Oddly enough, the old man has left me alone since he married Suzanne, but she continues to get bruises once a week. He doesn't beat her like my mother for every small screw up; after all, we still have the attention of the neighborhood on us... but nevertheless.

She stays with him, just like my mom, albeit she never lets him touch her kid.

Or me, come to think of it.

She just whispers that he'll change and once again become that loving and caring man who she fell in love with. I barely stifle my laughs any time she mentions it, because honestly, the fucker isn't capable of such emotion. However, he never gets as violent with her as with my mom, and I did wonder when his barely contained fury will once again spill all over our house.

Showtime is here, it appears.

"He's angry again," Kim murmurs, peeking from the blanket, and I look down at her.

She has the bluest eyes I've ever seen, and sometimes that pleading look begs me to do something I cannot refuse.

Maybe because I recognize myself in it. Only I had no one to beg back then.

"Please, no. Matt—" Suzanne doesn't finish, as another crash sounds in the distance, and I know what it means.

"He's hurting her," Kim says, ready to run and defend her mom, but I stop her and tuck her back in as I rush to the door.

I call over my shoulder, "Do not come. Stay put." No child should see his or her mom being beaten. Those scars would stay with her forever.

I take the stairs three at a time, only to see Suzanne on her knees in front of Dad who has wrapped his black leather belt around her neck, a smile gracing his features while she holds on to it, trying to free herself while gasping for air. Her face has turned blue, and she is barely keeping herself up.

What a fucking asshole. "Let go!" I shout, and he turns his attention to me, surprise reflected on his face, but then the wide grin comes back.

"Oh, you finally decided to come, huh?" Approval laces his voice as he drags her to the side, loosening the tight hold for a second as she gasps for breath but then tightening it again. "Do you miss me torturing your mom like this? Want to stay and watch just like old times?" He licks his lips while Suzanne's mouth gapes open, remorse and shock written all over her features as she gazes at me.

"Let go of her," I repeat.

"You are too cocky for your own good. You think I won't teach you a lesson since you've grown bigger and have the support of everyone?" True, slowly but surely, I've made friends with the popular kids, upped my grades, and generally built a circle of support around me so Matt won't have access to me.

But most importantly? I managed to convince the local biker who lives three blocks from school to give me lessons in boxing, so I'd know how to protect myself in case the old man decided to go back to his old ways. I knew it would happen sooner or later, especially when he had an available victim in his vicinity.

His interest in me allows Suzanne to slip away from him. She begins to crawl to the far corner of the room, aiming to get to the phone, but he stomps on her back and she falls on her stomach, groaning painfully.

"You are a monster," she says, breathing rapidly, and I want to add "Duh," but don't.

My father is scaring the kid upstairs though.

And I will always protect any kid from the kind of things he is capable of inflicting.

I see small droplets of blood staining the white carpet, taking me back in time to when it happened to my mom.

The piercing pain assaults me, and I cover my eyes, swaying from side to side, hoping it will stop.

The memories are too painful to ignore, but with that also comes a deep fury that demands to be let out.

So I don't think, just react, as I latch onto and raise high the baseball bat from under the couch that I put there in case of an emergency.

Matt just laughs. "Look who got brave. You asked for it, boy." He steps toward me, the leather swaying with his movements, and then the metal buckle hits the table as if he is warning me what is to come.

I don't wait any longer but lunge at him, hitting him on the back. Because he doesn't expect it, it takes him a second to react before he retaliates with the belt. First, he pushes me to the floor, and then he punches me in the back. He attacks with the belt, the buckle bruising my shirtless skin while he kicks me in the stomach. The baseball bat rolls to the side, and it only adds to his confidence it seems. He grabs me by the nape and pounds me against the floor, excruciating pain instantly traveling from my nose to my forehead. I bite my lip, trying not to make a sound, because I know that's what gives him the most pleasure. Nausea sweeps through me, but I wait, letting him add a few more blows before Suzanne slaps him on the back, screaming, "Matt, stop! You will kill him!"

What is she doing? I furrow my brows in confusion. Why can't the woman stay fucking put? I break free and get up, fishing for the knife I stuffed underneath the chair. I spin around quickly, flashing it in front of his eyes as he halts in the middle of throwing Suzanne on the table.

Everyone freezes while he tsks. "We both know you won't do anything about it, boy. Go back to your room. I'll forgive you this time," he boasts with a grin, scanning all my bruises.

Yeah, well fuck him.

I push the knife right into his liver and he bends in two, my action so unexpected he doesn't even have the chance to fight.

Suzanne screams, and I pull the knife out only to stab him in the stomach and then in his chest, making sure to miss all the arteries.

I want him to suffer, but not bleed to death. He falls to the floor, holding his wounds as the blood seeps through his fingers, and I pick up a tissue from the table and wipe my fingerprints from the knife, throwing it next to him. Suzanne trembles and dashes for the phone when I speak quietly, yet firmly. "You will call nine-one-one and tell them there was a dispute. In order to protect yourself, you had no choice but to stab him. Pick up the knife so they will have your fingerprints. Show them your bruises."

"You are insane, boy!" he hisses, but I ignore him, my gaze holding Suzanne's prisoner, who just blinks.

"Do you understand?"

At this moment, Kim joins us, gasping. "You are hurt, Shon." Then she hugs me close, but I don't return it. She is safe and it's all that matters.

That's enough as something shifts in Suzanne's gaze, and she dials the number before whispering into it. "Help, please, come to my house—" I don't listen to the rest, but sit on the chair while my dad chokes on his blood and a smile tugs at my mouth, this moment so profound and magnificent as power rushes through my veins, even blocking away the pain.

The old man might think it's the end, but it's not. I'll kill him someday, but only when it will bring him the most pain.

A quick death for this fucker is salvation and not a punishment.

*E*lla

It's been hours now since our last conversation, and I do nothing but sit on this fucking couch while he wanders around the house and does his shit.

First, he chopped wood. God knows why, considering it's warm, and then he stacked it himself too. After that, he cleaned the place, being very OCD about a little dust. Come to think of it, I consider myself a germ freak, but Kierian takes it to another level.

But then, he has to get rid of evidence, so he does have to be more careful.

Currently, he's reading a book in his chair, completely ignoring me, and this drives me crazy. I pace the kitchen back and forth and finally settle with resting my back against the wall near the bedroom, bored and confused out of my mind.

Who kidnaps a woman to do this? This unsettles me even more, because I have no clue what to expect from him.

"This place looks pricey." I can't believe I'm breaking the silence, and neither can he if the look he gives me above the book is anything to go by. "How can you afford it?"

He shrugs. "I have good friends and invested well a while back. Under a different name though." Just how many different names does he have?

"How come no one has found this place?"

"Because it's located in a field near the woods. No one wanders this deep, and besides, even if they do, it's not against the law to have property here. But you'd need a warrant to search the place."

"Those bodies... you were the one to call the police about them? Because you knew I'd be joining the FBI."

"Yes." He says it so freaking casually, like it's an everyday thing for a man to drop dead bodies as a ritual to woo a woman.

"Must be hard to live a double life."

"Not really. My two friends know about me, and women were there only for no-strings-attached sex. It's not like I needed to keep up a constant act."

Jealousy rushes through me, creating an unpleasant feeling in the pit of my stomach. He's repeated it many times, but I decide to ask anyway. Maybe his answer will help me hate him more or something.

Because at this point, my mind and feelings are all over the place. "You needed sex regularly, so you spied on me and fucked some chick afterward?"

The hand holding his glass of whiskey pauses midair, his stare intense as he swallows quickly. He drops the tumbler on the carpet and is by my side in a flash. He presses me against the wall, plastering both his palms on the wall on either side of my head while he leans closer, our lips just a breath away from each other. "Why? The idea of another woman displeases you?" He fixes his gaze on my chest rising and falling, his closeness still clouding my senses.

My hand is about to slap him, when he catches it and traps it against his chest. "What is it, Ella?"

What do I have to lose anyway?

I might die any day now, so fuck it.

"So you consider me yours and still stick your dick in every available woman? Great. Thanks, but no one needs this kind of obsession." The red haze is still present in my eyes, and I can't shake it away.

We weren't anything to each other, but it makes me sick to think that he probably didn't allow anyone to come even close to me while he whored around.

"I didn't," he replies, and I catch his drilling stare. "I haven't touched anyone since laying eyes on you. Truth be told, you were all I could think about. So there were no women."

I exhale in relief, and it doesn't go unnoticed by him. And that's when the mood shifts, bringing such familiar awareness, and when he leans closer, I whisper, "This is so wrong."

"Why does it feel good, then?"

I glare at him. "Because it's wrong!"

But in all the chaos that's blown up in my face, our physical connection is the only thing that binds us, the only thing that's familiar and, oddly enough, safe.

So why not use it as an anchor? Even if it's weak and irrational.

With determination in mind, I pull him to me, rise on my toes, and kiss him.

For a second, he is frozen, and then he answers the kiss, fisting my hair and angling my head back, plunging deep. Immediately, I taste the whiskey he was consuming earlier.

Except it tastes different on him, more rich, vivid, and makes his kiss even more intoxicating.

Suddenly, he pushes me away and spins me around, pressing my cheek to the wall as his hot body cages me in.

He murmurs harshly into my ear, "Where is the knife this time?" My heart stops and then speeds up as he slides his hand from my collarbone down to my stomach, and it dips from his touch. He doesn't stop and moves his attention to the sensitive skin of my core. He murmurs again, "No knife?" My raspy breath fills the space as he bites my earlobe, and a rush flows through me even though I hate it.

Shouldn't a woman have pride? Or common sense? The man practically admitted he wants to kill me and he is a serial killer. How can my body desire him? How can I still feel anything for that matter?

"I didn't have time to grab one on the way." Sarcasm coats my words, and he chuckles, the vibration from it dancing on my skin.

And then he is gone, once again.

"Tempting, but not enough. There is no escape from here, Ella, until I say so. And I'll never say so." I turn around, only to see his face void of any emotion as he gives me a crooked smile. "Maybe you shouldn't have joined the FBI after all."

He walks toward a room at the far end of the hall, and I call after him, "What's in there?"

"None of your business." He goes inside after he places some kind of card near it and then shuts the door behind him.

𝒫sychopath

Leaning back in the chair, I turn on the camera in the living room and study Ella as she runs around searching for cells or landlines, computers or internet, and coming up blank.

She huffs in frustration and then goes quickly to the kitchen, opens the drawers, probably searching for weapons, finding nothing but forks and spoons.

She screams while shaking her hands then rests her palms on the table, breathing heavily, clearly thinking of a way out, even though I've told her multiple times there is no escape.

Then she straightens, hugging her wounded hand close, and a wince flashes across her face.

It speaks to something inside me, because the idea of her in pain unsettles and displeases me at the same time.

She shouldn't have interfered; then she wouldn't have been hurt.

The stupid woman doesn't listen, ever.

What am I doing here really? From the very beginning, she was an experiment, a woman who could withstand everything and not give up.

But can she give up once the man she supposedly loves turns out to be, well, me?

She is trying to escape, trying to talk back to me as if she's not afraid, although I can taste her fear; it's evident in every move she makes. She chose a different tactic by acting compliant when she was plotting, so she's probably attending to my narcissistic nature.

Oddly enough though, I'm not a psychopath. I was profiled as one, of course, but psychopaths show violent tendencies no matter what their upbringing. Some even claim it's genetic.

Now, sociopath suits me better, since they're usually shaped by their environment.

In short, her tactic isn't working.

But my own feelings that do not want to hurt her?

They so fucking work.

Ella removes a small metal hook from one of the curtains, breaks it in two, and then twirls it in her hands while kneeling in front of the door lock. She gets it inside and wiggles it from side to side, her brows furrowing in concentration, and she constantly looks behind her as if checking for me.

A smile pulls at my lips at this. What a fighter.

She unlocks it, fisting her hand in the air, and puts on the socks she found earlier on the couch.

With one last glance in the direction of my room, she slips out, probably happy as fuck.

Too bad I'll rain on her parade sooner rather than later.

*E*lla

I can't believe it actually worked!

I'm free!

Not wasting any time, I check for Rex, but he is nowhere around, so I sprint as fast as I can despite the ache, needing to find the road and then escape this man.

My heart might love him and feel sorry for him, but that's about it.

Sacrificing myself for him? No fucking way.

I don't know what kind of tactic he has chosen. Maybe it's to drive me insane with waiting or confuse me with his bad and good persona, I don't know.

There is one thing I know for sure though.

I can't let him convince me that this is okay, and that's inevitable if I stay here long enough.

So I run faster and reach the forest, walking through the trees as the leaves crunch under my feet, and I wince in pain.

Shoes would have been better than socks, but none were lying around.

Resting my back against the tree, I gulp breaths while hurriedly studying my environment. It's dark and I don't see much, but I hear cars passing by so far away they're barely audible. I'm about to dash again, when he appears in front of me, wearing all fucking black and a smirk plastered on his gorgeous face.

No! How did he know? He wasn't even around when I left, and I was as quiet as possible.

"Ella."

"Stop saying my name!" It grates on my nerves the way he changes his tone to a dangerous-sounding one whenever he says it.

"I will do whatever I want, Ella." He pauses. "You don't call the shots here."

The annoying son of a bitch!

I raise my hand and slap him hard right across his face, the sound echoing between us and his cheek turning red from my hit.

My ears ring as fear washes over me, because his face changes rapidly from amusement to fury and then to complete indifference.

Maybe I've pushed him too hard this time, and this is my end after all.

He wraps his hand around my throat, presses me to the tree, then squeezes hard, cutting off the air to my lungs as I struggle to breathe. "Do. Not. Ever. Hit. Me." He emphasizes each word with a tighter squeeze while I grab for the tree, hoping it will help me to stand, although I feel myself slipping into oblivion.

He releases me and I gasp for breath. He catches me before my knees have a chance to buckle and squeezes me harshly. I whimper in pain as the fabric digs into my cuts. The skin already aches so much.

"Does this make it better?" he asks, as my brows furrow in confusion. "Making me show my darker side. Is it easier to act like the victim? Is that why you want to push my limits?"

"I want to get away from you!" I try to shout in his face, although it comes out as a hoarse hiss since my throat hurts.

"It's easier to hate me than to pretend like you don't want me."

This is so insane!

"No!"

"Yes! Then you can convince yourself that I take everything with force."

I open my mouth to protest, but then close it, because maybe his words have merit. Maybe I do try to do that so he will show me nothing but a monster and I won't have to be confused or feel guilt over it, a guilt I don't understand.

Kierian scoops me up in his arms, and despite my kicks and slaps, he continues to walk back to the house, and I wonder if it's always like that with the likes of him.

No matter how much you try, you can't escape.

We step inside the house yet again and he goes straight to the bedroom, dumps me on the bed, and I bounce on it with a hoarse squeal.

He disappears but comes back shortly stirring a steaming cup.

I warily watch him, rubbing my arms as he sits on the bed and hands me the cup. Giving it a suspicious look, I shake my head.

"Drink," he orders, and I huff.

"What is it? Some kind of sedative to make me more compliant?"

He snatches my hand and tugs me closer, and I have no choice but to lean forward. "Drink, Ella. I don't need to do much to make you compliant." He brings the mug closer to my lips and the smell of honey and tea register in my nose. "It will help you with your sore throat."

"If you didn't hurt it, I wouldn't have an issue in the first place."

He presses the cup against my lips, so I take a huge sip and instantly welcome the soothing sensation it gives me. Wrapping my

palms around it, I pull it to me and sit on the bed cross-legged while
he chuckles.

"You like it, I gather."

"Mom used to make it for me when I was sick," I reply quietly, and
he tenses, jerking his head. "That's what your mom did too?" I don't
remember having this drink after they died; in my opinion, it's such a
mom thing to do.

A beat passes, and then he finally says, "No. I made it for her whenever *he* hurt her, although it rarely helped her." Kierian glances at his
hands and then turns around, resting his elbow on his knees while he
breathes heavily.

"Did he beat her a lot?"

A humorless chuckle erupts. "I don't remember a day when he
didn't."

My heart aches for the little boy who must have lived through hell
and watched his mother suffer, and before I can even think about it, I
raise my hand and touch his back softly. If it's possible, his muscles
become even more tense under my touch. "I'm so sorry, Kierian. No
one should experience that."

"True. But rarely anyone can stop them." His voice is filled with
distaste and hatred. "I'll never apologize or feel remorse about killing
those men. They deserved it."

I've read the file on him, so I know what his father did. Convincing
him otherwise is pretty much a dead end.

But he doesn't know the whole truth, and I'm afraid to tell him,
because it won't bring him any peace. Yet maybe it will make him more
understanding toward his mom.

He stands up, spinning to face me, and I see different emotions
flashing in his eyes, but none that I can name. "No matter what he did,
she always stayed with him. Even when he moved his violent tendencies to me, she still stayed, although she loved me. Nothing, *nothing*
made her leave him, although she had all the chances in the world." He
hits the wall hard, and it's probably painful, but I just sit silently,
because what can I say to that?

In his mind, his mom betrayed him.

"And she just left me to him. So you were right. I was saving the kids."

"You don't know your mom's story."

"Spare me the explanations. This is not me saying victims are at fault for domestic abuse. I don't blame her for what *he* did, and she always protected me. But she shouldn't have stayed with him."

Silence falls over us as I ponder his words and finally speak. "But you want the same kind of love from me."

"At first, you were an experiment. I needed to understand how a woman could stay with a man who hurt her." My brows furrow, because that hardly describes our situation. "But then everything changed. Sleep now. I'm done talking." He leaves me alone, shutting the door behind him, and I hear the lock being turned. Well there goes his breezy attitude about me wandering around the place.

At first, you were an experiment.

What am I now?

I've never thought it possible to love and hate one man at the same time, but Kierian quickly proved otherwise.

Despite everything, I want to pull this monster out of the darkness and give him the light he so desperately seeks, even though he doesn't understand it.

Because all his confusing actions make one thing absolutely clear for me.

Kierian fell in love with me.

And that has become the greatest sin in his eyes.

*P*sychopath

Resting my elbow on the window, I study the night while Rex lies next to my feet, snoring loudly. The dog usually runs around the land freely, preferring to have freedom than be stuck with me. I gather even he has his psychological traumas.

All those conversations about my mother aren't bringing out the best in me, remembering what my father did.

Especially now, when I hurt Ella in similar ways.

Disgust crashes into me like an angry wave, spreading through my system, and I take a long sip from the water bottle, hoping it can wash the feeling away.

What am I doing with her? Turning her into a woman who will take whatever I dish out to her and still stay?

Isn't that exactly what I taught those men not to do?

But just the idea of giving her freedom unsettles me, awakening something dark and possessive inside me that roars.

She is mine.

And no matter how bad that fucking is, she will always stay mine.

With that decision in mind, I stroll to the room and enter, only to see her lying on the bed, sleeping soundly while the moonlight covers her in shimmering light, emphasizing her beauty that could have seduced even a stronger man than me.

There is no physical need; it's something else I can't explain as I lie down next to her and slowly trace my finger over her face. I would memorize it, if I hadn't already.

Her smell, her softness, her soft breaths that show me she is still alive and here with me calm me down in a way I've never known.

When we started our "relationship," I used to lie just like this at night and doubt myself, because she never looked more vulnerable and mine than during sleep. I've always been a light sleeper due to my past; I never know what or who might disturb my life.

In those moments, I want to do nothing else but protect her and keep her safe from all the bad things that can happen out there.

Which is kind of ironic, considering what she's had to experience from me.

Why do I feel like this?

Suddenly, her eyes flutter and her brown pools look at me with surprise, and I expect her to move away or scream or give me sass—that seems her best defensive instinct lately—but she does none of those things.

Instead, she shifts to her side, facing me as she extends her hand and softly cups my cheek, the touch so unexpected I jerk.

She rubs my cheek with her finger, and then leans closer and kisses me on the mouth, her lips lightly grazing mine, and then she rests her cheek back on the pillow.

There is nothing sexual about any of this, yet it does things to me I cannot name or understand.

Women loved my looks, strength, brooding character, and cock that did wonders in the sack.

But no one ever showed acceptance for the monster living inside me, while Ella did it just now, for a moment.

"Sleep, Kierian," she murmurs, bringing us closer while we are a breath away from each other. "I'll guard your sleep tonight. Sleep," she repeats, and oddly, I find peace in her words, and with her gentle touch and her body pressed tightly against me, I finally find sleep, lullabied by the knowledge that she doesn't run away from me.

Instead, she tries to speak to the monster inside me with a language I don't understand.

Love.

CHAPTER TWENTY

New York, New York

Psychopath, 16 years old
        Hiding behind the column, I tighten my hold on the knife in my hand as I wait for an approachable victim to pass by.

The familiar buzzing fills my ears as sweat coats my shirt from the prospect of taking a life. I fucking need it like a second breath.

After Matt went to jail, I studied all the serial killers and how easily they took care of their victims, and most of the stuff was gross as fuck, but the idea of focusing your anger on those you deemed unfixable?

It had a certain beauty to it, and whenever I thought about it, the feeling of complete power I felt while stabbing Matt came back.

Exploring those desires was out of the question in our small hometown. But here? In fucking New York?

It's a gift!

My football team played a game here, and while they have been busy making a list of buildings they wanted to visit, I've had other plans.

Killing someone seemed like the best of them.

So I sneak out in the middle of the night and go to the most dangerous street in sight, hiding my weapon under my coat, hoping to find an opportunity to use it.

Unfortunately, I've been doing it for the last few days, and every time, something gets in my fucking way, but tonight I'm determined.

Those fuckers are the lowest scum of society anyway; they probably come home and beat their wives, so it's not a big deal to get rid of them. I'll go insane if I don't settle this deep craving inside me that demands someone else's pain and fear and blood.

A man walks out of the bar, laughing loudly while he sways from side to side, with a beer in hand. He shouts into the phone, "Our team won!" Everything freezes as Matt's voice penetrates my mind.

"My team lost," he screams, throwing his bottle against the wall as Mother's eyes widen in fear, and she ushers me toward the stairs.

I don't want to go, but she silently motions for me to continue. However, it's too late as his heavy footsteps come closer and closer. So instead, she quickly pushes me in the pantry and closes the door right in time, as he bellows, "I told you not to fucking cook that shit, didn't I? That food brings nothing but bad luck." And then my mother cries out in pain as he hits her and continues doing so for some time.

I sit and cover my ears, rocking from side to side, counting the minutes when he'll get tired and I can run to Mommy and soothe her as best I can.

I no longer see a stranger. Instead, he transforms into Matt, and with raging determination, I dash toward him with a knife ready to stab him right in his fucking gut where he likes to put all his alcohol.

But then strong arms wrap around me, and I don't have time to scream as someone knocks me down.

The face of a dark-haired man is the last thing my mind registers before darkness overtakes me.

*L*ater than night

. . .

A splash of water wakes me up as I gasp for air and choke on the liquid while trying to see through my blurry vision.

I want to raise my hand to wipe the wet from my face, but I can't, as it's tied behind my back.

Finally, my vision clears and I see some kind of weird-looking room with several questionable devices. I notice two men standing right in front of me.

One of them is a dark-haired, tall, lean guy, who gives a "don't fuck with me" vibe as he crosses his arm and looks at me indifferently. He glances at the blond man next to him, who watches me with interest, although he looks weird in his three-piece suit while holding a cane.

A fucking cane with a metal top!

"Why is he here?" the dark-haired one wonders aloud while the weird one cracks a smile. Instead of answering him though, he steps closer to me, and I pull on my chains, but it's useless.

It's like I'm fucking glued to this chair!

"It's a fool's job really, boy. No one can get out if I don't want them to."

"What do you want from me? Let me go." Are they some sick fuckers who are into young boys and rape them?

I heard and researched a lot, and sometimes fucked-up shit came up. If they think they have an easy target, they have another think coming.

I won't surrender without a fight.

"The question is what do you want from our city?" This halts my movement as my brow furrows in confusion. The blond man exhales heavily, grabs a small chair nearby, and sits on it while propping his leg on another. What the fuck is this? Another century? "You see, this particular New York neighborhood belongs to me and my protégés. Yet you've been hunting for days now, and I tried to stop you in a good way. But you are stubborn." So they are the ones responsible for all my failures? Either the victims were called by someone or bouncer dudes appeared in my vision, stopping me from killing anyone. "While I like it, it creates problems for me." I stay silent, because frankly, I have no idea what to say.

So cities have special serial killers now roaming them and no one steps on someone else's territory? What the hell?

"Let me go." I finally settle on that, but he just clucks his tongue and opens a *folder on his knees. He clears his throat and starts reading, the information chilling my bones.*

"Shon Dawson. Sixteen years old. Mother committed suicide, father in jail for domestic abuse. Am I missing anything?" *I'm too stunned to reply, so he continues.* "This kind of stuff messes a person up. So you stabbed your old man, huh?" *He rubs his chin.* "And urges have arisen. You want to kill. Want to feel that power again. Where you rule the situation and have the control. The control that has been denied to you for years." *With each word, I scowl and scowl more, anger rising in me in spades.*

"Fuck you." *They might as well kill me now, so I don't have to play nice.*

The blond smiles, rises, and delivers a blow to my face. My head falls back as pain assaults my nose. "A little respect for the older generation, Shon. You kids these days don't know how to behave."

What the fuck? He looks a maximum of ten years older than me. Surely not a grandpa.

He clasps his hands. "I would have killed you because you have traces of uncontrollable psychopath written all over you. But you're a teenager. You can be trained. And you will be."

What?

With that, he walks out, patting the shoulder of the dark-haired guy and leaving us alone in the white-as-fucking-snow room.

"What did he mean by trained? Who are you?" *Do they run some kind of organization?*

"Sociopath. My nickname is Sociopath. That's all you need to know."

My eyes probably bulge out of their fucking sockets. The guy has a reputation already, killing off people around the country and leaving only notes with his name. He is a legend.

"Why am I here?"

He straddles the chair and holds my gaze. "You have urges to kill."

"Fuckers like Matt." *I wasn't hunting for innocent people.*

His chuckle fills the space. "The guy you wanted to kill today is a good family man. He is nothing like your father. But you don't see it. Something triggers you, and it's enough for you to snap. You will justify any violence just to feel that high again." *He pauses, while I contemplate his words.*

"I can control myself." *Control is everything to me in this life. He's wrong!*

"No, those urges will only rise faster and faster, taking over your sanity. They will control you, if you don't learn how to direct them properly."

"Properly?" How can killing and proper be in the same sentence?

"I will teach you an art that will help you control your urges and direct them on selected people. Then you will control your life, not the other way around."

This doesn't make sense to me. *"But why? Isn't it easier to kill me?"*

His eyes darken, but it passes quickly back to indifference. *"Consider it a debt. Lachlan and I are giving you a chance. Do not blow it."*

So the other guy's name is Lachlan? This is so fucking surreal. Who does this? Do they have their own academy or what?

"Who is he?"

"A man who doesn't like to be crossed."

"What will happen if I do?"

"We will kill you."

Well, easy rules to follow.

*E*lla

The machine beeps that the coffee is ready, and I pour it into a cup while gazing through the window, albeit through bars, and study the ever-changing nature.

Although it's summer, the wind is blowing quite strongly and even Rex doesn't feel like going out. He just whines and then begs for food, and since I find some meat inside the fridge, I give it to him.

Resting my back on the counter, I grip it hard and know I have to tell him the truth.

The truth he has no idea about, and it will probably destroy him, but how long can a person live a lie?

Loving a man has proved to be the biggest challenge in my life. He is perfect outside those psychotic tendencies of his, and even then, he can't hurt me. I know I should be afraid, but instead I feel sorry for the little boy he was who didn't know any better.

I hear footsteps behind me, as he says, "Ella, you're not asleep." Spinning around, I see him gripping the top of the doorjamb, leaning on it as he swipes his gaze over me, possessiveness flashing brightly in his silver eyes.

His jeans hang dangerously low, showcasing his six-pack and the little trail that will lead.... Shaking my head, I focus on the task.

If other women heard my thoughts, they'd probably consider me insane.

There is good in him, and he needs me. But I don't know how to be with him while he continues to do what he does, as it goes against all the principles I have in life.

"I couldn't sleep."

He slowly walks to me like an animal assessing his prey, but then stops right in front of me and picks up my hand, gently rubbing it with his thumb. "Your hand bothering you?"

"No."

He kisses it softly and I blink. "What's going on?"

"You probably have access to my e-mail." He doesn't say anything, but I know it's true. "Print out what Preston sent me about two days ago."

He frowns, gripping my chin, and demands, "What's in there?"

"Something you need to see to understand your mom."

He steps back, fury crossing his face. "If this is some great plan—"

"Check it, Kierian," I whisper and give him a soft peck on the cheek. "It's important." Placing the cup in the sink, I walk back to the room and get in bed, hoping his smell can calm me enough to prepare for the fury he will unleash soon.

CHAPTER TWENTY-ONE

*P*sychopath, 17 years old

"*Where are you going, Shon?*" *Suzanne asks, placing a plate in front of Kim, who munches on the french fries while giving me her toothy grin.*

I pat her head, still not liking the kid much, but she is the only person I can tolerate without getting anything in return. So there is that.

"*I have stuff to do,*" *I reply shortly, and she grits her teeth.*

"*I'd like to know more than that.*" *My brows rise as I grab the bottle of the water on my way out, but she follows me.*

"*You are not my keeper,*" *I remind her, hoping she'll go back to her things. My dad got locked behind bars for eight years after we fed the authorities our story, and everyone believed it easily. It was enough to see the state they found us in. Once again, the whole neighborhood showed their support. Suzanne got herself a job in the hair salon, working as a receptionist, while Kim was accepted at my school where I kept an eye on her.*

But since everyone knew she was my sort-of sister, although I loathed the word, no one dared touch her, and I was okay with that.

I'm protective of them, but I don't love them. We just use each other to have a normal life.

For the time being at least.

"*Shon—*"

Fed up with the bullshit, I face her as my car keys dangle from my hand. "Look, when Matt got put behind bars, what did we agree on? You can be my guardian and get to stay in the house, since you have nowhere to go." She winces at that, but I don't care. "And everyone here goes out of their way to help you. Right? Let's not disturb the status quo."

She crosses her arms, opens her mouth, and then closes it, and finally she exhales heavily. "I'm worried about you," she says gently, and I laugh bitterly, finding it fucking amusing while she frowns.

"Yeah? Well don't." I step outside, cracking my neck from side to side to remove the tension from the five-hour run this morning. Kathy leans on the hood of my car, winking at me as her jean shorts showcase her long legs that feel exceptionally good around my waist while I fuck her senseless on the backseat of my car.

Adding myself to the football team and with time becoming the captain sure elevated my status in school. From the nerdy, weird kid who everyone felt sorry for, I became the guy everyone wanted to be friends with. Parties, games, dates.

Life is nothing but a dream it seems, at least on the surface.

"Hi, baby!" she squeals, jumping in my arms and latching onto my mouth, but I quickly end it, hating the whole kissing thing.

Fucking—yes, but intimate kissing while she murmurs some romantic shit in my ear? No fucking way.

Truth be told, she's gotten too attached to me, but I can't break up with her. The only reason we started dating was because she's the daughter of our local sheriff. Being the boyfriend of his princess sure gives me a much-needed advantage and allows me to apply to the police academy, hoping his connections will help me to get there. With my family track record, it could be impossible, but I have a special plan.

And no one will stop me from accomplishing it.

"What are you doing here?" I ask, fisting her hair and inhaling her perfume that oddly always calms me down. I place her on the hood of the car, while stepping between her legs, digging my fingers in her sides, loving the soft curves.

Discovering sex could be an adrenaline rush where everything fades away was certainly a surprise. I was introduced to it by a girl from another town when we played a game there. She was a couple of years older than me, and she knew so fucking much. I thought I wouldn't be able to stop with all the blankness it brought to my mind, but also clarity.

After each fucking session, I knew exactly what to do and how, and more importantly, no conflicted emotions existed inside me.

But I had to be careful here, so the arrangement with Kathy worked. Although she called it a relationship.

"I thought we could spend some time together," she says, trailing her finger down my stomach. "Watch a movie or something." Her voice sounds hopeful, but I shake my head.

"I can't today."

She huffs, annoyed. "You never have time for me unless it has to do with sex." Before I can reply, my phone rings and I pick it up on the second beep while Kathy's eyes narrow in suspicion.

"You're late," the voice on the other end of the line says, and I can hear a muffled groan in the background. A smile spreads on my mouth. "Had to start without you."

"I'll be there soon." I hang up while Kathy practically screeches.

"Who was that?" Jealousy oozes through her every pore as she aims for my phone, but I quickly halt her by wrapping my hand around her neck, choking her for a brief moment, and she instantly calms down, while excitement shines in her green pools. "Shon," she purrs, bringing herself closer to me.

I lift her down, while murmuring, "I'll be back tomorrow and take you for a ride. How does that sound?"

She pouts but nods eagerly. She knows a ride in my car usually means hot sex by the lake. Her naivety has to be seen to be believed. "Daddy won't let me."

I barely restrain myself from snapping at her, but instead give her a harsh kiss while she moans into my mouth, but then I step back as she breathes heavily, her cheeks flushing as she touches her lips.

Guys my age would kill to have an opportunity to fuck a hot girl like her. Me though? I get hot by thinking about the torture Sociopath inflicts on his victims and learning from the best.

"I'll handle your dad," I reply, and walk to the driver seat.

With a last wave, I drive out of town while classical music is blasting from the speakers, calming me down and reminding me that these trips are the highlights of my life, allowing me to find comfort for the need to kill that's settled deep inside me.

Finally, I reach his warehouse, park the car on the side, and move toward the house, sliding in the key card and entering soundlessly as cries of pain echo through the space. I close my eyes, savoring them for what they are.

Music created by a master.

"Please," the man begs. He is chained on his chair to the wall. His face is bleeding, probably from a broken nose, as many cuts and bruises mar his body. A yellow pool is under him, and by the disgusting smell, it's urine. He trembles all over while his gaze focuses on Sociopath.

Sociopath puts on gloves and grabs the knife from his table, clucking his tongue. "Mercy is a funny concept. I don't remember you showing me any." This strange comment raises my brow, as he rarely speaks with them.

I'm not stupid enough to question him about his victims, but I do have Google. All of them are important men of society who have respectable reputations.

But then, a reputation is just an illusion created for people to believe in, and in most cases, it means nothing.

I should know.

The man finally registers my presence, and he kicks on the chair, trying to get out, although it's useless. "Help me."

Yeah, right.

Whoever the fucker is... he deserves his punishment.

"You finally joined us. You know what to do."

I nod even though he can't see it and quickly put on my own gloves, grabbing a similar knife, just with a slightly longer blade.

He goes behind the fucker's back and motions for me to come closer. He places the tip of his weapon on the shoulder, near the vein but not touching it. "You have to press it deep enough to give pain and draw blood, but light enough to scratch it with a name. This is different than just randomly stabbing someone. I'm showing you an art form." He then proceeds to slide the knife on the skin as blood slowly comes to the surface. The man cries out in pain as Sociopath writes names I have no clue about.

Once he is done, he does something unexpected. He steps back and sits on the chair nearby, grabbing a bottle of water on the way.

"Continue. You know my ways by this point. Let's see what you've learned."

Excitement builds in me, transforming into a rush of adrenaline that spreads through my entire system as I take a deep breath and stab him several times and then proceed with other methods of torture I've learned.

Once we are done, Sociopath pats my shoulder and brings me back from the heavenly place where nothing else exists. "You're ready."

Oh, I so fucking am.

But then he spins me around to face him, while he warns me, "But only those who deserve it, Shon. If you start killing for the hell of it, I will end you. Remember that."

I agree, but then I don't know what will happen in the future.

$\mathcal{P}$sychopath

"What's this?" I ask while shaking a file in my hands, and Ella sits up on the bed, holding my stare but not saying anything. I throw it on the floor, screaming, "Fucking answer me!"

She doesn't even flinch, but instead clears her throat. "The truth."

"It's not the fucking truth. How did you come up with this plan, huh? Discussed it with Noah? What the fuck is it?"

She gets up, stepping closer to me, but I don't allow her to touch me. Her touch can destroy any ounce of control I have left, and then only God knows what I'd do to her.

"I'm sorry, Kierian. But it's the truth."

Of its own accord, before the action even registers in my mind, my hand wraps tightly around her neck, squeezing the breath out of her while she struggles and tries to hit my arm—not that it works. Her beautiful pale skin slowly becomes red while her eyes widen with fear, and then I snap out of my raging haze, letting go as she falls on the bed, breathing hard and gulping as much air as possible into her lungs.

"Do not try to manipulate me with your lies."

She holds her throat. I see tears swirling on her lashes, but she doesn't let them go farther.

Instead, she croaks, "Your mother was Annette Grace, kidnapped at the age of sixteen on the way from school." She gulps one more time, but continues, "Your father raped her repeatedly for years until they found him dead. His wife finally told on him, and they scouted his location. But Annette was gone. No one could find her."

Everything she says makes no sense, doesn't match my memories.

Doesn't add up to the truth in my head, and I want to shut her up, but at the same time I long to finally have this door open.

"She probably ran away and met your stepfather. Who ended up being... well, him." She finishes, but not before adding, "All this came to light after you killed him. Your mom never had a chance, Kierian, but she tried once, for you. You just blocked those memories out as too painful to remember."

"Bastard."

That's why he always called me that. I was never his.

Instead, I was the evil spawn of someone else.

And with that, a flashback comes to me, penetrating every nerve in my body when I'm transported far away from my house.

*P*sychopath, 5 years old

"Mommy, can you tell me a fairy tale?" I whisper, and she smiles at me and places me on the mattress while lying next to me. I can't wait for the adventurous stories of trolls in the forest.

The room we live in is very small, just our bed, and a toilet a few feet from us. The smell is really bad, because all the trash lying around is only taken away by him once a month. Mama scratches her dirty cheek, but it doesn't make her less beautiful.

My mama is an angel with her golden locks that always sway softly while she dances with me to the tune she hums. Or when she plays around with me, teaching me to imagine stuff like we are in a different place filled with grass and trees. I've never seen them, but the way she talks about it, I can picture all of it in my head.

"Of course. Which one?" Before I can reply, heavy footsteps above us become louder and louder, and Mommy instantly tenses, throwing a blanket over me while she gets up. She winces at her bruised knees but quickly pats me on the back. "Darling, do not say a word while he is here," she orders, while wiping away a tear.

The monster is back.

Sinking deeper into the covers, I squeeze my eyes shut, hoping to pretend to sleep so he won't touch me or Mama again.

Seconds later, the door opens as he comes down the stairs, his alcohol-smelling breath filling the space.

Peeking through the blanket, I notice a bag of food and a small bottle of water in one hand, while smoke rises from the cigar he holds in the other. His white tee is stained with some brown substance and his shorts are ripped in half at his knees.

He came alone without that awful woman who hits me while calling me an evil spawn. She also doesn't like Mommy much either as she claims she is a sinner who deserves her punishment. I don't know what that means, but I hope there comes a day me and Mommy stop being one, because I hurt when she cries.

"Food is here." His voice is so scary, especially when he smiles and moves his gaze up and down, admiring Mom. "You know what to do," he says, and she pulls the blanket tightly around me.

I hear her as she shuffles, but then suddenly, he speaks again. "This time I don't want you. You are old. I need to get rid of you." What? Does this mean he will let me and Mommy go?

"Get rid of me?" she asks with a trembling voice, and I peek again to see him nod, as he grunts in disgust.

"You are not interesting anymore. The boy can stay. I know people who like pretty boys like him."

"No!" she shouts, and he hits her. She falls to the ground, but I don't get out, because she instructed me not to.

I silently cry, very worried for what will happen next.

"Shut up. Who asks you what you want?" He throws the blanket away, and my shoulders sag, hoping he won't touch me, but he grabs my hand and drags me out of the bed. "Have to get you out until Missy comes. She doesn't like looking at you." But Mom hugs me close, shaking while repeating, "No, no, no."

And then before I understand what is going on, Mommy takes the metal bat she's been hiding under the bed and hits him hard on the head, and he falls down with a loud grunt.

"Shh, Shon," she tells me, wiping away my tears. "Don't cry, okay? Mommy will get you out of this mess." She picks me up and I wrap my arms around her, hiding my face and hoping she will escape from this bad place.

She goes up the stairs and then outside the house. When we hear loud sirens moving in our direction, Mommy runs and runs and runs until she probably has

no strength left, as she sits by the side of the road, rocking me while water starts
to pour on us from above.

"What is it, Mommy?"

Her body shakes hard as she kisses me on the forehead, and whispers, "Rain,
that's called rain, sweetheart." Then she laughs, lifting her face to the sky. "And
this is grass." She points at the floor. I've never seen a grass-filled floor! "Every-
thing is going to be all right now, baby. I promise," she says, and that's when a
bright light flashes on us and I hear a man coming close to us, his heavy footsteps
scaring me as I burrow deeper into Mom.

He is very tall. He looks clean, not like that awful man who kept us. "Hey,
miss. You lost?" he asks, but Mom scoots back and he just raises his hands. "I have
a few blankets and stuff. Let me help you." They talk for a long while, and then
Mommy gets us inside the car where it's warm, and the man gives me a delicious
drink that he calls juice.

In a while, I fall asleep and everything feels good.

Until a few weeks, when the first blow comes and nothing is ever
the same.

Pulling my hair, I throw my head back and roar in agony while
rushing out of there. I kick and smash everything that is in my way:
the table, the blankets, the glasses.

Lies, I've lived fucking lies.

My mind goes crazy from the fucking truth that stayed hidden
within me for so long.

Rushing outside, I don't even bother to restrain her, because where
the fuck would she go?

Like father like son, right?

The realization hits me hard as I sink to my knees on the grass,
palming my head and shaking from side to side, trying to avoid other
flashes that come.

Us starving. Him raping her while I grew up. How everything always hurt,
because we didn't have water to wash ourselves. How my clothes were usually
too small and smelled like shit.

How he always grunted and laughed whenever my mother showed any
resistance to him.

The sound of belt buckles hitting the spine.

Matt was supposed to be her salvation, but instead became an even bigger nightmare, punishing her for the mistakes of another sick fucker.

It's a wonder she survived for so long in this fucking unfair life.

And what is my mother's legacy?

A son who does exactly like all those men who hurt her.

The padding of feet draws my attention as Ella gently kneels next to me, placing her shaking hand on my shoulder, but I brush it off, not needing the comfort she so wants to provide.

Her developing Stockholm Syndrome will probably make everything okay, but it's not.

What the fuck am I doing to her?

I have no remorse for all the men I've killed, because they deserved it. Maybe due to my help, fewer kids will grow up with the need for revenge like me. Fewer mothers will choose suicide or slowly dying inside while monsters continue doing whatever the fuck they pleased.

But then again, serial killers will always justify their actions. A kill is a kill. Right?

"Kierian, I'm sorry," she whispers.

"Are you?" She blinks in surprise at my question, and I turn to face her. The moonlight is shining brightly on us, highlighting every bruise I've inflicted on her. "Why do you feel sorry for me? For the man who kidnapped you and gave you this?" I point at all the wounds as she licks her cracked lips. "Or are you relieved, because my fucked-up past gives you an excuse to feel sorry for me and accept my darkness? Thinking that a little bit of love can fix all this," I question, while she shakes her head, but I won't let her run away from it.

"I made the bruises myself when I tried to get free. You didn't inflict them."

I grab her by the nape and bring us closer, my breath fanning her cheeks as she trembles in my arms. She slides her hands to my face as she wipes away the wetness from my chin, not that it matters. "I'm not the good guy, Ella." She closes her eyes at those words, breathing heavily while I continue to deliver my mental blows. "I will never be Prince Charming. This is me, Ella."

"You don't have to—"

"What? Kill you?"

She flutters her brown eyes at me and fists my shirt while determination settles on her face. "It's your choice. You can choose something else." With all her knowledge in psychology, does she truly believe a person like me can change?

Nothing and no one can stop me from killing.

A humorless chuckle slips between us. How has fucking simple torture turned so tragic? "I'll always be a serial killer."

Psychopath seems like a fitting term now.

I remove her hands from me and drag her back inside, where she stays silent, just watching me and expecting something.

I don't know what love is and have no desire to find out. But in that single moment as I went out of the house, all I wanted was to set her free so she could escape from a monster like me who only adds to her sorrow.

And maybe for a fuck up like me, that's love.

I have to give her a reason to hate me, because only then will she be able to survive.

CHAPTER TWENTY-TWO

*P*sychopath, 18 years old

       Pulling the car into the secluded area of Sociopath's warehouse, I turn the engine off while my hands grip the steering wheel tighter, my lips hurting as I bite them hard so no sound will escape them.

       "Why did you bring me here, boy?" Matt asks, shifting uncomfortably yet curiously gazing through the window.

       "Wanted to show you something." I barely restrain myself from snapping his neck right there, and keep my voice even, so there won't be even a hint of the emotion running through me.

       His mouth spreads in a smile as his chest lifts in pride. "That's my boy. Getting gifts for his old man," he says proudly, and gets out of the car, still flashing me a grin.

       What a dumb fucker.

       Because law enforcement didn't have much on him, just the one assault, and his great behavior and ability to deceive people, he ended up in jail for only a few years, and then he was released.

       I destroyed half the living room when the news got to Suzanne, who quickly packed her bags and took Kim, fleeing the city. I highly doubted he would trail after her, because the authorities would keep an eye on him.

I got offers from the police academy and had my entire future in front of me. They advised me to leave too and never look back.

But how fucking could I, when I knew he'd go back to his old ways? He'd charm some clueless woman who'd be stupid enough to fall in love with him, and he'd make her life a living hell.

He giddily paces the place, and I try to concentrate on my breathing, remembering all the teachings about torture, but I come up blank.

I don't want to play with him. I don't want to show my art to him. I don't want to see excitement in his eyes as he sees what I've become, because that was probably his single-minded goal.

To make me as fucked up as he is.

So with that comes a decision, as I shout from the window of the car, "Matt, get back. Change of plans. I have a surprise for you at home." He frowns, not liking it much, and opens his mouth to protest, but that's when I have enough.

I drill him with my stare, and he blinks rapidly and gets inside. "What kind of surprise?" he asks, but I ignore him, not feeling the need to play a part in this charade any more.

We are going to end it where it all started.

In the fucking house where my mother killed herself.

$\mathcal{E}$lla

Pacing the room back and forth, I wonder where he went to be gone such a long time. He hadn't left my side in the last two days, and I thought maybe I could convince him to change his mind, but I understand now that I thought with the mind of a woman in love, not a psychologist who knows better.

People like him do not change; they are too broken by the past to get beyond it. Most grow stronger through their experiences, but some use those experiences to define and lose themselves in this life.

The sound of the door shutting snaps me from my stupor and I walk to the living room and gasp in shock.

Kierian has a man on his shoulder. He dumps him on the floor and punches a security code into the keypad on the wall so no one can get in or out. The man is unconscious, a gash on his cheek leaking droplets of blood.

My first instinct is to help him, so I take a step in his direction, but Kierian's harsh "Don't" stops me midway.

He grabs my elbow painfully and I wince, but he ignores it and drags me to the far end of the hall, to the place he's never allowed me to enter.

He presses a keycard near the door and it instantly opens. He throws me inside and I barely keep myself from falling.

What has gotten into him?

Only then do the computer screens showing different angles of his torture basement register in my mind. He presses on my shoulder, forcing me to sit in the chair in front of the screens, giving me a good view of what will happen.

"Kierian—" He takes out handcuffs and chains me to the chair so I can't leave, even if I want to.

"You will stay here and see firsthand what it looks like when I torture a man." He puts a blue file on the table, barking, "You can read all the information I have on him while I prepare him. Enjoy."

So this is how he lashes out at me for telling him the truth?

"Don't do this, please." I promised myself I wouldn't beg, but what else is left?

Please, don't put me through this. Don't make me see this part of you that will forever shatter my illusions of you.

At the end of the day, life makes me face the hard truth.

It doesn't matter if you understand psychology or not; when you love a man, you expect him to get better or change.

Even if you know he never will.

He leans closer to me so that we're only an inch away from each other, as he says, "No illusions, Ella. You'll see who I truly am." With that, he turns and leaves me alone while I close my eyes and pray for him to change his mind.

Because in this small room with the ten monitors and high-quality equipment, it will be impossible to hide from the truth.

And I'm afraid the truth might destroy me.

Flipping the folder open, I see the man is Mark Dacke, a doctor who has been married to his wife for the last twenty years.

They have a young son, and based on pictures in the first pocket, you'd think you couldn't have seen a happier family.

It all changes though the minute you flip to another page, a report gathered by Kierian.

Medical treatment. The haunted eyes of his wife and son. Screams in the middle of the night. He must have spied on them, since these are his notes.

Throwing it back on the table, I cover my face with my hands and wonder what he will do to him.

In previous crimes, he didn't have to prove anything to me, and he didn't know the full truth about his biological father. Now though, all this pent-up rage will burst out onto this guy.

Is the doctor innocent? Of course not. But it's not Kierian's right to proclaim himself the judge of bad people. He could have spent his life catching people like this guy and let the justice system handle the rest.

That's the right thing to do.

But how can I explain it to him?

Psychopath

Splashing water on the fucker, I watch him gulp for air as blood oozes from various cuts and stabs I've inflicted, and he barely holds his head up, exhausted from an hour of torture.

This one is more resilient than most. He hadn't asked for mercy for an hour before he finally caved.

They all do, after all.

Watching him now, I know it's time to move to my final stage of things and cut him open, but I can't.

There is so much more I know to make a person feel sorry he was ever born. Half of them I've never used, because I had neither the patience nor the desire to spend so much time on the victim.

But maybe it's a good opportunity to show Ella who she is dealing with.

I grab the brass knuckles, and I'm about to hit him, when Ella's face appears in my mind, the fear in her eyes of what she'll see, and I can't go through with it.

For fuck's sake! I shouldn't be conflicted. I shouldn't think about her. She is nothing but the prey.

But my egotistical self considers her mine, and as odd as the concept is to me, I don't want to hurt what belongs to me.

Grabbing him by the shirt, I place him on the table and strap him to it while turning off the cameras, so she won't have to see the grand finale to my sick hungers.

I think she's had enough anyway.

And for the first time ever, killing a person doesn't zone me out of reality. Instead, it reminds me that it's the straw that will break Ella's back.

CHAPTER TWENTY-THREE

Psychopath, 18 years old

The birds are chirping loudly as I sit down on the bench, resting my arms on my knees while Sociopath paces back and forth in front of me. "What the fuck were you thinking, Shon?"

"I didn't." How the hell could I, if the fucker got out of prison? I could have lived with the satisfaction that he was rotting in there. But to have him on probation so he could find someone else to torture?

Fucking never.

My hands shake just as I remember torturing him. His cries of pain and his blood pooling under my feet reminded me of all the times when I was the victim and he felt himself the king of the world.

"They are searching for you. You killed him in your house, Shon! I hope you're fucking satisfied." He takes out a phone, probably to call Lochlan while I think about his words.

That's the thing though; I don't fucking feel satisfaction or pleasure from the fact he is gone. He is dead, which means he can't suffer, and what's good about that? If only I'd shown more restraint, I could have kept him alive for a month, torturing him every day, creating awareness in his body with each step so he'd know what I felt. What my mother went through when he made our life a living hell. But the chance is gone.

Because the fucker is dead! I gave him an out, and he took it.

Roaring in fury, I get up and push over the bench that should be too heavy to move, and it falls on the ground. I kick it with all my might, needing to get out my frustration as familiar anger prickles my skin.

With one irrational decision and lack of control, I jeopardized my future and became a killer. My life will bring no justice to anyone, and I just wasted everything I've worked so hard for.

"Help me get out of town," I whisper, even though I know I don't deserve it. He trusted me when he took me under his wing, and I failed the first time around.

But as odd as it might sound, I don't want to die or spend my days caught. I want to do something in life. Something that holds fucking meaning for the likes of me.

Sociopath stays silent for a beat and then comes closer, stopping next to me as he lights up a cigarette and exhales a cloud of smoke. "I've taught you self-control. Not this mess."

I stay silent because what can I say to this? He's right. But nothing could have stopped me in that moment.

"But I understand. In a way. There is one man in this world who I wish to choke with my own hands. And if I had the chance, I probably wouldn't let it slip either." He doesn't elaborate, not that I expect him to. He never talks about his past... or present for that matter.

"Help me," I repeat, and he exhales heavily.

"One last time, Shon. One fucking last time, I will help you. But if you break my trust, I will kill you myself. Don't let it destroy you." He pokes at my chest painfully, and I sway back from his strength. "Stay focused."

Sociopath with his connections got me a new identity, a new passport, and a new chance.

And I used it well.

Catching serial killers is an exceptional job, because I help save people, most of whom don't deserve cruelty. And a few times a year, I act like a judge, jury, and executioner, choosing my own victims and getting pleasure from it.

Back then, I thought no one had the power to break the status quo.

If only I knew that a dark-haired beauty would have the power to put me on my fucking knees.

*E*lla

    I sit on a chair, rocking back and forth with my legs raised and my head propped against my knees.

I tried to avoid looking at the monitors or hearing the cries of a man who begged to live.

Tears stream down my face as nausea swirls in me, but I can't make a sound. I want to scream or shout or defend or try to get free, but I don't do it.

I just numbly sit there, still remembering the monster he becomes while he is alone with his victims.

The picture will be forever imprinted on my mind.

At some point, he turned the cameras off, maybe an hour ago. Plenty of time to finish.

I hear a sound and then the door opens. Kierian is standing in the doorway in different clothes and smelling like shower gel.

Right.

He doesn't want to have traces of his victims left on his skin.

Will he wash me off too?

Silently, he uncuffs me from the chair and gently rubs my wrist, but I snatch it back. "Don't touch me."

His lips thin at my words, but surprisingly he doesn't object. Instead, he waits for me to get the hell out of there and I gladly do, hoping to never end up here again.

But once I'm in the living room, I wish I hadn't left the media room.

Because a black garbage bag lies near the main door, waiting to be disposed of. "I'll be back soon. Don't do anything stupid," he warns, and I sit on the couch, ignoring him and all the sounds associated with him as he finally gets the hell out.

Loud laughter echoes in the space, grating on my nerves, and it takes me a moment to realize it's coming from me.

Did I think he'd change for me?

How can he choose light if he's lived in the darkness for so long?

Stupid, naïve Ella. A woman becomes a fool in love hoping to soothe all the edges of her man, not understanding that sometimes all those edges just hurt her.

Knowing all he lived through, can I demand something else from him? Knowing myself, can I expect a future with him?

A love story that was doomed from the very beginning.

Why did I think we would have a happy ending?

He told me himself.

He is not Prince Charming.

CHAPTER TWENTY-FOUR

*P*sychopath

The music is blasting through the speakers as people dance wildly when I enter the New York club. John, the bouncer, raises his chin in greeting, as he is used to seeing me here.

With a green light, I stroll through the sweaty bodies, bypassing a few women who throw seductive glances my way, letting me know they won't mind repeating the performance just for me.

Sadly for them, I came here for a specific target, who is leaning on a barstool, explaining something to the bartender as she points at the whiskey bottle behind him. The guy shakes his head, huffing, but takes out the silver shaker and gives her a thumbs up, clearly preferring to give her what she wants instead of refusing.

Her two best friends join her, squealing loudly and jumping excitingly, clapping their hands. Then with a shared mischievous look, they say, "Tada," and place a large box wrapped with a red ribbon on the barstool while Ella's eyes widen.

She smiles brightly at them, blinding me for a moment when I see utter happiness displayed on her face as she hugs them close, tightening her hold on them for a second.

Will she still smile after the torture I long to inflict on her with my knife collection? I'll use the new equipment for her, made out of the finest steel.

From the moment my gaze first landed on her in that running park, the mental clock has been ticking inside me, counting the minutes and seconds until I can finally introduce myself and come one step closer to achieving my goal.

It's not about the end result with her; it's about the hunt.

She needs to answer a question for me that has driven me crazy through the years, and no amount of studying the likes of me has brought me any relief.

Is it out of love or desperation that a woman stays with a bad man who repeatedly hurts her?

The time has come to find out. I know Noah has called her and she'll work with us soon. I could introduce myself now, but based on the report I've collected on her, she would never agree to this.

"Your favorite song, Ella!" her friend Chloe says and then tugs her to the dance floor, while she stumbles slightly on her heels and sends daggers to her friend, who just shrugs. But then she allows the music to guide her as she becomes one with it, and each of her movements is filled with grace, sensuality, and confidence.

One of the nearby men grabs her arm, spinning her to him while she gasps in shock. "Hey, beautiful, care to dance?" He slurs his words, having had too much to drink. I quickly scan his expensive gold watch, designer wear, and rather egotistical approach.

Ella pulls at her arm, but he doesn't let go. "Come on." He brings them closer, and she fans her face as she winces from his breath. Without warning, she pushes him away, and since he is not sober, he stumbles back, splashing his beer and staining the perfectly white shirt. His friends next to him, not in any better condition than he is, snicker. "Fuck it. No bitch is worth it," he snaps at the girls, who roll their eyes. He walks in the direction of the bathroom, and although I hate letting Ella out of my sight, I trail after him, my hands fisting.

No one else is in the bathroom and he leans on the sink, wiping the beer away with a tissue before he registers my presence.

"What are you starting at?"

Without replying, I grab him by the nape and slam him to the nearby wall, hard, as a painful groan echoes through the space.

"You do not touch what's not yours," I say calmly and repeat the action, but

this time a sinister smile spreads as blood slips from his nose while he is plastered against the wall, trembling.

"Sorry, man, an honest mistake."

I want to hurt Ella in all the ways possible except one, but no one else has this right.

Never will.

She is mine.

Rinsing my hands, I get out of there, closing the door, and a giggle erupts when something soft bumps against me. "Sorry." Her voice freezes me in my tracks, and I allow it to wash over me then spin around. My sudden movement sways her to the side, and I manage to catch her right in time, pressing her tightly against my chest.

Ella blinks a few times in surprise, her breath hitching as her hands rest on my shoulders.

A surge of energy runs between us, creating an awareness I'm not used to, and based on her lost look, she's not either. An unfamiliar emotion threatens to erupt, confusing me, and for a second I consider letting her go and disappearing from her life.

She can be happy with her fulfilled dream, and maybe along the way meet a man who will chase all the monsters away.

But I quash it hard inside me.

I'm not capable of anything except being selfish.

"Kierian," I introduce myself, and she nods.

"Ella." With that, the plan is set in motion, and I wonder how long it will take her to catch me.

But most importantly, I ignore the part of me that screams to not do it.

What did Sociopath say all those years ago to me?

I'm a monster, and they don't have hearts.

Back then, I hadn't realized the deep, set-in-stone truth of those words.

*P*sychopath

Stepping inside the house, I immediately search for Ella but don't find her anywhere.

Frowning, I go to each bedroom and bathroom, but there is no sign of her. She couldn't have escaped, as she doesn't know the alarm code and I would have been notified.

Hitting the table, I shout, "Ella!" But she doesn't reply, probably hiding somewhere from me and licking her wounds.

But then it hits me that there is a place I haven't checked, and sweat drips down my back as I rush downstairs to the basement, hoping I'm wrong.

She's standing near my weapon wall, running her fingers over various devices as she focuses her attention on the kitchen knife with a sharp serrated edge. Although it's not as big as most blades, it brings piercing pain to the victim and always leaves scars.

Her hair is mussed and her bare feet rub against each other; she is acting as if in a trance.

I curse inwardly, because I should have seen the signs when I went to the media room, but I was so deep into my own agony I didn't see her stunned state.

I finally broke her.

Why doesn't it bring me pleasure? Isn't it the proof I so desperately needed?

"Ella," I address her gently, but she doesn't move, doesn't even turn to face me.

"It's all so clean, even though you just killed a man," she whispers softly, her voice raspy.

Does her throat hurt?

"I cleaned it up." I always do, not wanting to have their blood or smell present in my life.

A laugh slips past her lips, but it sounds hollow and lacks any humor. "Yes, you are all about control and killing those who deserve it." She clicks with her fingers. "That's how they taught you, right?" She finally faces me, and only then do I see her wet cheeks and cracked lips, dry blood on them. "How will you clean it once you kill me?" she asks, and I freeze. "I mean, I'm innocent." She places her hand on her chest as her lips tremble. "I'm innocent of any crimes. How will you get rid of me?"

Desperation runs through me. I need to soothe her, to get her the fuck away from here, but emotions are still raw between us, and she steps back from me. "Ella, come on." She shakes her head, cries racking her body as she tries to control herself.

"End this, Kierian. Just do it. Enough. We both know you will never change." She raises her chin. "Finish what we came here for."

"You are hysterical," I say, but fear rushes at me, because I've never seen her beautiful brown eyes this blank.

I can't kill her. For whatever reason, I long to keep her and have her in my life, maybe bring a little light to it.

She said she loved me. What is it like to be loved in this life? People called it a gift.

I wouldn't know.

But she doesn't want *this* life, and how does it make me different from my fathers? Sick bastards who used a poor, young woman for their twisted desires?

How do I save her from myself when she is already here?

"This is important to you, right?" she screams and picks up the knife swiftly. "Hurting me is what brings you pleasure. Mentally or physically, it makes no difference to you." She raises it and is about to stab herself in the stomach, when I snap out of my shock and manage to halt her movements.

Wrapping my hands tightly around the weapon, we breathe heavily as we press against each other. Tears are sliding down her cheeks, as she cries out, "Let go of me. That's what you wanted! To test me. Then do it. No matter how much pain I will be in, I won't give up." She finishes on a sob and turns around as the knife drops with a loud clatter on the floor. "Let go of me. You've already done this anyway." She spins around, but I lock my arms around her waist and hug her from behind. I close my eyes, breathing in her scent, while she cries in my arms.

Her shampoo reminds me of a green field where I used to go as a child and my mom would teach me how to dream while gazing at the clear, blue sky. Dreams that never came true.

Bringing her closer, I don't know what to do with her. With us.

Part of me hates her.

Part of me loves her.

Part of me wants to hurt her.

But the bigger part of me wants to free her so she will forever forget this nightmare.

She was never supposed to be an attachment, just an experiment.

When did she become an obsession?

If I could be someone else, if I could have had different childhood experiences, then maybe we would have a different ending to this story.

But we can't. It's impossible to fix me, and she won't love me while I continue to do what I do. And I can't ever stop.

It's in my blood.

She's right. She will never give up; she even loves with dignity, having herself as a priority.

The decision is made in my head, but before doing it, I need to feel her one last time, giving us what we so desperately need in this moment.

With that thought in mind, I shift her to face me while she whimpers, her eyes shut. Sliding my hand up her neck, I bring us closer and without warning slam my mouth on hers as she struggles in my hold. For the first second, she doesn't welcome my touch, but then she relaxes in the embrace, fisting the front of my shirt while our mouths engage in a deep, probing kiss that is filled with desperation and doom. Without speaking it aloud, we both know it's our last time together.

My lungs burn with the lack of air, but I don't let it deter me from continuing my assault as she sways a little to the side, and I follow, pressing her against the wall. She gulps as much air as possible while I hike her hoodie up, wanting to feel her skin, when she whispers in my ear, "I hate you. You destroyed me." And this time, these words are not said in the heat of the moment, but it's the God's honest truth I see shining from her eyes.

We have no illusions that this isn't the last time.

But I won't have our last time be tainted by the presence of all the ghosts of those I've killed in this place.

Sliding my palms under her ass, I pick her up and she circles her legs around me as we go upstairs, not for a second taking my eyes off her while she rests her cheek on my shoulder, breathing evenly.

It takes several minutes, but I finally place her on the bed and she scoots back, her brown eyes exceptionally vivid against her pale skin as she wipes away the tears.

She's never looked so broken or alone, and I hate myself for it.

"I can go, Ella."

She doesn't say anything, but then rises to her knees and comes closer, motioning for me to do the same, and I comply immediately. She places her hands on my shoulders and exhales a heavy breath. "This is all we'll ever have, isn't it?" she asks, and I don't know what to say.

We have no future; we didn't from the very beginning.

Her name means the light—how fucking ironic?

The light never mixes with the dark, because it can't be tainted by it.

But I tainted her in a way she will never forget, in a way no man should.

And every dark part of me loves it, because it leaves my brand on her.

How fucked up is that?

"Yes," I reply, and she closes her eyes, wincing, but then opens them again, giving me an intense stare that awakens the familiar rush between us.

I start to think that nothing and no one can ever extinguish it.

"Then tonight is our last night? Everything will be different tomorrow?" She doesn't wait for my answers, but instead asks, "Can you be truly mine tonight, then?" My brows furrow, so she continues. "Give up your control that's ever present in all our encounters. Can you do that for me?" Her words freeze me on the spot, because that's the one thing I vowed never to give away.

To give it away means to trust a person to never turn their back on me or hurt me with that power. How can she ask me for it?

But then she pleads. "Please. For once, let me pretend I have all of you. That it was worth it, however long it lasted. I leaped and I lost, but at least I will know I had it all." She puts her hand above my heart, whispering, "I won't do anything bad."

How can I refuse that?

Without saying anything else, I step back and tug on my shirt, removing it quickly along with everything else.

Her breath hitches, and she does the same with the hoodie, showcasing the beautiful body that was always supposed to be mine.

Too bad not for long.

Not taking my gaze away from her, I wait for her next move, because she wants to run the show, and I'll let her.

Just for once.

She grabs my hands and pulls me on the bed, and as I get to it, she flips me on my back while looming over me, her eyes roaming all over my body.

Her fingers trail down my scars and her breath hitches, as if in pain. "They are old." I feel the need to reassure her, and she smiles sadly.

"They aren't if they still have the power to hurt you." Her words stab me like a fucking knife in the heart that suddenly knows how to beat for another person, but she shakes her head. "This has no place for bad memories." Ella captures my mouth with hers as we entwine in a wet and needy kiss that leaves us alone with raging desire between us spiking the flames.

The kiss awakens my strong need for her that I barely restrain myself from taking back my control and entering her easily, finding the oblivion only she can give me.

I fist her hair, mashing our mouths closer, but she pulls away as our panting breaths fill the space. "My rules, remember?" she says while taking my hand and placing it above my head, leaving my other one to rest by my side.

She nips on my chin, slides her lips down the column of my throat, and then licks my collarbone, paying attention to each scar inflicted by *him,* and I wish her mouth had been with me when it all happened.

To soothe it all better in the darkest moments of my past so I could hold on to her and never let go.

But what I have is now, and it's fucking magnificent.

She trails kisses down my abs after taking a bite of each pec as she slides lower and lower, and I can feel her wetness slicking down my leg.

My cock throbs painfully, needing her to soothe the ache, but I don't rush her. She wanted fucking control; she's got it. But serious as fuck, she is driving me out of my mind with her slow seduction and desire to please every part of me, despite me being a monster.

Her breath fans my cock and I hiss.

*E*lla
        In this moment, I don't think or dwell on the future. I just exist with my lover in our make-believe world where everything is perfect and I can run away from the truth.

I don't think I'm weak or broken, or even heartbroken for that matter.

I just concentrate on Kierian and his desire-filled eyes, and fear too that shines from him because he doesn't know what to expect.

He doesn't have to expect anything but loving from me.

His cock demands attention and I grip it, running my hand up and down his length, wiping away the precum and tasting it on my tongue. "Ella," he warns, but I just grin.

"Not your rules." In rare instances when he's allowed me to touch his body, it's usually been at his demand, and I'd kneel in front of him, asking permission to pleasure him.

Not this time.

Blowing a little on the head, I take him in my mouth as his groan fills the air, and he grabs the headboard tighter, clearly not wanting to dictate the show.

I suck on him with a hungry urgency, sliding my mouth up and down while paying extra attention to the head, nipping on it from time to time, and tightening the grip of my hand at his base, while more cum spills into my mouth. I'm hungry and wild for him, as my core throbs with urgency to have him inside me, but I ignore it and focus on him as he pushes a little forward, and I open my mouth wider to accommodate him better.

But then I still his hips with my hands, and he slips out of my mouth with a loud pop as I scatter kisses down his length, pressing the tip of my tongue on his underside, making him jerk again.

He growls this time and grabs my chin. As our eyes meet, he lifts his hips up and makes me take him again. While I suck him with newfound desire, I slip my hand down to my core, wanting to calm the fire that spreads through me.

I want to taste him and make him crazy with my mouth so he will lose all control.

But he has other plans it seems.

Psychopath

Fuck me.

It's not that women weren't paying attention to my body or were on top of me or didn't suck my dick. But no one ever did it bringing so much peace, showing me with each touch that I'm loved, despite everything.

That I can trust without having this trust thrown back in my face.

She is moaning around my length, the sound sending vibrations through me, and I can't take this any longer. I can spill in her mouth, but I don't want that for our last time. I need to feel her squeezing her tight pussy around me, reminding me that for a short time this woman belonged to me.

Even if she didn't want it.

So, fisting her hair, I tug her up until finally our mouths collide and I taste myself on her, while she groans into me. Her hands wrap around my neck as she rubs her nipples against my chest like she needs the pressure that only I can give her.

She is hot and needy, grinding on me, seeking relief, but she can't find it.

Not without my help.

I flip her onto her back and she yelps, but then it turns into a groan as I push her legs apart and find her dripping pussy begging for some attention from me. "Don't tease," she orders, lacing her hand in my hair and pulling me closer to her heat. I comply easily, because clearly sucking me off turns her on.

I lap through her folds, feasting on her unique taste that is so fucking sweet to me I think it's a crime.

She jerks her hips, closing her thighs around my head, but it doesn't stop me from devouring her—licking her from side to side, dipping my tongue inside her and pushing, fucking her with my tongue while she groans and moans and possibly bites her fucking lower lip. That always drives me crazy.

She clenches around me, and I stop, to her loud protest. She trembles as I run my face against her heated flesh. I wonder, *Do my whiskers scratch her sensitive skin?* Trapping her clit between my lips again, I suck on it gently while she tugs on my hair with both hands and her loud scream echoes through the room as more flavor enters my mouth.

She is about to come, and I bring myself up to her chest rising and falling as she watches and pleads with her eyes for me to get going. "Does my Ella need me?" She nods and then thumbs her nipples, moaning. I scoot up, slapping her hands away, and squeeze them with mine, feasting on one nipple and then on the other while her legs wrap around me and her nails scratch my back, demanding more.

Moving to her other breast, I lavish it with the same attention while two of my fingers slide between us and I enter her, stretching her for me although she is so fucking ready that she grinds on them, trying to come from them alone.

"Won't work, Ella."

Her brows furrow, as she snaps, "Then get to it already!" With that, all games are off. The electricity rushes through me, and neither of us can take it anymore.

With one final suck to her beautiful nipple, I push my arms under her knees and thrust into her so hard the headboard hits the wall.

She cries out, but it quickly turns into a moan as I pull back and push in again, digging my fingers into her hips as hard as possible so she'll be marked by me.

I expect her to close her eyes and get lost in the moment as she always does, but instead, she brings my head closer. Our gazes clash for a moment and then she hugs me, giving me a hot kiss that flames my desire even more.

Relentlessly, I pound into her over and over again while enjoying every breath, every moan, every fucking sensation that is so familiar, yet so different this time around.

But this isn't what she asked for, is it?

My thrusts change. They become deeper and slower as I let go of her thighs, and instead slip my hands under her waist as she wraps me close, not an inch between us.

My lips and lungs burn from the kisses, but I don't give a fuck.

I intend for it to last as long as possible, as long as I can control my need, as long as she can take it.

She groans with each push, as her heels dig into my ass and she urges me to speed up, but I don't. We are entwined like this for what seems like an eternity, when Ella palms my face, bites my lower lip, and whispers, "I love you, Kierian." And this ends me.

No one ever told me they loved me, not that I can remember anyway.

I thrust into her hard with one swift move, and her pussy clenches around me, bringing a scream tearing out of her throat as the familiar tingling in my spine signals my own release is imminent. My balls draw closer, my ass clenches, and I spill inside her with a loud growl, breathing heavily.

We lie locked with each other while she rubs her hands up and down my back, not saying anything.

Because the minute someone speaks, it will break the fragile cocoon that exists around us, and unfortunately it's fake.

So I lie on my side while she does the same, facing me and trailing her fingers all over my face while tears stream down her cheeks, but she says nothing.

And hugging her closer and basking in our connection, I wish I was different and could give her what she so desperately wants from me.

But I can't.

We fall asleep lullabied by the peace that for a short time settles over us.

* * *

Slipping from the bed, I gently roll Ella to her side, and she mumbles something in her sleep but hugs the pillow instead. I put on black jeans and a shirt, because this has to end.

Glancing one last time at her, I kiss her softly on the cheek and breathe in her scent, forever memorizing it.

If things could have been different, life would have been different. We've both suffered enough.

There are only two more things to do, because I know danger is around us. I can feel it like a prey feels its hunter.

In my basement, I create a specific plan that will put an end to this charade.

CHAPTER TWENTY-FIVE

*P*sychopath

Parking the car near the Hudson River cliff, I slowly step out onto the ground and inhale deeply, closing my eyes and lifting my face to the bright sunlight streaming down on me.

My lungs fill with the river's air as I step closer to the cliff, peering down to see it's fucking high. If one should ever fall, he probably wouldn't recover.

I hear footsteps behind me, but make no move to face the person as he finally speaks. "Kierian."

"What's your real name?"

He chuckles, joining me on the edge, but instead of answering, he asks, "Why did you call me here?"

Removing my sunglasses, I search for words but fail, because I've never felt like this in my entire fucked-up life.

A woman changed everything, and it shouldn't have happened to the likes of me. It has never been written in any textbook that men like me can love, but then why are they denied such emotions? They say they can form attachments.

But I can call her everything but.

Whenever she doesn't give up after yet another fight, my longing is even greater. Hatred unlike anything assaults me to the point of me barely holding on, to ignore the guns in my house and not shoot myself on the spot.

For all the emotions she makes me feel, I'm not supposed to love, yet what can explain this obsession?

She is a walking reminder that a person can hold on for dear life, even if she has nothing left to live for.

But I will bring nothing good to her.

"I'm going to kill an innocent soul tonight." My mind immediately protests; it screams at those words, the unfamiliar emotion of regret.

I can't function with this anymore; whenever she cries in pain, I want to soothe it and then inflict even more pain. This fucked-up dual thinking only confuses me, and a psychopath who loses control is one step closer to dying.

I have to save her, because she deserves to be happy.

Sociopath freezes next to me, and nods. "Who is she?"

"It doesn't matter. I thought you should know our deal is no longer valid." If there is one person I respect in this world, it is Sociopath. The man helped me survive all those years ago, teaching me a torture method that allowed me to stay sane through all the nightmares.

The only authority in my life, like a fucking older brother I never had.

Too bad, he shouldn't have trusted me either.

Since there is nothing left to say, I walk back to my car, when his voice stops me. "This need will never go away. But if you cannot control it and see straight, remember my promise to you." With this, he goes straight to his car without turning back even once.

A killer without control is a dangerous person. There is a mission and there is killing for sport. The minute you cross the line, Kierian, I will kill you.

No matter where you are.

He didn't have to worry about that.

That's exactly what I want anyway.

. . .

*E*lla

I hear the security code being dialed then the door bursts open, and I quickly rush to it, hoping to see Kierian. When I woke up, he was nowhere in sight, and considering how I lost my shit last night, God only knows what he's going through.

I pushed him too hard when he discovered the truth about his past, and as a result, he lashed out with his torture on that man. But maybe it was a necessary evil, although it sounds now as if I'm justifying him.

No matter that what he does is wrong, it doesn't change the variables in our equation. I love him, plain and simple, and he loves me too. He just doesn't know what to do with it. But this knowledge brings no peace, since it doesn't solve the problem. He will never change, and I don't think I can accept his little hobby.

Blinded by the sun, I shield my eyes from the light and adjust my blurry vision. The man standing in front of me is not Kierian.

It's Preston!

My brows furrow as my jaw drops. How is he here? No one has access to Kierian's house!

"Preston? What are you doing here?" I come closer to him, but slip on the floor and fall on my knees, a gasp of pain escaping me. "Please help me!" He was always with me on cases, and all along, he got all the stuff right. He probably figured this out on his own too and then trailed after Kierian.

After all, he is a computer wizard. How hard would it be for him to hack the security system?

I expect his immediate help, but instead, he cocks his head, seemingly mesmerized by the vision I provide for him. "Ella," he says with wonder while moving his gaze to my bruises and licking his lips, "you are magnificent." To my horror, he trails his finger down my cheek, and I can almost taste my repulsion as I try to evade his touch.

"No," I whisper, refusing to believe what my eyes clearly show me. A tear slides down the side of my nose, while realization threatens to turn me insane. "No, Preston."

His face falls as he caresses my cheek. "Shh, Ella. Don't cry. I don't want to hurt you."

What is it about me that attracts serial killers? It's as if they have a contest among each other for who will manage to kill me first, but everyone fails, because they find my suffering more amusing.

"Don't touch me." I slap his hand away and he frowns, anger flashing in his eyes, but he keeps smiling when he reaches for another touch. I scoot farther away, my back hitting the wall painfully as he crawls after me, wrapping his hand around my ankle and tugging on it. I kick my foot to get away and it connects with his nose, halting his movements.

He grunts, blood slipping through his fingers, and he kneels and sits back on his heels while I breathe heavily, ready to fight.

I might be helpless and doomed for death, but I'll be damned if I go down without a fight.

"You are sick."

He shakes his head, one blond curl lying on his forehead messily as he exhales heavily. "You're mad. You shouldn't be mad at me for lying. I couldn't tell you until I was sure." His jabbering makes no sense to me, so I stay silent while he continues, taking a tissue out of his backpack and wiping the sweat away from his upper lip. His hands tremble as he adjusts his glasses on his nose. "What if you judged me? But when I figured out your past and Kierian's... it was like an epiphany. You'd never turn your back on me." He slides his palm to my thigh, gripping it painfully, and I cry out as he digs right into the fresh cut Kierian left behind. Only, Preston brings nothing but pain. "Beautiful," he whispers.

Hysterical laughter echoes through the room, and it takes me a moment to understand it's coming from me as I hold my stomach, tremors shooting through me while the hilarity and desperation of my situation finally register in my mind.

No one is going to save me, so the responsibility falls solely on my shoulders. Out of the two evils, Preston is the greater one, because I cannot predict his next move. So I have to keep talking with him and not agitate him, just hold him off till Kierian comes.

Kierian will never allow anyone to hurt me, because he considers me his. I know that with deep, set-in-stone certainty. People can call it Stockholm Syndrome or stupidity, but for me it's love. A love he has no clue about, because he simply never lived with it.

Inhaling deeply, I throw aside the victim and leave only the criminal psychologist who studies her unsub.

Preston bites his lip, opening his mouth and closing it as though he's searching for words, and I can see how he nervously glances at the clock over his shoulder while his hands can't help but reach for me again.

No control, shyness, creating me as this big ideal, a person who never had understanding. Demanding for me to listen to him and not comprehending that my no means no.

Connecting all the other pieces about him, the profile is formed in my head. "It was the book."

He whimpers, crawling closer, and I do my best not to show my revulsion as he nods eagerly. "Yes! I knew you'd remember." He snatches his backpack that's next to him, grinning at me like a fool while shaking the book in front of my face. "The minute you told me that the book will make you understand the suspect, I knew you got me."

Since Kierian wanted nothing to do with this case, I mostly spent my days discussing the book with Preston, who was always eager for interesting conversation.

Yeah, and we all read it. Noah likes Hector, which fits him, always the protector. And Preston is into Paris, God knows why.

Paris was the most cowardly of them all, when he left his brother to deal with the problem.

"Our research was foreplay for you," I conclude, and even though I want to block it all out, I can't. "Who was she, Preston?" He whimpers again, palming his face while casting his gaze down. "Preston, look at me." He raises his eyes immediately. "Who was she?"

"Alana," he says, sitting on the floor. He locks his knees close to his chest and rests his cheek on one of them. "She was so beautiful."

Lowering my voice to a steady and soothing one so he'll stay in the trance, I continue to probe deeper. "You loved her."

He nods eagerly. "More than anyone."

"What happened to her?" She was Helen in his mind, which means either he had to kidnap her or she belonged to someone else.

In the next second, he proves my theory right; he shifts as if in a trance and tells me his story, which makes me sicker with each word.

Next to him, Kierian doesn't seem so bad, and how fucked up is that?

"My father fell in love with her, and they started dating. She didn't want it, but she knew he'd hurt me if I spoke up about our relationship. She always protected me." A relationship that existed only in his head. One gesture of kindness can evoke this kind of reaction with his insanity. "She suffered, cried all the time, and he screamed a lot." He tightened his hold on his knees, zooming into space. Reliving all the events from the past. "Then my brother came back from college. And I decided to strike," he murmurs, and I dread his next words. "Dad beat her up all the time, and I couldn't take it anymore. I took the knife and aimed it at him, but I only managed to surprise him as he knocked it out of my hands."

I don't have to listen to know how this ends.

Or who suffered in the end.

He exhales heavily. "Father would have done something to me, but my brother saved me. Came between us and Dad killed him." He finishes in a whisper, "Right in front of my eyes."

Oh my God.

But I can't lose my focus now, so I ask, "What happened to Alana?"

His face transforms into a mask of indifference and disgust, if that's possible. Harshness laces his voice. "She blamed me for the entire thing. Goes to visit him every month and claims he is the love of her life."

"And since then, have you loved anyone else?" Just how many people has he killed? All women would be surrogates for Alana, who he never had and could never save.

"Besides you? Five more girls. I saved them," he says with a crazy look in his freaking eyes.

I'm in a house in the middle of nowhere with a serial killer whose MO are girls my age in a relationship with someone else.

How long can I stall him before it's enough?

"You know about Kierian?"

He shrugs. "Not at first, but yes. He became careless with you. And it's not hard to track him down if you have my resources. I only joined the FBI for fun. I never gave up the old ways. But when he started a relationship with you, I knew it was a sign to act fast. But you understand why he had to kidnap you first, right?" He pinches my chin, raising it higher, and although I wish to pull away, I can't, because he might be in a violent state. "Otherwise, I wouldn't have been able to save you."

Two different men grew up in similar circumstances where their father essentially destroyed their lives. But where one learned from others to direct his anger and psychopathic tendencies for the so-called greater good, the other killed people in his misguided attempt to save them, but in truth, he relived the final moments of his brother's life all over again.

And each time, he wants the girl to be grateful for what he does, because then he thinks he will find peace for indirectly causing his brother's death.

Looking at all this now, does it make it so impossible to love Kierian? How many more lives could have been destroyed if he didn't kill those men? Granted, most kids don't grow up with such tendencies, but a lot have unhealed wounds that affect their entire lives.

Can I be with him and accept all this, knowing he will never stop?

I don't have much time to dwell on it as the door bursts open and Kierian walks in. Immediately, Preston lifts me up off the floor and settles behind me, pressing my back to his front. He places a knife to my throat, and Kierian freezes in place, awaiting Preston's words.

Closing my eyes for a second, I bask in the emotion of relief as my monster comes after me.

And he will fix it.

"We need to kill her, Kierian. Only the stronger one can take the prize and honor." Preston's words chill me to the bone as he continues. "She deserves it for what she put you through!" he screams in my ear, and I understand then, that's another fantasy he wants to play out.

He and his big brother punish Alana for betraying them. His ultimate fantasy that he probably didn't have the chance to experience through all those years.

This nightmare will never end!

*P*sychopath

My heart is racing in my chest as I assess the image in front of me.

Preston holds a knife to Ella's neck, and she winces in pain from his pressure on her shoulders.

Fisting my hands, all I want is to grab the fucker and kill him on the spot, but he knows his job. He holds the steel right next to her artery, and the minute I make a move toward him, one cut and she will be gone.

My beautiful prey I intended to set free once and for all won't die at the hands of Preston.

I never thought the overpowering fear I'd felt in my childhood would ever come back. Nothing scared me, because a person can be scared only when he can lose something.

But in this second, fear unlike anything I've known before enters me and penetrates every part of me, ordering me to come up with an idea to save her.

Oddly enough, fear is absent from her features. Only relief is flashing brightly right at me, as if she knows I will save her.

Like she waited for me to arrive.

Despite the hell I've put her through, she still trusts me. And in this moment, I can admit the pressure in my chest has nothing to do with desire and everything to do with love.

Emotions I can never speak of or enjoy, but it's there.

Unfortunately, it changes nothing for us or this story.

It will end today.

I just have to alter my plan.

"Of course we will kill her. What was the point of bringing her here, right?"

Preston frowns, throwing me an accusing stare. "But you were ready to attack me."

Fuck. He would notice that, considering he grew up with a monster.

This is a surreal experience to say the least.

The last thing I ever wanted to do is hurt a kid who suffered through his childhood. But he threatened what is mine, and no one harms what belongs to me.

*E*lla

Opening my heart to love certainly filled my life with vivid emotions as Chloe claimed.

Now I'll have to pay dearly for choosing my love over killing Kierian when I had the chance.

"Then how?" Preston's knife slips as he loosens his grip on me to lean forward, not wanting to miss Kierian's words.

"What's the fun in it? Let's start the hunt."

I close my eyes, willing the tears to stay inside them and not concentrate on how my heart painfully pangs against my ribcage at his statement.

I thought he'd save me, but apparently my stupidity has to be seen to be believed. There is no good in him.

And I'm so desperately in love with him despite everything that I still search for it in him.

Live and learn.

"The winner takes it all?" Anticipation laces Preston's voice, and for a second, I notice fury crossing Kierian's face, but it's so quickly gone I think I've imagined it.

"Right. Everyone has a chance."

Preston throws me to the side, and I stumble a little, barely keeping my balance. Kierian is at my side at once, grabbing me by the shoulder and steadying me.

"Listen to me very carefully, Ella," he whispers in my ear, his breath fanning my cheek while he inhales my smell as if memorizing it. "Run as far away as you can. If you want to live, run." His voice is harsh and devoid of any emotion, which contradicts his silver eyes that flash with possessiveness and determination unlike anything I've seen in him.

Even in this moment, where he feeds me to the wolves, the wolves being their sadistic desires, I can't help but feel utterly safe in his arms. Nothing is dangerous to me except him, but he betrayed me, right?

Chose his psychopathy over me. Although it's not like he can control it. I'm just one of those women who believed he could.

My *Beauty and the Beast* story doesn't end with the beast becoming a prince.

His thumb wipes away a single tear from my cheek while he pauses, and then pushes me to the door. "Preston, she has a five-minute lead, and then we can follow."

"And do whatever we want?" he asks excitedly, while his frantic gaze sweeps over me, and I shift to the side, despising the implication it has.

"Yes."

Kierian stands between us, blocking Preston's view of me, and our gazes clash for the last time, as he whispers, "Go." But for some reason, I'm frozen to the spot, hating to leave him here even though I know he'll most likely catch me soon and kill me. But running away seems like giving him up to the darkness that's followed him since he was a child.

But there is no solution, is there? He will always be bad, and I won't ever accept it.

So ignoring the blinding sun and nausea, I dash outside, running and running, my feet burning from touching the rocks and grass that cut into my bruised flesh.

The wind blows into my face while tree leaves slap me, and my raspy breath is the only sound that accompanies me.

My lungs burn from the exercise, my legs getting weaker, but I will myself to go on, remembering my life is at stake and I won't let a serial killer win. Even if only Preston enters my mind.

Why doesn't Kierian come to it too?

It's funny how life had no meaning for me through the years, but now I desperately try not to give up.

Since I'm not watching where I'm running, I don't see the glass until I step on it. Screams of pain leave me at the exact moment strong hands wrap around my waist from behind, lifting me up. I shout, "No!"

and struggle in the hold, kicking the person with all my might, and it takes me a second to register his hands do not feel familiar.

Before I can dwell on it, he pushes me down on my stomach and covers my back, and orders, "Stay low. Do not move." The voice is laced with authority and harshness, but I don't recognize the man. Who is he?

The minute the thought enters my mind, there is a loud blast, reverberating through the forest as birds fly up high, circling widely, and pieces of wood rain down around us. A surge of energy washes over me, freezing me on the spot for a moment while I think about the source of the blast.

"What is it?"

The stranger stands up, and I can finally sit up. I turn around and a gasp of shock slips from my lips.

Even though I thought I ran far away, in fact it was only a few hundred feet, and I can still see Kierian's house, or what's left of it, behind all the smoke that surrounds the destroyed building. Fire creeps along the grass, and flames consume what's left of the house as acrid black smoke fills the forest with its disgusting smell.

What the hell happened?

I cough into my hand and the stranger removes his jacket, throwing it over my shoulders while dialing on his phone. "Nine-one-one? There's been an emergency..." He proceeds to give the address while I numbly study the wreckage, and only once the shock disappears do the memories of my captivity come back.

"You need to leave. They are coming after me," I croak through my dry throat, but the glance he gives me makes uneasiness settle in the pit of my stomach.

This man could easily be mistaken for the angel of death with his black hair, tanned skin, amber eyes, and the aura of danger surrounding him.

"They stayed inside, Ella. Kierian saved you." He pauses, then he mutters, "He knew I'd come after him and save you."

I'm smart, Ella. I can predict everything.

Could he have predicted Preston's insanity? That's why he insisted on me running away—he chose love in the end.

He chose me, but by doing that, he sacrificed himself?

"No!" I scream, darting to the building, but the man locks his arms around me once again, stilling any movement I might have made.

"Kierian." My whisper is barely audible, but he hears it nevertheless.

"Dead, Ella. Your nightmare is over."

Oh, no.

My nightmare has just begun.

How will I be able to live with it?

Sobbing uncontrollably, I sink to my knees and weep into my hands at everything that could have been and everything that won't ever be. Love and hatred entwined when it came to Kierian, but to think he is no longer with me?

It kills everything inside me.

The sound of sirens echo and the stranger pats me on the back. "The help is here. Good luck, Ella." With one last glance, he leaves me alone, and I don't even bother to ask his name, because it doesn't matter in the grand scheme of things.

In a few minutes, paramedics are at my side, wrapping me in tight blankets while tending to my wounds and asking me millions of questions to which I mostly nod.

Firefighters do their best to stop the flames while police shake their heads in disbelief but make notes anyway.

They put me in the ambulance but quickly administer sedatives when I thrash around the minute they want to strap me down.

In seconds, everything goes blank, and for the first time in my life, I welcome the oblivion with open arms.

Maybe all the wounds in my soul will stop hurting and bleeding like they do now.

CHAPTER TWENTY-SIX

*E*lla

Resting my back on the pillow, I gaze through the window of the bare hospital room and completely zone out of conversation at hand.

Chloe quickly brings me back though. "Ella?"

I don't react, because I don't care about anything else but the things that have happened to me in the span of seventy-two hours.

Finding out that Kierian stayed in his house to die with Preston broke something inside me, and I'm not sure I'll ever be able to mend it.

Why does my love always have to revolve around serial killers?

A serial killer took my parents away. The serial killer was a man who I considered an uncle. And now the man I fell for and opened myself up to ended up being one too.

Even Preston, who I considered a friend, as much as you can be a friend in the short amount of time with a coworker, turned out to be insane.

"Ella."

Finally, I snap my attention back at her and nod. "Yes."

"Yes, what?" she asks, confused, while Simone gives me a concerned stare.

"Whatever you want, it's a yes. Look, I'm just not in the mood for this conversation, okay?"

Chloe exhales heavily and then sits down next to me, her palm covering mine, and I try to snatch it back, but she holds it firmly. "Ella, Kierian—"

"Don't," I warn, and they share a look, but frankly I don't care. I wasn't sure I wanted to discuss him with anyone, let alone with my best friends. They would know I lied.

I couldn't let anyone know what I did.

Everyone waited for my statement, to put the final nail in the coffin, so to speak, and close the case. I got so many flowers it felt like a floral shop here.

"Okay." Chloe doesn't push me, but then when did she? "Your landlord understands your situation and is fine with you prolonging the lease once you are out," she says cheerfully, as if it's supposed to lift my mood or something.

"I'm not going to renew it."

She blinks several times and then clears her throat. "We are talking about your dream apartment, Ella. You said you'd never move." Yeah, I fell in love with my apartment that opened to the best city view and it reminded me every day I had accomplished everything on my own.

But now this place will remind me of nothing but Kierian. Some of his clothes are still there. I can't imagine continuing to live there anymore.

"Dreams can change."

Simone opens her mouth to say something, when they are interrupted by Noah, who enters the room with a frown on his face.

"Didn't know you had visitors. I'll come another time." He practically walks on eggshells around me, wary of my reaction or bringing up the case, although I know he has to.

If I were anyone else, he'd be questioning me and taking my statement the minute I could talk, but because I was under his protection and he failed me, he lets me do it in my own time.

This has to end, maybe because I won't have the courage to do it all over again.

"Please come in, Noah. Girls," I address them, and they get up, but not before Chloe flashes me a look that says we will continue our conversation later. I just roll my eyes as she kisses me on the cheek, and they leave, the room enveloping in silence that is disturbed only by the traffic sounds coming from the streets.

Noah shifts from side to side, and I wait for him to ask a question, wondering with whom he'll start.

Or if he knows I've lied.

He curses and then sits on the edge of the chair next to me, still keeping his distance though. "I need to ask you."

"Go ahead." I know the protocol.

He cracks his fingers, and then asks, "Did he rape you?"

I shake my head, focusing my attention on the bright billboard that faces my window. Sometimes lying in bed and gazing at the ceiling, I wonder if he had then maybe I would have been able to hate him and cross off all the good parts that happened with him. "No."

"For how long did he keep you?" My brows furrow, as it's a bit stressful for me, but then I finally find the words.

"Around four days. Maybe less." I see him making notes on his iPad, and then he continues.

"What did he do to you?"

"You've read the doctor's report, Noah." My soft voice seems to snap something in him as he swiftly gets up and paces the floor, going back and forth, his fingers tangled in his hair.

"I can't believe I didn't seen his insanity. I mean, he was just a good guy. Why would he do this?" He exhales heavily. "Although I know perfectly well why he did what he did. But still, it makes no sense that such a good kid like him would do this." He grips the edge of the bed's rails so tightly his knuckles turn white. "I should have protected you from him." He leans forward, defeat marking his every action, but I don't reassure him.

Because truth be told, I don't know what to say to that.

We are humans too. We are allowed to make mistakes.

"Noah, he had a plan, and he executed it. Please don't beat yourself up because of it."

A humorless chuckle slips through his lips as he tugs on his hair, holding my stare. "You could have died."

"Yet here I am." My life has to be seen to be believed. Twice, serial killers aimed to kill me.

Twice, they've spared my life.

How ironic is that?

"Will you come back to work?" His abrupt change of subject throws me off, and I shift uncomfortably; I didn't expect this question so soon. "I've been in this job for a long time. It's okay to want an out."

Fumbling with my fingers, I pull the blanket higher as suddenly shivers run down my spine. "I think my professors were right. There is no place for me in the FBI." Or in psychology. I should have never sacrificed my life to catch serial killers. I only proved to everyone who objected that they were right.

What would my life have been like if I'd stuck with photographic journalism? Would I have been happier? Would I have married Kierian and lived with him without knowing his secret desires?

"I'll get the papers drawn up. For better or worse, you've managed to destroy one serial killer in this world. It's an accomplishment, Ella." He pats my hand gently and clears his throat. "We will all miss Kierian."

Adrenaline pours into my veins as my breathing speeds up, sweat drips down my back, and my eyes widen in fear that he'll notice.

That he'll know I lied.

He thinks only one serial killer died that night.

No one has any idea who Kierian was, because I kept my mouth shut.

For them, he died a hero trying to save the woman he loved.

Let it be my final gift to him for saving my life when he didn't have to.

A gift freely given.

Even if it probably makes me end up in hell one way or the other.

· · ·

*R*ichmond, Virginia
    One month later

*E*lla
My feet step soundlessly on the emerald-green grass as the breeze fans my cheeks lightly. I inhale the familiar scent of home, and somehow along the way, the cemetery became my home since my family lies there, and I exhale a heavy breath.

Walking closer, I pick up the nearby hose and spray water on all the different flowers planted on the gravestones, then remove the dust that has collected from all this time.

Done with the task, I place a single red rose on each stone then sit down on the small step, resting my back on Mom's grave, and close my eyes, searching for words I cannot find.

I thought coming here would ease my pain, but it only becomes stronger. "I'm sorry I haven't been here in a while." More like years. I usually made sure to visit them once a year on the anniversary of their death, but with each year, with each new accomplishment, it became harder and harder. So at some point five years ago, I gave up altogether. "I'm not even sure why I'm here now," I murmur into my hands, as I press the heels of my palms on my eyes, but I do know.

Kierian.

With the truth and captivity, I should hate him.

But I can't, because I fell in love with the man first. All the monstrous things he did haven't managed to extinguish this love.

And I hate it, because the pain in my chest stabs me every time his face flashes in front of my eyes. It's because living without him is unbearable.

"He's dead, Mom." I wipe away the single tear from my cheek and then laugh, although it's strained. "I got my dream job, only to realize everyone was right all along. It's not what I want to do." I fist the soil and then slowly let it go. Taking a deep breath, I spin around, placing my hand on the stone, ignoring the burning sensations from the hot July sun shining brightly on it. "I always felt guilty for being alive, and I had to repay it. So I ventured into criminal minds, but truth be told, I only understand now how stupid it was." Rubbing the headstone gently, I wish she were here with me so I could share all my deepest secrets with her.

But life decided differently. "It's a gift. Me staying alive. Because somehow part of you is still here. And I will use it wisely, Mom." I kiss the stone soundlessly and get up, only to blink in surprise when I notice a white dove landing on my sister's stone, so beautiful I long to touch it.

A bubble of laughter escapes my mouth, and I look up, appreciating this kind gesture letting me know it's okay to finally let go.

The peace that settles inside me is unexplainable, as if a heavy weight has been pulled away from my chest. I'm twenty-nine years old, but it feels like I've just started living. I'm never going to be completely good with what has happened to me, but I don't have to live in an illusion that I'll get justice for my family.

I never will, and that's probably the hardest truth I've had to accept and always ran away from.

Oddly enough, I have no one else but Kierian to thank for this realization.

Dusting my hands off, I saunter back home, to the house I haven't visited since that tragic day.

No one ever sold it, as I still had the rights, but there were no interested people either. I imagined not many wanted to live in a house where a murder was committed.

With the serial killer's house a few feet away.

Stopping in my tracks, I stand in front of the two-level wooden house. The grass is freshly cut and nourished, and it doesn't seem like an abandoned house. I have to thank Miss Kara for that, since she made it her mission to take care of it. God only knows why.

Each step that takes me to the door feels heavier and heavier as vivid images dance in my mind.

Sarah's laughter when I spun her around in the backyard.

Dad's scowl when he didn't appreciate our wet-from-the-hose clothes.

Mom calling us for dinner and winking as she baked a delicious cake. My nose can still smell her cinnamon masterpiece.

Shaking my head from all this, I insert the key and unlock the door, the echo of my shoes greeting me as I step inside. All the furniture was thrown away since it was all covered in blood and I saw no use for it. I'm about to check the rest of the house, since I've planned to stay here for a while, when the hair on my neck prickles and my heart rate speeds up.

There is barely audible breathing behind me, but my ears catch it nevertheless.

Slowly, I turn around as the keys fall to the floor with an annoying jingle, and I come face to face with the man.

He rests his back against the wall, relaxed, as the silver blade shifts through his fingers. He catches my stare and then shuts the door, forever deciding my fate.

Death finally came full circle with me.

It's ironic how I'll face my death in the same house that once allowed me to escape it. But then you can't cheat destiny after all, right?

"Ella," he says, still drilling me with his stare. "I told you I always win."

EPILOGUE

*S*omewhere in the world...

*E*lla
 Inhaling the fresh scent of coffee, I go out on the deck, enjoying the view of a magnificent sunset over the ocean, the orange light reflecting in the misty blue water that calls for you to enter it and never get out.

The soft breeze touches my skin, giving much-needed cooling as my white summer dress sways around my legs.

Laughter on the beach snaps my attention and my eyes land on the two-year-old who chases the small husky dog. The puppy jumps from side to side barking, circling around his feet and licking them from time to time. The boy laughs joyfully, clapping his hands, and then lands on his diapered behind as the puppy jumps on him, nuzzling his neck.

Rex sleeps next to my feet, snoring loudly, and I shake my head at him. He got old and lazy, but still plays with Dean from time to time.

The familiar twitch in my hands creates uneasiness in me, and I know how to soothe it. I grab my camera from the hook nearby and snap a picture of Dean, capturing this perfect moment in time that will never happen again.

Focusing my lens on him, I notice how the man leans next to him and helps steady him, and the child grins, raising his arms.

The man complies easily, placing the child on his shoulders. I'm finally busted, and the man raises his brow.

"Mama is watching us," he says to Dean, who waves at me joyfully.

"Mama!" Pride laces his voice as he tunnels his tiny hands in his father's hair, and my man doesn't even wince.

I think at this point he is just used to it. Our baby boy is fascinated with his hair, maybe because they share the same color. Mine never has the same appeal for him.

"Hi, honey." I walk closer, meeting them half way and, with a smile, place a soft kiss on my husband's cheek while patting my son on the back in a soothing motion when he senses the tension between us.

I've been avoiding them the whole morning, knowing full well today's date and hating it at the same time.

Because I know Kierian will go out to hunt and disappear for an entire week until his dark desires are satisfied.

This will never get better; he will never change.

But then, he never hides the truth from me, not anymore.

He gave me a choice five years ago, and I chose him for better or worse.

After he was declared dead, he managed to have new passports made for us with our new identities, and we left everything behind. He found us a piece of heaven where we could live and enjoy every minute of it. Despite him being a monster in a well-understood sense by the people, I couldn't have been happier and never regretted my decision.

We'd been two lonely souls drifting in this world without much purpose, seeking things we thought were right. But truth be told, our childhood shouldn't define us or dictate our life choices.

Our love story makes no sense for most people and never will. After all, how can I be so weak and love him? For whatever reasons he does what he does, it's still wrong. He still touches me with his blood-stained hands, and I know if he ever feels I'm a threat to our child, he will kill me at once. His protective instinct is what defines him.

While he loves our son with everything he has, it doesn't change him.

And never will.

Although it scares me on most days, and even though I have nightmares of him ending up in jail and the police coming to my door asking me how I could live with him all these years, it doesn't stop me from being his.

Because I can't imagine a different life. My heart forever belongs to him, and love is not an emotion that can be dictated.

It'll always be wrong. But it's a choice I make nevertheless.

Resting my forehead on his, I inhale his smell, and whisper, "I love you." He doesn't say anything back. I think the concept's too far gone for him to understand or want to acknowledge.

Kierian is silent for a moment, but then his arm locks around me, bringing us closer together, as he murmurs in my ear, "I know." These words he says with gratefulness, and the smiles he gives our son are the reason I stay.

The reason I don't run away. He needs us. He longs for acceptance and love, for a peace his restless soul can never find.

I've become Psychopath's prey that he decided to keep.

And somewhere along the way, the prey fell in love with the hunter, and they lived happily ever after.

Kidding.

We don't have a happy ending, but we have the only ending that suits our story.

And I'm okay with that.

The End
Turn the page to read excerpts from Lachlan's Protégé and Sociopath's Obsession.

LACHLAN'S PROTÉGÉ EXCERPT

Valencia

My eyes snap open. I look straight ahead and take a deep breath, then step into a pose. I'm illuminated by the moonlight shining brightly into the room from the glass-like ceiling above me. This silent space is filled with a mysterious atmosphere, creating an almost-perfect setting for a romantic evening.

The familiar first notes of Tchaikovsky's *Swan Lake* echo through the room, and I assume the position, rising on my toes and swaying from side to side while slowly moving to the corner. I hop on my toes again, owning the stage as if nothing matters, blocking the outside world away.

To each dramatic note, I perform with my hands and facial expressions, giving away all the hopelessness of the swan, the beautiful young woman Odette, who's been captured by the dark sorcerer and can't be reunited with her lover.

The pain and heartache fuel her desire to fight against him, so she feeds on them even if they threaten to destroy her.

I swirl and swirl, rising up and down, up and down, and then a cry of pain slips past my lips as my feet land on glass. I halt my movements, barely breathing from the glass digging into my skin.

I glance down to see my white pointe shoes slowly coating in blood from all the scattered glass covering the floor; if one is careful enough to avoid it, he is a master.

My feet agonizingly throb. I can barely stand on them. My rasping breaths help me to concentrate on something other than the pain.

I've been doing nothing but dancing for the last hour. I've never performed for this long without a break in my life.

The sound of the lighter flicking fills the space as he lights up his cigarette, takes a deep breath, and exhales it in my direction while resting comfortably on the chair right in front of me. "Ah, Valencia. You know the rules. Never stop." His deep, dangerous voice raises goose bumps on my skin, reminding me once again that the monster never sleeps.

He just feeds on my misery.

He tugs on the rope wrapped tightly around my waist and I stumble forward. I can't help the groan of pain when he directs me onto the big pile of glass. The air freezes in my lungs while I pray for the hurt to pass so I can continue.

But I can't.

Instead, fear unlike anything before spreads through me. Injuries like this may ruin a dancer's career forever, and if I don't have dancing, I won't have anything in this life.

But he knows that.

Another tug. This time, I can't keep up. I land on my knees, biting my lip hard so I won't groan when the bare skin on my palms and knees land on the glass.

"Get up," he orders, but I don't.

He can dish any punishment he wants. God knows the cuts and throbbing skin are an indication of that. But I won't let him taint the one thing in my life that I love the most.

He's already taken everything else; he doesn't get to have ballet too.

He exhales heavily at my disobedience and rises, straightening his perfectly ironed three-piece suit, then walks to me as his expensive Italian leather shoes make an unmistakable sound against the floor.

With each step he takes, my heartbeat speeds up faster and faster to the point of feeling it in my throat. He places the metal head of his cane under my chin and lifts it up.

I meet his stare head on. I hate everything about this man.

Or at least I hope it's hate.

"So that's your choice?" he asks as his lazy gaze roams over me, but I say nothing.

I won't give him the last part of me that matters.

Even if it seals my death tonight.

SOCIOPATH'S OBSESSION EXCERPT

Sociopath

The man in the chair was pinned to the wall with several straps across his chest. He cried out in pain as I relished the exquisite torture my hands inflicted on him. It was truly a work of art to make a man suffer agonizing pain, but not enough to die.

I'd mastered it for many years, learned everything there was, and practiced my craft religiously.

Knives, guns, chains, wires.

Nothing was off limits for me.

I loved this—the feeling of power and knowledge that I could play with my victim for days, and sometimes, if the mood struck me, for weeks. When I finally had enough, and it was always about me, I'd kill the fuckers quickly. They tended to get on my nerves with all their whining.

The most boring part in the whole process was disposing of the body—not much work there—and then covering my tracks so the traces would never bring anyone to me.

However, the idea of anyone suspecting me of such things was laughable.

I was the one who sent condolences to their wives and families, if they had any, and the one who actively participated in police searches.

People were very naïve sometimes. They had no idea appearances could be deceiving.

What they thought was good, might be dark.

What they thought was dark, might be the only salvation to human kind.

"Mercy." The fucker was choking on his own blood; his voice was barely a whisper, and his eyes were wide with fear. It made me chuckle.

"Never." I held the knife, small but sharp, and engraved small patterns on his back, which earned me another cry of pain. The familiar, disgusting smell of urine filled the air. How many fucking times could this guy piss his pants? Adjusting my nose mask better on my face, I continued to write the names on his back, so he would know what the fuck he suffered for.

You'd probably think I was a monster.

Well, you wouldn't be wrong.

I loved torture and pain, but only when I was the one to inflict it.

I was the witness, judge, and executioner all at once.

No one knew better than I did what it was like to be in their position.

Helpless.

Afraid.

Starved.

Neglected.

And in pain.

Always in fucking pain.

No one was born a monster.

He made me the person I was, and I was glad for his '*gift.*'

Sociopath took care of men like him, made sure they suffered to death. They would never get an easy death from me. I'd make them suffer for all the shit they'd done. It was fun and well deserved.

Mercy. What a funny concept.

I would never have mercy for anyone in this world, let alone for people who were the same monsters as I was.

Life wasn't that generous.

I was not that generous.

No one knew about it; no one knew my name. They only knew a nickname.

Sociopath.

And those who received an e-mail with that name knew the end was coming.

It was part of my high, to watch them for weeks being cautious, uneasy, and frightened of every step. They knew why they would suffer.

Life was fucking great.

It thrilled me.

And I never wanted more.

Women were interchangeable, and I only used them when I needed a cover.

I never wanted to touch them, never wanted them to touch me. Fucking hated any physical contact with them longer than what was necessary. I never allowed them to touch my dick, or any other part of my body. I had to learn how to please them, so they wouldn't try any stupid moves.

Sex was a chore, a necessary weapon to use when information or access was needed. Nothing more, nothing less.

Until I met her.

Meeting her changed something inside me, and my control snapped.

She was a target, just like everyone else. One touch from her, and she became my everything.

Instead of being repulsed by her, I yearned to touch her, and for her to become undone under me. My head was filled with images of our bodies covered in sweat when she was spread on the mattress in my dungeon, her body covered in my bite marks of ownership.

I never wanted to hurt her, but I wanted to own her. Brand her as mine for the world to see and accept me as I was.

She had the bluest eyes I'd ever seen; it was like looking into the clear blue sky.

They were warm and beautiful.

Sapphire.

My Sapphire.

If I were a better man, I would have left her alone and never made her part of my life.

But I was a monster.

And monsters didn't have hearts.

ACKNOWLEDGMENTS

First, I want to thank God and my family for allowing me to write and make this dream possible. The support means so much to me, and I understand that sometimes it drives you crazy, especially when I try to meet my deadlines and seem unavailable to you. But I love you guys and appreciate everything you do for me.

This was not an easy book to write. The idea about a love story between a serial killer and criminal psychologist came to me on one summer afternoon. The prologue scene popped in my head and I wrote it down, not really knowing where the story would lead me. From that day I'd add several scenes from time to time to manuscript thinking that they would work perfectly only to delete them several days later. Something was missing. But finally several months later I had a clear picture of their story in my head and wrote it down. I hope you enjoyed reading it.

Huge thank you to Hot Tree Editing team for helping me with my editing process. Especially Becky, Donna, Peggy, Kayla and Mandy. Plus beta readers and final eyes, who gave me valuable feedback and made sure I covered any plot holes I had.

Thank you to Hang Le, Olivier Lachance and Rusty Blade for the fabulous cover.

Heather Roberts and Lauren Rosa, thank you for being with me during this release every step of the way.

L. Woods PR thank you for hosting my cover reveal and release blitz.

Thank you to Ena and Amanda from Enticing Journey Book Promotions for hosting my release blitz as well. It's always a pleasure working with you, ladies!

Thank you to my reader group, ladies you are amazing!

Thank you to all the bloggers for spreading the word about Psychopath's Prey and leaving reviews.

And finally to all the readers who took a chance on this journey of love between Psychopath and Ella. Thank you to each one of you.

ALSO BY V. F. MASON

Dark Romance

Sociopath's Obsession

Sociopath's Revenge

Lachlan's Protégé

Micaden's Madness

Callum's Hell

Madman's Method

Madman's Cure

Mafia Romance

Pakhan's Rose

Pakhan's Salvation

Sovietnik's Fury

Brigadier's Game

Kaznachei's Pain

Free Books

His Broken Princess

CONTACT

Website: http://vfmason.com
Newsletter: http://eepurl.com/bTq66n
Reader group : http://bit.ly/2iXZdol

Made in the USA
Middletown, DE
19 May 2023

30846073R00175